At a Time Like This

CATHERINE DUNNE is the author of five previous novels (*In the Beginning, A Name for Himself, The Walled Garden, Another Kind of Life* and *Something Like Love*). She has also written about Irish immigration in *An Unconsidered People*. All of her work has been published to both critical and popular acclaim. The novels have struck a chord in several countries and have now been translated into many languages and optioned for film. Catherine Dunne lives in Dublin.

Acclaim for Catherine Dunne

'A wonderful and utterly convincing evocation of friendship over the years'
Irish Examiner

'Elegant, lucid prose . . . with depth, intelligence, and a few surprises'
Irish Times

'Dunne's Dublin dialogue is deft, her writing sings'
She

'Warm, funny, persistent, poignant and feisty . . . [Catherine Dunne] is a fine story-teller'
Irish Independent

'From page one the reader is won over . . . Brimming with raw emotion'
Bookseller

'An outrageously good read'

Catherine Dunne

At a Time
Like This

PAN BOOKS

First published 2007 by Macmillan

This edition published 2008 by Pan Books
an imprint of Pan Macmillan Ltd
Pan Macmillan, 20 New Wharf Road, London N1 9RR
Basingstoke and Oxford
Associated companies throughout the world
www.panmacmillan.com

ISBN 978-0-330-46385-0

A CIP catalogue record for this book is available from
the British Library.

Typeset by Intype Libra Ltd
Printed and bound in the UK by
CPI Mackays, Chatham ME5 8TD

Visit www.panmacmillan.com to read more about all our books
and to buy them. You will also find features, author interviews and
news of any author events, and you can sign up for e-newsletters
so that you're always first to hear about our new releases.

Here at the frontier, there are falling leaves,
Although my neighbours are all barbarians,
And you, you are a thousand miles away,
There are always two cups on my table.

Anonymous (Tang Dynasty, AD 618–906)

Acknowledgements

The author gratefully acknowledges the travel and mobility grant awarded by An Chomhairle Ealaíon, the Arts Council. Such practical support made possible the acceptance of a residency in an artists' retreat in the village of Mojácar, Almería, Spain.

Sincere thanks, too, to the Paul Beckett foundation – Fundación Valparaíso – in Mojácar. The kindness of Beatrice Beckett and the staff and residents at Valparaíso meant that parts of this novel were written in the most memorable and magical of circumstances.

To the members of Novelshop, without whom this book would never have been written in the first place: Lia Mills, Celia de Fréine, Mary Rose Callaghan and Ivy Bannister. For the careful reading of many drafts, for critical insight and practical support and, above all, for friendship. Thank you all.

To my friends, Antonio Gomis Noguera and Beatriz Gómez Ygual – heartfelt thanks for providing a place of light and space and peace in which to work. Happy memories are anchored beneath the blue skies and purple shadows of the mighty Ifach.

To all the team at Macmillan: Imogen Taylor, Trisha Jackson, Emma Grey, and the unbeatable duo of Davy Adamson and Cormac Kinsella. Many thanks for that special combination of professionalism and enthusiasm that both cheers and sus tains.

Thanks to Shirley Stewart, Literary Agent, for just about everything.

And finally, to my father, whose support remains constant and unwavering throughout all.

Prologue

So. This is how it happened.

It's Friday morning, five o'clock. I'm standing in the porch, suit-case at my feet. Cold air radiates from the glass doors and crawls beneath my clothes, but I haven't time to go back inside and get a coat. I can already see the taxi as it swings around the corner and then slows, almost at once. I watch its measured approach, see it climb the ramp and then descend, headlights glaring up and down like semaphore.

I step outside at once. I decide to carry the Samsonite: its wheels make too much noise on gravel this early in the morning. By the time I reach the gate, the driver has already leapt out and has the boot open.

'Mornin',' he says, reaching for my case. 'That all the luggage?'

I nod. 'Yes,' I say. 'That's all there is.'

He heaves it into the boot and slams the lid shut. I don't wait for him to open the passenger door for me. Quickly, I slide into the back seat, tugging at the seatbelt until it releases. When I glance out of the window, I catch sight of Raffles, picking his way across the frosty grass. Each delicate paw is placed only after great deliberation. Raffles doesn't trust the cold. For a moment, I imagine I can hear the tinkling of the bell that hangs from his collar, but of course that's nonsense. Carla's 'bird-warner'. I look away.

'Airport, 'nt tha' righ'?' the driver looks at me in the rear-view mirror. He's in his fifties, balding. Crankiness clings to him like a wet vest.

'That's right,' I say.

The interior of the taxi smells of pine air-freshener, sad upholstery and stale perspiration. The driver turns up the radio to listen to the weather forecast: '. . . And little change expected for the capital city this morning. Rain and sleet until early afternoon, temperatures reaching a high of three degrees celsius. Driving conditions treacherous . . .' I can see that the sky is now a dirty orange, the Atlantic cold front already stomping its way towards us across the midlands.

'Fuckin' city,' the taxi driver says, trying to catch my eye.

I can see his expression reflected, hear his eagerness for conversation. I peer instead into my handbag, busy, distracted, in search of something urgent.

'It'll be gridlocked now, within the hour.' He keeps talking anyway, his tone one of satisfied disgruntlement. He shifts in his seat and runs one hand through what's left of his hair. Then he turns up the heat, blasting the foggy residue on the inside of the windscreen. Wipers scream suddenly across the outside of the glass. My stomach shifts towards nausea.

'Dunno why people in this country can't drive in the rain,' he says, shaking his head. 'We get enough of the fuckin' stuff.' He turns left then, on to the main road, and swerves immediately into the outer lane. Horns blare behind us and beside us, a cacophony of early dawn road-rage. 'See what I mean?'

I don't answer. I don't want to be a memorable passenger, one too easily distinguished from all the others he'll meet today. As it is, I am his first fare and that is bad enough. I keep my mouth shut.

'Goin' anywhere nice?' he asks, after a polite interval.

I lower my head. 'Funeral,' I say.

'Ah, sorry, missus.'

2

And that's that.

I shall not miss Dublin. Of that, I am certain. But there are some things I *will* miss, some people. Maggie, for example. Well, perhaps my other friends, too, but Maggie most of all. She and I go back the farthest. I won't be with her this evening, won't be there to share in the festivities. Nevertheless, I can still predict how it'll all go. It's Claire's turn to be the hostess. At about eight o'clock, she will take the first bottle of Prosecco out of the fridge. She'll stand it in the functional but elegant ice bucket that she once brought back from Copenhagen. She'll drape a white linen napkin about its neck. All her movements will be graceful, unhurried. Then she'll probably enlist Maggie's help to check the four place settings, making minute changes to the position of the cutlery, or the wine glasses, or the angle of the flower arrangements: just as I've seen her do on countless occasions over the past twenty-five years. A special night, a night of celebration, she'd said, one to mark all our years of friendship. *A silver anniversary of girlhood.* Even then, the phrase had made me wince.

'You're all excited by the idea, aren't you?' I asked her, on the evening she handed each of us an embossed envelope. Style was a matter of honour with Claire. The invitations were on handmade paper, the black letters glossy as Chinese lacquer. Her smile was broad, her eyes sparkled with mischief. But some instinct drove me to burst her bubble. 'Do the four of us really need to be reminded about how old we're getting?'

Maggie shot me a warning glance then. One of those that I've become accustomed to over the years. But I had no intention of taking back what I had just said. I had no intention of softening it, either. Maggie knew when to give up. She'd learned way back how to recognize when such efforts were useless.

Claire's colour heightened at my jibe, and she tilted her head to one side. I thought she looked at me a little coyly. 'Don't be mean, Georgie,' she murmured, and changed the subject.

I suppose it was mean of me, but by that stage I'd already withdrawn in all the ways that counted from my friends, my family, and the way they lived their lives. From the way we'd *all* lived our lives. Twenty-five years is a long time: long enough for some things to change and too long for so much else to stay the same. I've been thinking a lot, particularly over the last few weeks, about what friendship is and what it means to me now, what it has meant to me over the years. I can still remember the night we made our pact: a bit like the three musketeers, but there were four of us. One Four All. All Four One. Our motto, until things fragmented. Well, nothing lasts for ever.

It happened shortly after the birth of Nora's eldest son, Robbie. Maggie and I were sitting together on the overstuffed, buttoned leather sofa. Nora was upright in the armchair, holding court. Claire was in her favourite place, on the floor, her arms wrapped around her knees. Her red hair was backlit to perfection by the faux-Tiffany lamp on the nest of tables behind her. She looked glorious, like one of Titian's saints about to be assumed into somewhere a lot more interesting than Nora's suburban living room.

'Why don't we make a pact?' Nora was saying, nursing her one glass of wine of the evening.

'What sort of pact?' Claire asked drowsily, tipping her head sideways to see Nora better. The glow from behind sharpened her cheekbones, made her eyes luminous. Maggie nudged me then. She made the faintest of gestures in Claire's direction.

'Wouldn't that make you sick?' she whispered. I grinned. I knew exactly what she meant.

Nora kept on talking. 'Why don't we arrange to meet every month to six weeks or so – I mean a real arrangement, a date we put in our diaries? Then we'll make sure it happens and that way, we won't lose touch.' She gave each of us in turn one of her brightest smiles. None of us spoke.

'I'll cook for us here,' she went on, and I felt how her eagerness was almost a fifth person in the room. 'You're all still students, and you don't have the space. It's so much easier for me.'

'Oh, but that wouldn't be fair,' objected Maggie. At the same time, her leg jerked and the tip of her shoe glanced off the wine glass I'd set on the floor beside me. Dear, clumsy Maggie with her two left feet. I watched as the red stain spread out in slow motion across the beige carpet, acquiring the contours of a rather tipsy Australia.

'Oh, shite, shite, shite – sorry, Nora. Here, let me mop it up.' Maggie was struggling to free herself from the sinking embrace of the sofa. But by then, Nora was gone, racing for the kitchen.

'Oh God, oh God,' Maggie muttered, shaking her head. 'Why does it always have to be me?'

Nora was by now on her knees, the kitchen roll in one hand, the drum of Saxa salt in the other, holding them like six-guns. She was more tight-lipped than usual. Maggie continued to grovel until I nudged her to stop. Enough, already.

Dab, dab, sprinkle. Dab, dab, sprinkle. Claire looked on, fascinated. The soggy paper towels gathered on the sheets of newspaper and looked like the aftermath of a massacre.

'Oh, but I don't mind cooking,' Nora said. She ran her hand over the pile of salt, pressing it still further into the carpet. We all watched as the wine began to bleed into it, lifting the stain from the beige surface as if by magic. 'I love entertaining. And with a new baby, well, I can't get out much. You'd be doing me a favour. I mean it.' And she looked Maggie right in the eye.

Game, set and match, I thought. I may have been only nineteen, but nevertheless, I recognized Nora's skill. I couldn't help but admire it. Kind-hearted Maggie was caught in that dangerous net of hospitality: she knew that resistance was futile. Any further struggle would pull the filaments tighter, enmeshing her all the more. So she just nodded, looking from Nora to me for confirmation. 'Oh, well, in that case, then, yeah – yeah, that would be really great. It would be lovely to meet here.'

'I think it's a wonderful idea,' Claire interjected, softly. I don't know which of them glowed more at that – Nora or Claire.

'So it's settled then,' said Nora, as she knelt beside Australia. She couldn't hide her delight. 'I'll get the calendar.'

And so it came to pass. A quarter century of monthly meetings. Occasionally, one or other of us had to cry off. I never felt as though I was missing out on anything spectacular. But I have to say that each of us was afraid that those present would speak of many things, including the absent one. And for that reason, if for no other, nobody ever wanted to be the absent one.

I take out my purse as the taxi pulls up outside the departures terminal at Dublin airport. I glance at the meter and hand the driver twenty euro. He starts to scrabble for my one euro eighty cent change.

'That's fine,' I say, and open the rear door. He pops open the boot and is by my side in an instant.

'Thanks very much, missus,' he says, placing my luggage on the ground, snapping the handle upwards and into place for me. 'I hope your day isn't too sad.'

I look at him in surprise. What on earth can he mean? Then I stifle a smile with difficulty. 'Thank you,' I murmur, taking hold of the proffered handle. I settle the strap of my bag more comfortably on my shoulder. 'Thank you very much.'

He nods and slams the boot closed. 'No problem,' he says, and I walk away. All at once, I see myself through his eyes and experience a sudden surge, a rush of pure elation. If only he knew.

I approach the check-in desk. There is no queue. I hand my passport and ticket to the smiling young woman who asks me all the usual questions about sharp objects, bombs, dangerous weapons.

'Is Frankfurt your final destination?' she asks.

I shake my head. 'Florence,' I say.

'Would you like me to send your bag straight through?'

'No, thank you.' I realize my tone is firmer than I intended. In the recent past I've had far too much experience of lost baggage. 'I'll collect it in Frankfurt, just in case. I've lots of time between flights.' I don't want to arrive to where I'm going unprepared. Not on this occasion. I don't want to be caught without all the things that make a woman's life civilized.

'Have a nice flight,' she says. But I hear 'Have a nice life.'

Will I? I wonder. It's not too late to pull back, to go home, to pretend that this is the result of a momentary madness. It's strange, this sudden tension I feel between wanting and not wanting. I feel the pull of old intimacies, followed almost at once by the push of alienation. I think about tonight at Claire's, with Maggie and Nora. Of course I won't be with them: I have chosen not to be with them. But I'd love to *be* there, nevertheless: a presence, a shimmery ghost sliding in and out among the chairs, finally settling at the one empty place, listening.

So. I can see the contours of their evening spread out before me already, like a well-worn pattern, undemanding, easy to follow. I might need to make the occasional nip here, a cautionary tuck there, but by and large, I have the evening's measure. Of course, I do accept that I shall never really know: instead, I'll have to be content with imagining. And I shall miss that knowing, miss those comfortable, predictable endings. I'll raise my glass to them all this evening and take great pleasure in this, our final gathering.

I buy a newspaper, coffee. I settle into the traveller's sport of waiting.

Georgie, Porgie, pudding and pie. Kissed the boys and made them cry.

Well, let's see who's crying now.

1. *Claire*

I can still remember the day we met, as though it was only yesterday. The day that changed everything. The day after which things were never the same again, not for me, anyhow.

I saw her first in Front Square. She was tall, fair-haired, standing very straight. That day, she had her hair up, and I admired her long neck and the silver earrings she wore. They caught the light, like fish gleaming silver under water. Her presence was commanding: that was the first word that came to mind. Even back then, even as a teenager, she had that air of ownership that continues to define her as Georgie.

She was talking away to a guy seated at one of the Freshers' Week tables and from where I was standing, I could tell that she was giving him a hard time. He looked as though he was trying to disappear under the scarred wooden surface, or at least, to hide further behind it. I could see that he wanted to be somewhere both safer and quieter. That spindly table reminded me of primary school, of copy-books smelling of chalk dust and low-ceilinged rooms filled with books and certainties.

'Well?' the girl who would soon become Georgie asked for the second time, just as I approached. Except that it sounded more like a demand than a request. She pulled a leaflet from the bundle in front of her. 'What other reasons could there possibly be for joining?' Her voice was crystal, full of confidence. It made me conscious of my culchie origins. I decided I'd better keep my mouth shut.

The young man began to fumble with the leaflets, tidying them. It was an attempt, and not a very effective one at that, to try to ward her off. He was really doing his best to show his authority. But he didn't have a chance. Strangely for me, I didn't feel the least bit sorry for him. I remember thinking that he was almost a caricature with that shabby tweed jacket, those heavy black spectacles and a row of cheap biros straining from his breast pocket. 'Eng. Lit. Soc.' was stapled crookedly across the pitted wood in front of him. I took one decisive step forward, surprising myself. I'd never been much of a joiner before, but somehow this girl's brashness gave me courage. The world owed her and she knew it. Maybe, just by my being with her, it might realize that it owed me, too.

'Hello,' Georgie said, sensing my presence. Then she turned to look at me. No, she *really* looked at me, as though she was interested in what she was seeing.

'Hello.' I didn't know whether I felt disconcerted or pleased.

Her gaze swept over me. Head to toe. No attempt to hide her appraisal. 'Pure English?'

I shook my head. 'No,' I said, trying not to let the Clare cadences slip through. (I know, I know, Claire from Clare. I've heard that joke a million times and do you know, everyone who makes it believes that they are the first to have thought of it.) 'Not Pure English. I'm doing French as well.'

She nodded, her blue eyes unblinking. 'My name's Georgina, but everyone calls me Georgie.'

'I'm Claire. Nice to meet you.' I wasn't exactly sure what we were supposed to do next. Shake hands or something? I decided that I'd take my cue from her.

'Shall we go ahead and join and put this guy out of his misery?' The young man sitting behind the wobbly table hadn't said a word throughout our conversation, and now he looked from one of us to the other. His head was like one of those nodding dogs you see in the backs of cars – except that his nod was horizontal, rather than vertical.

'I should close my mouth if I were you,' Georgina – Georgie – advised him. 'Lots of wasps dying, this time of year. You could get stung.' She signed her name with a flourish and handed me the pen. I did the same.

Everyone calls me Georgie.

I remember how struck I was by her comfort inside her own skin, her familiarity with *Everyone*.

'Been to the Buttery yet?' she asked, hoisting her rucksack over one shoulder.

I shook my head. 'No. I've only just arrived.'

'Fancy a coffee? Or a tea?' she added hurriedly.

I suspected that there had to be only one right answer here, and I already knew that I knew what it was. Coffee (urban, sophisticated); tea (provincial, dull). As it happened, I have never liked tea, tea and sympathy. But still, my answer made me feel like a fraud. 'Yeah. Coffee'd be good,' I said. We crossed Front Square and made our way down the Buttery steps.

'Your accent is lovely,' Georgie said. 'Where are you from?'

'Ennistymon. County Clare,' I added, in case she hadn't heard of Ennistymon.

'I know Ennistymon well,' she said. 'And Kilkee. And Doolin. My last boyfriend was a traditional music nut.'

Her *last* boyfriend?

Somehow, I knew that Georgie's experience of boyfriends was the real thing: cool, sexy, grown-up. I bet she'd have lifted her well-defined eyebrows if she knew anything about my couple of blunderers. I thought of Jamesie's shy, adolescent fumblings, the hopeless tangle of his fingers in my bra straps.

By then, I was really hooked. Georgie's ease with the world

was seductive. It helped, too, that she'd been to Doolin. She'd crossed into my territory, and that somehow expanded my small childhood world and gave my home place a measure of significance. 'And you?' I asked. 'Where are you from?'

She opened the glass door to the Buttery, waving me in ahead of her. She grinned. 'Oh,' she said, 'I'm from the centre of the universe. Ballsbridge.'

I said nothing. What was I missing here? What secret language was I not able to speak?

'Don't worry,' she said, 'you'll get it soon enough.'

It was only when we were sitting down I realized that I hadn't spoken those words aloud. 'You read my mind,' I said to her. The coffee was awful. It was weak and burnt-tasting and bitter all at the same time. The tables were crowded and the blue air was humming with cigarette smoke and conversation. A dumpy, bad-tempered woman with misapplied orange lipstick swept by us. Her greying hair was curled tight and angry: an exact match for her face. She loaded dirty crockery on to a trolley, but not before she glared at us and swiped at the table with a less than clean cloth. We waited until she'd moved along before we dared to speak again.

Georgie made a face. 'I know,' she said. 'I'll have to stop doing that. It makes people nervous.'

'Does it always work?'

She shook her head, tucking a strand of fair hair behind her ear. 'No. But your expression said it all. It was easy to know what you were thinking.'

I decided right then that I liked her.

'Can I ask you something?' Georgie said, pushing her cup away from her. She didn't wait for me to answer. I liked that, too. 'Your hair. Is it . . . naturally like that?'

I wasn't sure what she meant. 'The colour?'

She shrugged. 'Everything – the colour, the curls, the . . . exuberance. The whole deal.' She nodded at me, waiting.

I sensed that something hung on my reply. I wasn't sure what it could be, but I was taking no chances, not with this girl. The truth, the whole truth. Nothing but the truth.

'Yeah,' I said. 'It's naturally like this. It's mine. All mine.' And I tugged at a curl above my right ear, just to prove it. I decided that today I could be whoever I wanted to be, miles and miles from Clare. 'My mother's legacy. She abandoned us for the local doctor when I was twelve. I shaved all my hair off when I found out, and when it grew back, it looked just like this.' I waited. This was where *I'd* decide.

Poor little lambs, and they so young. And Claire's so like her mother. Same shape face, same slender frame, and now, with that mane of red hair . . .

Would Georgie be curious? Shocked? Would she, too, define me by my mother?

'It's stunning,' she said, shaking her head slowly. 'Absolutely stunning. I'd say that Eng. Lit. guy still has his mouth open.' She pulled a packet of twenty Carrolls from the side pocket of her rucksack.

I remember thinking: how extravagant.

'Smoke?' she asked, offering me one.

I accepted. I rejoiced. I inhaled. The right answer, I thought, as I savoured a blast of nicotine and delight. She'd chosen the right answer.

And that was how Georgie and I met. After a whole miserable month of getting lost on my own in Dublin, I felt, finally, that I'd found a way home. I'll go further and say that I dated the beginning of my grown-up life from the minute that Georgie offered me one of her cigarettes.

Being with Georgie changed everything. The College lawns

were greener, the sky looked bluer, kinder. It was as though some-one had just adjusted the focus. The picture shimmered into clarity. It felt as if I had just met, and instantly recognized, myself. My other, more assured, more daring self. The one I hadn't met before and whose existence I had never even suspected.

'Where are you staying?' Georgie asked, as we climbed the steps from the Buttery and made our way towards the New Arts Block. We'd decided to check out the English Department, to see what our timetables were like for the following week, when Michaelmas term would begin. Despite myself, despite my wari-ness of elitism, and urban sophistication, I loved the names. I loved the oldness of everything, the shabby, ruddy splendour of the Rubrics, the gnarled ancientness of trees.

'In Rathfarnham,' I said. 'In digs, with a friend of my aunt's. Just until I find my feet,' I added, aware that I'd just sounded old-fashioned.

Georgie looked at me. 'How long do you have to stay there?' she asked, having seen right through me.

'Until Christmas,' I replied miserably. Such safety, such pre-dictability already felt like a prison sentence. I knew that I'd found my feet now and that Georgie would keep me grounded.

'I have a place in Rathmines,' she said. 'I'll be sharing with Maggie. We've been friends for ever. You'll like her.'

'I'm sure I will,' I said.

'There's room for three, but so far, there's only the two of us. Someone else let us down. Her parents made her stay at home for first year.' Georgie settled her rucksack again. There was an unmistakable ripple of irritation as she did so.

I was very glad that it was the other girl Georgie was mad at, and not me.

She continued. 'Apparently, if you live at home for first year, you're safe. You won't have *any* opportunity to have sex. Did you know that?'

I laughed. 'I think that you should talk to my dad.'

Georgie looked at me, interested. And I remember thinking: *she's* interested in what *I* might have to say?

'Go on, then,' she said.

I shrugged. 'Well, d'ye know, where I come from, nothing bad ever happens before midnight. Be home by ten, and you'll never be a pumpkin.'

The blue gaze stayed level. She waited.

'It means you can hang on to your virginity for ever. My father calls it "The Cinderella Syndrome". He says it's absurd.' He did indeed say that, but I wasn't sure he'd have expressed it as boldly as I'd just done. I was beginning not to recognize myself.

Georgie grinned at last. 'A sound man, your father.'

I nodded. 'Yeah, yeah, he is.' And suddenly, I missed him. But why should I? He was the one who'd kicked me out, after all, the one who insisted I had to 'spread my wings'. I'd fought him, tired of always having to do those things that were supposed to be good for me. I can hear myself now. Why is it 'good for me' to have to do the things that make me feel bad? To leave my friends? My home? My wings are quite happy as they are, thank you very much and I'll spread them as much as I like. Home gives me enough room to stretch, and, if we want to extend the metaphor, just enough to feel the bars of my cage if I push too hard.

But he wouldn't listen. I tried to avoid it by using every trick in the book. I'd even hoped that fate and poor exam results might bring about a happy accident and let me stay where I was. Local. Located. I prayed for a marriage between hope and circumstance: hopenstance. Well, happenstance is a word isn't it? But it didn't work.

And so, here I was. Standing in late September sunshine with the first person under forty years of age I'd spoken to in a month. Well, except for children, and they didn't count, not in the way I meant.

Georgie was looking thoughtful. 'So, your father mightn't mind you giving up your digs, then?' she persisted. 'We hope to move into the flat at the beginning of November. That's almost five weeks away.' I could feel her watching me. 'What do you say? Long enough to convince the old man, do you think?'

I smiled. 'Old man' he was not. Not in any sense. 'Yeah,' I said, feeling brave. 'I'll talk to him at the weekend. When would you need to know?'

Georgie shrugged. 'Two weeks? If you can't take the room, we'll need to look for someone else.'

I felt stung. I desperately wanted to be part of this imagined life that Georgie and Maggie already shared. I didn't care what the rent was. I'd earn it. I didn't care what the consequences were. I'd put up with them. I wanted Rathmines, friends my own age, freedom. Bugger the suburbs, the number sixteen bus, the fifteen hours of babysitting every week. My father wanted me to spread my wings, to stretch myself? Then watch out. The bars of the family cage were about to get a beating.

'Yeah,' I said, casually. 'Two weeks should be fine. I'll let you know.'

Georgie nodded her agreement. 'Great.' By then, we'd arrived at the English Department noticeboard, and I still have no idea how we got there. I remember nothing other than floating along on this girl's promise of a life I had never known. She pointed to the timetable. 'Look,' she said. 'We share lectures at least twice a week. That's good.' She smiled at me. 'I'm meeting Maggie tomorrow night for a pint. In O'Neill's of Suffolk Street. You know it?'

I was embarrassed to admit that I didn't. I decided I'd find it for myself. 'Yeah,' I lied. 'I know it.' Tomorrow's Thursday, I remember thinking. I'm babysitting Friday and Saturday. 'Tomorrow's fine.'

'Okay, then,' she said. She glanced at her watch. 'I've got to go now – I'm meeting up with Danny, my boyfriend. See you tomorrow evening around nine?'

I nodded. I had that cold feeling, again, that I'd just been a useful opportunity – that I'd filled some kind of a gap in a busy woman's schedule. But Georgie smiled at me then, a warm, genuine smile, and all my reservations faded away.

'Great to meet you, Claire. I know that you and Maggie will get along. Start working on that father of yours. Tell him you'll always be home by ten.'

We both laughed.

'Okay, then,' I said, my lightness of heart safe again, restored. 'See you tomorrow night.'

I decided to arrive at O'Neill's well before nine. I wanted to be there when the two of them came in, wanted to see if they'd arrive together or separately. I suppose I wanted to be sure that Georgie had room in her life for another friend, that she and Maggie wouldn't always be two against one.

I settled at a table in the corner, one where I could keep an eye on the door. Georgie arrived first and by herself. I was relieved. There was no conspiracy, then; no whispering campaign about the red-headed culchie. I was about to wave, but she'd already spotted me. Georgie had one of those effortless glances that took in a whole room at once. I learned quickly, too, that she could identify where the creeps hung out. And more: she could tell where boredom lurked. She used to say that she preferred creeps to bores. The 'undesirables', as she called them, were reduced to jelly by her sharp tongue; the bores were not. They, she said, were impervious. That was why they were bores in the first place.

'Hiya, Claire. No sign of Maggie, then.'

I looked at her. I felt completely stupid. But then, it wasn't a question, after all.

'Just got here myself, right this minute,' I lied. There was no half-empty glass on the table to give me away, no smouldering cigarette in the ashtray. I hadn't wanted to drink on my own, anyhow, so I'd hidden away and read my book. But Georgie didn't know that. She would never know things like that unless I told her.

'Ready to order now?' An eager young lad in a cheap white shirt and a tired bow-tie stood before us, his sticky tray held out in front of him like an offering.

Georgie looked at him for a moment as she took off her jacket and I noticed that her gaze made him blush. I felt sorry for him then. He was all awkward angles, all bony elbows and knees. He couldn't be more than fifteen, a new sixteen at the very most.

'Yes,' said Georgie. At that moment, the pub door opened and a small, dark-haired girl entered. She trailed a cloud of astonishing energy in her wake: even the tired, middle-aged men at the bar looked up from their newspapers as she passed. Georgie grinned. 'Yes,' she said again. 'We're ready now. Three pints of Guinness.'

Even if Georgie hadn't ordered (and how was I going to drink a whole pint of that stuff?) I'd have known at once that this was Maggie.

'Hi, Georgie,' she said, flicking a wave of dark hair away from her face, back over one shoulder. Then she looked at me. Her eyes were a translucent green, her lips painted bright scarlet. 'You must be Claire from Clare. Nice to meet you.'

But she didn't laugh at her own joke and I forgave her. 'And you're Maggie,' I said.

She nodded. 'That's me. Don't believe everything *she* says about me, though.'

I smiled. 'Oh, she didn't give anything away. You've nothing to worry about.'

Maggie snorted. She settled herself more comfortably on her

stool. She was dressed for maximum impact and I admired her panache. A crimson shirt, an exact match for the shade of lipstick she was wearing, and a pair of tight, black Levi's. Her curves were evident. Her whole attitude said: if you've got it, flaunt it. I wouldn't have had the nerve, not in those days. Anyhow, I didn't have the curves, not like Maggie did. I still hid behind flowing dresses back then because somehow, I believed that they camouflaged my thinness.

'Wouldn't I love to have something worth telling,' she said, throwing her eyes up to heaven. 'Life's much too quiet at the moment. Isn't that right, Georgie?'

Georgie said nothing.

Maggie had just begun to fumble in her bag for cigarettes. Now she stopped, reacting to Georgie's silence. She looked across at her friend, her green eyes huge. 'Georgie – you haven't, have you? Not again. Tell me you haven't?'

Although Maggie's tone was full of urgency, I felt that I was watching a well-rehearsed double act, where each person had already practised their lines and knew them off by heart. I was the audience, but I didn't mind. I liked being entertained.

Georgie closed her eyes, lifted her elegant shoulders ever so slightly and spread her palms towards us. Maggie shook her head. 'Who is it this time?' she demanded. 'Isn't one fella at a time enough for you? God knows it'd be enough for me, if I could *get* one.'

But Georgie made no reply. Just then, the lounge boy returned and placed three nervous pints on the table in front of us.

'Any matches?' Maggie asked him. There was a cigarette already lodged between her fingers. I noticed that it looked at home there.

'I'll go and see.' He disappeared in search of them. He hadn't been able to keep his eyes off her. I remember thinking that his cheeks had flushed to a fair match for her shirt.

'Don't terrify him, Maggie – I think it's his first night. Never seen him before, have you?' Georgie took out her own packet of cigarettes.

Maggie shook her head. 'Nah. Don't worry, I'll be gentle with him. He looks like someone's kid brother.'

Yes, mine, I thought, with a sudden, sharp prod of memory. Ruaidhri, with his long and awkward arms and legs, his sticking-up hair. The lounge boy delivered the matches to Maggie. I noticed how he averted his eyes. She smiled and handed him, grandly, a tip of twenty pence. He sloped off, pleased with himself.

Georgie raised her glass. 'Here's to us, then.'

'It was nobody we know, right? Nobody I need to avoid?' asked Maggie. She held the glass to her lips, delaying the first sip until Georgie answered her. They were very good together.

Georgie sighed. 'No, it's nobody *you* know. Just someone I met over the weekend. He was fun. So who cares?' And she shrugged again. I would get to know that dismissive gesture. And the tone that hovered somewhere between weariness and boredom. The tone that would make us – Maggie and me, that is – laugh and eventually forgive whatever it was she had just got up to.

'Well, okay, then.' Maggie lifted her glass. 'To the three of us, right?'

We all chinked obediently and drank. I tried not to breathe because I did not want to taste the yeasty liquid as it prickled and fizzled its way across my tongue. It was my first pint and I didn't know what I might be letting myself in for. Up until then, pints were for farmers and mountainy men who guzzled themselves to a standstill every Saturday night in the pubs of Ennistymon. Guinness was not something that girls drank. I also decided that I had better not to ask who, or what, they were talking about. I didn't feel, then, that it was any of my business.

'Well,' said Maggie, turning to face me. 'You'll be joining us in the flat, right?'

I opened my mouth to speak, about to be cautious. But Maggie's bright, open face and Georgie's amused one somehow gave me courage. 'Yeah,' I said instead. 'I will. As long as it's affordable. That okay with you?' And I smiled at her, having the impression that I was beginning to gain ground. She made me feel that I might be able to hold my own, placed somewhere appropriate and agreed between the two of them.

Maggie shrugged. 'Yeah, 'course,' she said. 'It's hardly a palace, though. Has Georgie told you?'

'I'm sure it's fine,' I said. Not that I cared. 'When can I see it?'

'I'll find out,' said Georgie. 'The other tenants are still there, but I'll see what I can do. Maybe we can get in at the weekend.'

''Course it's affordable,' said Maggie, putting down her glass. I noticed she was almost half-finished, Georgie too. I'd barely begun. 'Georgie's daddy would never try and rip us off, would he, Georgie?'

'Wouldn't dream of it,' she said easily. 'Besides, this way, he gets the best of both worlds. I'm out of his hair and he has three careful tenants. We'll keep things ticking over till he's ready to sell. And then off he goes and makes a fortune.' She turned to me. 'Simple, really. And that's another thing to tell your old man: you'll be a friend of the family, no possibility of eviction. Cheers.'

And she drained her glass, followed by Maggie. I said 'no' to another one just then – although there was a pleasant lightness dancing between my ears. Something was nagging at me, though: was Georgie just being careful, waiting for Maggie's seal of approval before telling me that her father was the landlord? Or was this how people at the centre of the universe behaved, by keeping secrets?

I didn't care. Possibilities were everywhere. I had a surge of anticipation about the future, one I had never even dared to imagine. The distance between the me right then, and the me of my other life was growing as we spoke. And it blossomed with only a little guilt to season it. I remember asking myself: is this all it takes? Are you really that shallow, Claire from Clare?

It seemed that Maggie was talking to me. More glasses littered the table-top, the ashtray was full and the bar was suddenly crowded with people. The evening had been slipping away from me and I hadn't noticed.

'Claire?'

'Sorry – Maggie, miles away.'

'Fag?'

I hesitated. The lightness inside my head was changing to something fuzzy and dark. It was unpleasant, like the dizziness you get just before you faint. 'No, thanks. Not now.' I needed to keep my hands very still.

'You okay?' She was looking at me closely. Georgie was trying to catch the lounge boy's eye.

'I'm fine. Just a bit wrecked.'

'You don't need to stick it out till the bitter end, you know.' She grinned. 'We won't talk about you when you're gone.'

'Really?' I asked.

'Well, no,' she admitted. 'But you have nothing to fear. I've never known Georgie to take so kindly to anyone before. And,' she said, lighting her cigarette and leaning towards me while Georgie was busy ordering another round, 'I should know. We've been best friends since our first day at primary school. Nobody knows her better than I do.'

I nodded. 'That's a long time to be friends,' was all I could manage. Maggie's face was friendly, but her tone had an edge to it. Territory was being staked here. She was warning me what the boundaries were. Or perhaps it was the Guinness. I've never been any good at drinking. It makes me paranoid. 'And you?' I asked. 'Are you happy enough that I'm moving in?'

''Course! It'll be fun. I'm looking forward to it.' But she turned away from me as Georgie handed her her pint. I didn't know what to think.

Maggie and Georgie walked me to the bus stop, three pints of Guinness sloshing around inside me. They shared a bag of chips. I couldn't even look at them and the vinegar fumes didn't help my restless stomach, either. But I felt as though I'd completed a rite of passage. It seemed that Claire the Responsible had left herself behind, somewhere between the Buttery, the English Department and O'Neill's pub. The Bermuda Triangle where family baggage came to sink and die.

Even then, I thought about how strange life is, how random the coincidences are that shape our lives. I watched the welcome approach of the Rathfarnham bus.

'You sure you're okay?' Georgie's face loomed in front of mine.

'Fine.'

'We'll see you Monday, then, right?' Maggie said. 'Unless we can get in to see the flat at the weekend. Here's a phone number in case you want to ring us.' She pushed a bit of paper into the pocket of my jacket. I didn't bother trying to explain about the babysitting. I stepped up on to the platform of the bus.

'Take care, Claire – okay?' Georgie called.

I waved. Maggie waved back.

I sat on the long seat at the side, one hand clutching the cold, stainless steel pole. I remember hoping that I'd make it home in one piece. I was afraid of making a show of myself by getting sick on the number sixteen bus.

Half an hour later, I straightened up. The bushes on either side of me snagged on the material of my jacket. I had no tissue, so I used the back of my hand. My mouth felt sour and hot but I felt a whole lot better. I was grateful for suburban roads and quiet cul-de-sacs. No one wants to puke in public. As it was, the only witnesses were abandoned tricycles, the occasional scooter and a couple of legless dolls in an overgrown front garden.

I felt free and happy and empty. The unruly grass had just accepted, without complaint, almost six years' worth of loss, sadness, and the hot, bitter bile of guilt.

I stepped it out then, all the way back to my digs, feeling that with each foot forward, the best of my life was just beginning.

December the eighth. The Feast of the Immaculate Conception. And my birthday. I was on my way to our housewarming. I say 'our', although I hadn't yet moved into the flat at number 12, Rathmines Road. That would happen after the weekend. Carol, my landlady, was less than pleased. But my Aunty Kate had told me she'd get over it.

'Never apologize, never explain,' she'd said to me when I rang her. 'You're only eighteen once. And Carol might be an old friend, but she's had enough free babysitting. Do whatever it is you want. It's your life.'

I always listened to my Aunty Kate. She said the things I most wanted to hear. And I figured that she knew what she was talking about. That year, the year that I turned eighteen, Kate was already forty-six. She was the only unmarried daughter on my father's side, the one who'd looked after an endless succession of elderly relatives, the sort of burdens every family seems to have, and no siblings want to share.

First Kate took care of her own parents – my grandparents – then a sad and terminally ill brother, and finally the ailing and distantly related Uncle Mick, who'd arrived out of the blue years back. His own son, 'young Michael', who had to have been about sixty at the time, literally dumped him on Kate's doorstep. 'For the weekend, just. Me an' the missus need a break,' and then never came back to collect him. Fucked off to England, was Kate's verdict, and without his missus, too, she said, grimly, but unfortunately *with* someone else's. By the time Uncle Mick had 'shuffled off his mortal coil', according to Kate, the years and the wrinkles had both caught up with her and she ended up forty and lonely. She was the only one in the family – in fact, the only one in the whole town and county, I used to think – who consistently refused to blacken my mother's name after she abandoned us. Even when her own brother, Don, my father, threatened never to speak to her again.

When Kate said, 'It's your life,' she meant it. Mostly because she had never had one of her own. I had already decided that mine was going to be different. All it had taken was less than three months in the company of Georgie and Maggie to teach me what I no longer wanted. No turf fires for me, no elderly men sitting in corners smelling of stale tobacco, no suffocating neighbourly concern. On that December night, I could feel my mother's startling presence at one shoulder and my Aunty Kate's at the other. The twin goddesses of rural disappointments. The one who got away and the one who didn't. The smallness of their lives pushed me forward that night, across the Rathmines Road, up the garden path of number 12, up the steps to a door that led on to light and space and rooms rocking to the beat of sound and freedom.

My new boots might have pinched a little, but my black maxi skirt was thrilling. My cream silk gypsy top was clingy and ribbony and frothy. I was showing a lot of cleavage, too, for me. I could hardly wait to plunge headlong into that party.

Maggie hugged me as she opened the door. Her eyes were huge, glinting; her face looked even livelier than ever. 'Claire,' she said, reaching for my hand, pulling me towards her. 'We've missed you. Come on in. Things are just getting going!'

I followed her down the hallway. I had to step carefully

among the bikes and bags of coal and the long blue-jeaned legs of what seemed like dozens of boys sitting on the floor. They were all deep in conversation. I remember how intense the atmosphere felt and how badly lit the hallway was. Maggie had said they were going to keep the lights turned low as the downstairs hadn't been painted in years. I heard words like 'Marxist-Leninist', 'proletariat', 'capitalism'. It wasn't easy to look as if I belonged, but I did my best. Claire from Clare: just-born, confident, woman of-the-world. My first real party. One that didn't involve twelve pots of tea, second cousins and home-made cakes and buns. I felt that the whole house had a pulse-beat that night. My mouth had dried up and my heart had begun to pound, keeping time with Sting whining not to stand so close to him. Just as Maggie was about to go into the front room she paused, her hand on the jamb of the door. I stopped abruptly, almost running into her. Her bare shoulder was about level with my elbow.

She looked up at me. 'If you don't wanna smoke, just say it makes you sick, right?'

I nodded, having no idea why she was so concerned, why she was whispering like that. I still didn't feel at ease with Maggie, although on nights like tonight, I could feel the atmosphere thawing. And as for smoking or not smoking: it never bothered me, one way or the other. Besides, I was saving hard and cigarettes were still easy to give up.

'Okay,' I said, wanting to humour her. I followed her inside. 'I'll just leave this beer in the kitchen. Give me a sec.'

The kitchen table was crammed with bottles of Pedrotti and Hirondelle, Blue Nun and Black Tower. Cans of Tuborg and flagons of cider crowded across every other surface: the counter, the draining-board, and even the floor. Someone had filled the stained stainless-steel sink with cold water, and emptied the contents of the ice-tray on top of bobbing cans of Carlsberg Special. There was also the occasional naggin of vodka, flanked by bottles of soda water and Rose's lime cordial. I realized that I was starving – but there was no food to be seen anywhere. I felt a pang of regret that I'd refused Carol's spag bol in my hurry to be gone. I followed Maggie into the living room, which was heaving. There were bodies everywhere: standing, lying and hunkered down. The air was silver and thick and sweet-smelling.

Maggie shrugged her shoulders at me. 'Oh, yeah,' she said, 'and emmm . . . just ignore the Midnight Cowboy, right?'

I can still see him if I close my eyes, and to this day, I have no idea what his name was. A big guy, wearing a cowboy hat – and precious little else. That is all I saw when I looked at him first, and it's what I remember best now. The dark, brim-curling cowboy hat that hid all his features, and seemed to cast a shadow over half the room. His chest was bare-white, wisped here and there with ginger hair. Then I saw the underpants. And the tooled-leather boots. He looked up briefly as the door opened. Almost immediately, his chin drifted down towards his chest again. His grip on the can of Tuborg never loosened, though, never faltered. He was splayed in one of the chairs in Georgie's and Maggie's – and soon to be my – flat. His skin was pale, almost translucent, and it stood out luridly against the greenish-mustard velour of the sagging armchair. Party guests drifted in and out, moving around the bizarre cowboy-hatted spectacle as though they'd seen it all before. And maybe they had. Gradually, the traffic between the rooms became more purposeful. Then it dawned on me that there were maybe a dozen people there, passing around the thin cigarettes that I quickly learned were dope.

I do remember that I'd felt a bit shy at first as I settled myself on to the floor, until I realized that there was no need to be. I was as ignored as the silent, ginger-haired Midnight Cowboy.

'Try some.'

I heard Georgie's voice, sounding somewhat strangled as she passed me a soggy joint. I hesitated, but she nodded. 'Test the

Cinderella Syndrome,' she encouraged. Her boyfriend, Danny, waved at me, then put his arm around Georgie's waist. He was taller than she was, his dark hair long and thick, dragged back into an untidy pony-tail. He wore a black T-shirt with 'The Clash' stretched tight across his broad chest. For a moment, I couldn't take my eyes off him. His physical presence was intense. I remembered feeling the same way, too, the first time I'd met him, sitting in O'Neill's with Georgie. He'd burst through the door that afternoon, and I was immediately reminded of Maggie making one of her entrances. All heads had turned in his direction. As he approached, it was clear he had eyes only for Georgie. Then he turned and saw me and seemed to quieten a little. But I couldn't help feeling that there was something edgy about him, some restless undercurrent I had never come across before, but was still able to recognize. Tribal memory, perhaps. Some sort of genetic warning to women, telling us to steer clear of dangerous men. I think I probably stared at him on that afternoon. I couldn't help it.

'Danny, meet Claire,' Georgie said. 'Claire, meet Danny.'

Her voice had been almost expressionless. It took me a second to recover. And I knew that Georgie had seen me looking. I turned towards her and she returned my gaze, one eyebrow lifting. See? Her expression seemed to say. Told you I only went for the best specimens. On that night, the night of the party, Danny looked away from me almost at once. He pulled Georgie towards him, his mouth softly and insistently at her ear. That gesture spoke to me of ownership, reassurance, the sort of intimacy I had never had. Watching them both, I felt a knife-edge of exclusion, a reminder that I was still single, still the naive and inexperienced girl from Clare.

'I'm afraid it's too late.' I laughed, waving away Georgie's hand. I was trying desperately to hide my self-consciousness. 'It's already well after ten o'clock.' But Georgie didn't move. She kept holding out the joint, looking at me. 'Oh, what the hell?' I said finally, and took it from her.

'Remember – it's not like a fag,' she warned me. 'Hold the smoke in your lungs for as long as you're able. Then, let it out slowly, as slowly as you can. And then you can pass it along. I'm finished. You look fab, by the way.'

I smiled my thanks and took a long drag – longer than I intended. My throat began to burn, my eyes watered almost at once. I had the most tremendous desire to cough, but I did as Georgie had told me. I held the smoke in my lungs, feeling as though something inside me was about to burst, hot and gritty and lava-like. Then I let go, not very slowly, it has to be said, but more by way of a hoarse bark. I took a minute to recover, coughing and rasping. But nobody seemed to notice, except Georgie. She was watching me and I shrugged. 'Nothing's happening,' I said, as I passed the joint along to eager fingers on my right. I felt strangely disappointed. In my new frame of mind, I expected every experience to be explosive, life-enhancing, spectacular. I did not want to deal with the bland or the pedestrian. Give me wonder or give me tragedy.

Georgie grinned, her eyes now as wide as Maggie's. 'Wait a minute, Claire,' she said, her head nodding sagely. 'Be patient. Just wait a *wee* minute and you'll see.'

I did wait. I can't say that I was patient, though. I had toke after toke, probably more than my share, but nobody commented. By that stage, most people had begun to inhabit a private universe of one. And then, without warning, all was revealed. My head seemed to part company from the rest of my body and it became light and free and insubstantial. I heard somebody laugh and realized that it was me. I looked around. I wanted to see how things had changed in the longest time it had taken for me to inhale, exhale and sit back, resting my loose and exhausted shoulders against the wall behind me. Then I closed my eyes. I had to.

The last thing I saw was Georgie's face smiling over at me, her expression full of meaning and her blue eyes brimming with significance.

I heard slivers of conversation and the shrapnel of argument. Almost at once, I was consumed by the notion that those around me, the whole room, even Georgie and Maggie, were talking about me and pointing the finger in a way I hadn't experienced since I was twelve. At the same time, the world – my own, physical world – started to lurch alarmingly. I snapped my eyes open, except that the snapping seemed to take a very long time indeed. I hadn't eaten since lunch at twelve, so my stomach couldn't be churning, but it was. I tried to stand up, but my legs wanted to crumple and I needed to laugh in that tearful, hysterical way that made my chest tighten in panic and my palms begin to sweat.

Anyhow, after what seemed like hours, maybe even days, I felt Georgie on one side of me and Maggie on the other. They hauled me to my feet, staggered me out into the kitchen, over to the back door. I took in great gulps of air, but the smoke and soot suspended in the calm and frosty night made me want to retch. I felt the awful dizziness that meant I was going to pass out. Black spots darted across my eyes and a buzzing began in my ears. Above its noise I could hear myself moaning softly. Someone called Paul unfolded himself from a kitchen chair and I was put sitting on it. Someone else, and here I think I sensed Maggie's gentle palm, pressed on the back of my neck and my head descended towards my knees. I found myself admiring the black swirls on my new skirt. A glass of water found its way into my hands and by then I was able to sit up and sip. Little by little, I began to feel better. Georgie was smoking a cigarette, her eyes a startling navy in a wide, pale face.

Maggie shook her head at me. I noticed that her lips were beautifully defined, the scarlet lipstick glossy and sensual. 'I told you it would make you sick,' she said. Which was not quite what she had said, but never mind. I was grateful to her anyhow. And now, someone else again, Georgie, I think, was rubbing their hands up and down my back. Inside my head quietened and my stomach began to settle, retreating from my ribcage. Paul – he of the kitchen chair – handed me a rather dirty white cup with a teabag floating in scummy water. Once Maggie poured the milk in, though, it began to look better. She fished out the teabag by one protruding corner. 'Ouch,' she said, 'it's hot. Here, drink this.'

And I did. Hot, sweet tea. I felt comforted, happy even in the middle of my sickness. I felt as though I'd come home, that these people would look after me and wouldn't abandon me. It was as though a great expansiveness had just wound its arms around me. I had fallen in love with the whole world, and the whole world had fallen in love with me.

'You're looking much better now,' Georgie said, and smoothed my hair back from my forehead with one cool, competent hand. 'Think you'd better stick to the Guinness, though,' she whispered, bending low towards my ear so that I was the only one who could possibly hear her. Her grin was wicked, and I knew that she was remembering the night of our first meeting.

I didn't tell her that all that Guinness had ended up on the grasses of suburbia. I was in Dublin six now, much closer to the centre of things and much more in the midst of the action, the thick of life. It would have to be my secret. And after the party, we could all pretend that dope didn't suit me. Nobody would mind. All the more for those who wanted it. No force, no flatter, what the hell matter, as my mother used to say when we were children.

And anyhow, despite it all, I was content. My friends, my flat, my freedom and never mind the small embarrassments. And Paul was hovering. He had a nice face. No. The word 'nice' was banned. Georgie did not allow it. It was a nothing word, she used to argue, a sit-on-the-fence word, a lazy, useless kind of adjective. In the same way, she didn't allow 'I don't mind'. 'Decide!' she'd say. 'Stop hedging and say what you want!' I decided that Paul's face was both strong and angular with something familiar about it. I didn't know him. I was sure I had never laid eyes on him before – but wasn't that the whole point of a party, so that you could get to know the people you hadn't known before? My stomach settled, my vision cleared and finally, my head stopped racing in front of me. I turned to Paul and smiled.

'Thanks for the tea,' I said.

I watched as his whole face brightened. Even I could see that he wasn't able to take his eyes off me. I felt Maggie and Georgie begin to draw away, could sense that they had already returned to their party. My new-found sense of my own self was urgent and important. I could already feel the pull towards this – what – boy, man? This young man who knew nothing about me, about my past and all my family baggage. This tall and handsome man who took me as he found me. A little the worse for wear, perhaps, but still sexy and fashionable, at her ease around people like Georgie and Maggie. In short, someone who didn't really exist – or hadn't, up until then. Until *right* then, right at that moment.

'Look after her, Paul, you hear? Or you'll have us to deal with.' Georgie's drawl was clear again, crystal, just as she had been with the Eng. Lit. guy on the first day we'd met. The one she'd warned about wasps and autumn weather and getting stung.

'No problem,' I heard Paul say as he smiled down at me. 'More tea, Claire, or are you ready for a beer?'

I hesitated. 'I think I'll stick to tea, for now,' I said, 'if that's okay.'

'Why wouldn't it be okay?' His manner was easy, friendly. He took my cup and plugged in the kettle, and at the same time reached for one of the cold beers from the sink for himself. I liked the way he moved. I liked his long hands with their tapering fingers, his dark curly hair.

'My name's Paul, as you've probably gathered,' he said, the ring-pull on the can of Carlsberg suddenly hissing. 'I'm Maggie's brother.'

'Pleased to meet you,' I said. Now I knew why I'd found something familiar in his expression. It felt as though I knew him already, that Maggie linked us in a way that made each of us already intimate with the other. He grinned at my ridiculous formality. 'Sorry' I slapped my palm against my forehead and shook my head in disbelief. 'But I am pleased to meet you. You look like Maggie.' I hoped that that was the right thing to say.

Because I couldn't say any of the things that I was thinking. I was imagining myself lying beside Paul, his body strong and warm and close to mine. I was already falling for the long-limbed, practised air he had about him. Here was somebody alive, confident, *manly*. This was as far removed from Jamesie and his blunt, awkward fingers as it was possible to get. 'I'll be moving in with Maggie and Georgie in a week or so,' I added lamely.

He nodded. 'I know. In fact, I know all about you.' He jerked his head in the direction of the main party room. 'Maggie's told me you've all become thick as thieves. God help us men. A new force of nature. Something else to be reckoned with.'

I laughed. 'Well, yes, it seems that way.' I was beginning to feel completely recovered, apart from the delightful and uncomfortable hammering of my heart.

'Hope you know what you're letting yourself in for,' and he took a huge swig of beer. 'They're a pair of witches, those two, d'you know that?'

'Well, now there's three of us, so we can be wicked together, like the witches in *Macbeth*.'

'"When shall we three meet again?"' he declaimed, striking a dramatic pose: back of hand to top of forehead. 'Did it for my Leaving Cert. That's about the only bit I can remember.'

'"In thunder, lightning or in rain."' I said. I was aware that I was flirting madly now.

'Pure English?' he asked.

I shook my head. 'No – English and French. What about you?'

He grinned. 'Medicine. Though I don't know how anyone could ever want to be a patient of mine. I'm in third year. Maybe I'll get better.'

I knew that I was already thinking: third year. That's good. At least he's got a few more years to go. I was already feeling his loss, that gnawing anxiety that one day he'd walk away from me and I'd never get him back. On that night, I knew without knowing that here was someone I would always need, someone I'd never want to let go.

This is where I came in, I thought. This is how my life began: first Georgie, then Maggie. And now this. Paul and I were about to begin, too. I knew it, I could feel it. So many beginnings. So much that happened over and over and over again.

There was movement in the hallway. We both watched as the Midnight Cowboy pulled on a full-length army coat over his bare chest and underpants, opened the front door and lurched forward in his boots, disappearing down the garden path out into the cold night beyond.

Paul raised his can. 'Welcome to madness,' he said.

I poured milk into my cup and stirred the tea carefully. Then I threw away the teabag. It was all I could do to stop my hands from trembling.

Welcome, indeed.

To madness.

What I remember next is that the party room seemed to empty all at once. Paul and I were the only ones left that could loosely be called guests. We had stayed in the kitchen, and now we stood at the door, both of us observing the after-party slump in the living room. Georgie was half-asleep on the rickety sofa, while Danny sat on the floor between her feet with his head resting in her lap. I'd noticed that the more stoned he became, the more his physical presence seemed to deflate. Now, snoring gently, he looked pale and spent, somehow. Ordinary.

Paul nudged me to look over at Maggie. She was kneeling by the stereo, flicking through one of the cardboard boxes that contained her collection of vinyls. On the floor beside her was a half-finished glass of beer, flat and tired-looking, with white froth clinging to the sides.

'Watch her,' he said. 'You'd better get used to this if you're goin' to live with her.'

As though she'd just heard us, Maggie turned towards where we were standing and waved a psychedelic record sleeve in the air. I recognized it at once. 'This one's for you-hoo,' she called. My chest tightened.

Paul looked at me. 'She means you,' he said. 'I was never big into the Beatles. More a Stones man myself. Fancy a beer now? Or a glass of wine?'

'Yeah,' I said, 'why not. Wine, please. White, if there's any left.' Maybe if I could be alone for a moment I'd have the time to gather myself. I'd told Maggie I loved the Beatles, told her how John Lennon had saved my life, dying on December the eighth. He had lain spent and bleeding on a New York pavement, five years to the day after my mother abandoned us. My brand-new seventeen-year-old self had rejoiced. Not because he was dead, but because he gave me a reason to be sad, a reason I could live with. Now, I remember thinking, now I can mourn. I'll have all the companionship of loss, a worldwide community of grief. I won't have to do it on my own any more, won't have to confess my mother's treachery. When I weep, I weep for John Lennon and the end of innocence. My mother doesn't even have to come into it. Callous, I know, but that's how I felt.

I took the wine Paul offered me and drank half of it as quickly as I could. It was vile – warm and sickly sweet, but I didn't care. I'm lucky that alcohol doesn't take the pain away. I know it does for some people, but for me, it simply blurs it at the edges. Makes it sit around the heart a little more easily. Anyhow, it worked that night, just enough. That, and Paul's arm, warm around my shoulders. I leaned into him and he bent down and kissed me. *Sergeant Pepper's Lonely Hearts Club Band* belted out 'She's Leaving Home' and all the words came flooding back to me.

I listened as the Beatles sang about an ordinary Friday morning; I listened as their nameless young woman made her way towards her second-hand car salesman and the disaster that her life was about to become. And then I saw her, my mother, dancing around the kitchen in Ennistymon, her face flushed with pleasure, a tea-towel flung over one shoulder. I remembered feeling how incongruous the sight was even then, and I must have been only a small child. This woman didn't suit her surroundings, she didn't fit into her life. She was willowy, her red hair was wild and gorgeous and her hands were floury up to the elbows. Her body seemed strangled by an old-fashioned pinny, tying her down at neck and waist. I know that I was shocked when she abandoned us, but I don't think I was surprised.

I pulled back from Paul for just a moment. He looked at me, his green eyes questioning. I put my hand around his neck and pulled him towards me again. I'd made up my mind. I remember thinking that my Aunty Kate hadn't been surprised by my mother's departure, either. 'Helen must have had her reasons,' she'd told me again and again, in the early years after my mother left. 'My brother,' she'd once said, very dryly as she lit one untipped Craven A off the other, 'was never the most exciting of men.' As a twelve- or thirteen-year-old girl, I couldn't be sure of what she meant, and was too shy in those days to ask. But even then, I knew it had to have something to do with sex.

John and Paul's mournful tones sang goodbye goodbye as their girl tiptoed away from a life that had become too small for her. Not that my mother left *us* for a man from the motor trade. No. That was just another one of life's tired little jokes. My father *was* the man from the motor trade. Not the seedy salesman of the Beatles' song, but the town mechanic, complete with overalls, dirt under his fingernails and skin that smelt faintly of diesel, no matter how often he washed. Mother's sights were set higher.

I felt angry: could she not leave me alone? Tonight of all nights?

Paul squeezed my hand. 'You okay?' he asked, brushing my hair back from my eyes.

'Yeah,' I said, as softly as I could. He continued to stroke my face. All I wanted was for him to kiss me again. 'This record brings back a lot of memories.'

He nodded. 'It's John Lennon's anniversary. Did you know that?'

I smiled. I didn't want to tell him the whole sad history of my mother, my youth, my dubious moral genes. Not yet. 'I think I must have forgotten.'

'My sister,' he said, 'is a music nut. Watch her. She knows every word of every song of every album – well, of the ones she keeps playing, anyway. This could turn out to be a very long night. She's got Otis Redding and Marvin Gaye already lined up. Knowing her, things'll go downhill as the evening goes on. It'll be something like Gladys Knight and the Pips next.' He stood, and pulled me up after him. 'Come with me,' he said.

And it was as easy as that. I followed him into what would become my bedroom in a few days' time. The air was freezing, the bed sheetless, but it didn't matter. None of it mattered. Still fully dressed, we huddled under the blankets that the previous tenant had either forgotten or left behind. They were pretty threadbare, anyhow. At first, we clung to each other for warmth and then, as our bones defrosted, we played a game, whose rules I can no longer remember. What I do recall is how we stifled our laughter as we threw off one piece of clothing after the other. There was the delicious, intimate shock of skin, finally, on skin. And then there was the sudden ambush of guilt like a sledge-hammer, mixed with fear and longing and all the impossible terrors of pregnancy.

'Paul, I—'

He kissed me into silence. 'I'm not going to do anything you don't want me to do. Relax. We're not going to go all the way. Trust me.'

I tried to read his face in the darkness. 'It's my first time,' I whispered. I could feel him grin at that. I saw the contours of his face change as he brushed my hair back from my eyes.

'Oh, really?' he said. 'I'd never have known.'

I could feel myself blush and I was glad of the darkness. 'Don't tease me,' I said, my breath warm against his ear.

'You'll have to trust me.' He stayed very still, resting one hand on my face. 'We can make this really special, but you'll have to trust me.'

I had a sharp snap of memory. My Aunty Kate, standing in her kitchen, fag in one hand, glass of Rioja in the other. She'd been to Spain on holidays and had come back believing that red wine was very sophisticated. The fire crackled in the grate, late October winds howled in the chimney, forcing the smoke back down into the hazy kitchen. I remember how she shook her head in disbelief, heard her hiss at Mo, her best friend – whom she called Maureen only if she was very angry – 'For Christ's sake, Maureen, how many times do you have to be caught? You've got five kids already and they're all "trust mes". Brendan would say High Mass if it'd get you into bed. And you're expecting *again*?'

I can't remember how many seconds it took for me not to care about Kate, or Mo or any of them. To dismiss the village voices and the gossiped tales of ruined women and abandoned babies, all the backwoods horrors of what would happen to people like me, people who refused to know their place and obey their God.

'I trust you,' I said.

'Good girl.'

The first devil-may-care moment of my life. It was almost pure in its recklessness. I managed to brush it all aside: that here I was in bed with a medical student – a definite no-no for good girls from the country. Their reputation was legendary. They were known to be fast and fickle and dangerous. That I was trusting my whole future to someone I had known for only four or five hours. That I was being seduced by someone about to become a doctor. The irony was not lost on me, Mother, oh no. Not even then.

'You okay?' Paul's kisses paused for a moment. The liquid pleasure that we'd been swimming in for what seemed like hours was suspended gently around us. 'Happy?'

'Oh, yes,' I said, pulling him closer. I remember feeling that I would never be able to pull him close enough. 'Happy and happy and happy some more.'

It must have been some time around four in the morning. The whole house had grown silent. I couldn't even hear Marvin Gaye any more. Strangely, my bedroom seemed to have grown brighter and I remember that I took that as an omen. I know now of course that my eyes had just grown used to the dark. But I didn't know that at the time. I was thrilled that Paul and I could see each other, that our faces were real and warm rather than shapes shifting in and out of the shadows. I know that I had been thinking, *this is so nice* – and then stopped myself, remembering Georgie's rules about lazy adjectives, no matter what the . . .

But I never got to finish my thought. Suddenly, I gasped,

slammed from drowsy arousal, from sensual restfulness into full-on, wide-awake wonder. Paul's fingers were inside me again, but this time, they made me feel powerfully alert and alive in a way I had never been before.

'What are you doing to me?' I whispered, my heart hammering, my soul racing, my mind speeding. My new, eighteen-year-old body was caught in a clutch of delight I had never even imagined, could never begin to imagine. All my nerve endings seemed to flood, to flush with heat and feeling. I no longer knew myself.

Paul leaned forward and took one nipple between his teeth, rolling the other between thumb and forefinger until I thought I might be just about to faint.

'I think I've found the switch,' he said. 'That's what I'm doing to you. I've just turned you on. Sergeant Pepper would approve, don't you think?' And he slid away from me and bit me, gently. Ever so gently. 'I told you you could trust me, didn't I?'

But by that stage, I was beyond speech.

I had never known it could be so easy: such fluent matching of bodies, of tongues and hands and legs and arms. There had been no awkwardness here, no fumbling at my bra, no hot breath on the back of my neck and no painful surprises with teeth and jagged fingernails. No. Paul was all easy movement, his hands tender and sure. He had surprised me, that first night. I'd been prepared for pain, discomfort and at the very least some unpleasantness. But there was nothing. Nothing but pleasure.

Sleep had become impossible. I lay as the dawn light filtered through the grimy curtains that had once been tweed, although I couldn't make out what the original shade was supposed to have been. We lay like spoons, Paul's arm over my shoulder, his hand cupping one grateful breast. A small, white breast; long, square fingers; the dip and swell of our thighs under a blue blanket. I wished that my eye could be a camera.

I couldn't stop myself thinking of Kate, of how right she had been about so many things. There *is* life after whatever the shit is that happens to you. But this was beyond Rioja and Craven A, beyond the sad lace curtains of a country kitchen and self-knowledge that was hard won, hard bought. Now, I thought, at last: *now* I understand my mother. This was love. And I wanted it. No, more than that, I craved it and needed it and breathed it in like oxygen.

And yes, I wanted its madness, too, perhaps. Although I was aware of its clear and present dangers. Or thought I was.

But when has that ever stopped us?

2. Georgie

And now, outside, the day's blue light is already slanting away from my balcony. Volterra has just begun to recede into the evening, sliding towards night. A low-key murmur begins in the grasses below. How do I describe it? As shrill droning or musical chirping? I can't tell any more, because I've just decided to close my windows against the possibility of mosquitoes. I don't entirely trust the screens. Anyway, who cares? Even if the windows *were* open, I couldn't tell the difference between a cicada and a cricket. They tell me that one colonizes the afternoons, the other the evenings. But one bug is very much the same as another, in my eyes, even in Tuscany. Especially so if they bite.

Tuscany, indeed. I can hear Nora's voice even at this distance, can discern all the nuances, can imagine her eyes ablaze with her customary indignation. I can see the three of them this evening as they gather around the table. Maggie, Claire, Nora. My friends, my oldest friends; my very best friends in all the world. Nora will, of course, arrive first. Among her other uncanny instincts is how to arrive just in time to interrupt a conversation belonging to other people.

'Hope I'm not too early,' she'll say, with the little tinkling laugh she has perfected over the years, the one that makes me grit my teeth. 'Frank insisted on giving me a lift, although I said "no". But he said he didn't want me catching cold.' Neither Maggie nor Claire will exclaim over Frank's sweetness in this instance –

nor in any other – so Nora will just raise her innocent eyebrows and ask: 'Is everything okay?'

Claire will relent before Maggie, as she always does. Just as Maggie has always relented before I would. She, Claire that is, will offer her cheek to Nora and give her a warm, if brief, hug. Maggie will do the same.

'Of course everything is okay. Why shouldn't it be?' Claire will say.

But Maggie will have stayed silent, and Nora will have noticed. She'll look from Maggie to Claire then, with those glittering eyes, that penetrating gaze she has when she suspects that she's being kept on the outside. 'Maggie?'

Maggie will shrug and look down at her fingernails. I've told her often enough that such talons don't suit her, but Maggie has held firm on this. She will have her vanities, even if one or two of them are not very subtle ones. 'It's just that I haven't heard from Georgie,' she'll say. 'Neither has Claire. It's probably nothing, but I'm a little worried, that's all.'

There will be a silence. To smooth over it, Claire will ask Nora: 'Have *you* heard anything from her since the last time we met?' Knowing, of course, that such a thing was unheard of. Me? Contact Nora if I didn't have to? Or even if I did? Nora will have the grace to realize the impossible kindness of Claire's enquiry.

'No,' she'll say. 'No, I haven't,' in that tone of voice that implies she would discourage any such contact, even if it were forthcoming. Nora likes to take the high moral ground, and pitch her tent there.

'Well,' Claire will say, 'maybe she's just been delayed. Let's sit and chat for a while and just hope that she gets in touch. It's not like her.'

And so the three of them will take their glasses into Claire's new conservatory. They will sit among her fragrant plants and her tasteful water feature and her elegant, comfortable furniture. The conversation at first will be quiet, intimate in the ways of people who know each other a long time, where silences are valued as much as speech. Then Nora will get going, convinced that she is being deliberately kept in the dark. Sometimes she pouts, other times she lets her lip tremble.

'You're keeping something from me,' she'll say.

And Maggie and Claire will exchange one of those swift, intelligent glances: one of those in whose orbit I should be included – had I been there. Nora's neediness will have demanded a response. But I have noticed Claire's increasing ability to handle our Nora, the last few times we've met. She has always got away with saying more than I ever could, given her gentle tone. But there is a new firmness to her now, a willingness to stop Nora in her tracks if she threatens to disturb. Claire's latest mantra when anything displeases her is that 'life's too short'.

'Too short for what?' Maggie asked her the last time we met, when it was just the delight of the three of us.

'For putting up with crap,' Claire replied, with uncharacteristic vehemence. Maggie looked quickly over at me, but neither of us said anything. We both suspected that there was a new man in Claire's life, but she was being very tight-lipped about him. Knowing Claire, we knew it was useless to ask. She'd tell us when she wanted to, or when it was over.

Anyway, her new philosophy meant that Saint Nora was permitted to hand down fewer and fewer judgements on the nights when the four of us met. But I doubt whether that will be the case this time. I have no idea what Claire will say to appease Nora tonight. Particularly as Maggie's unease is bound to grow throughout the evening, and Nora is gimlet-eyed when it comes to the emotional upheavals of others, given that she has never experienced any herself. I feel badly about putting Maggie under the spotlight, but it can't be helped. And there is always the fact that Claire's is the most soothing of all our households; the best, most comforting space for such small dramas to be played out.

I remember the first time that we, Maggie and I, arrived at Claire's new home. We got there, by prior arrangement, an hour before the stated invitation. Nora had exhausted all of us the last time we'd met – even patient Maggie – so we'd agreed that an hour together, just the three of us, was needed in order to fortify ourselves for the night ahead. We'd done this from time to time before, particularly in the early days. I'd have taken it further and not included Nora at all, but the other two always voted me down. Something to do with Nora's loyalty and good-hearted-ness, and too many years and so much water under too many bridges. All clichés, as far as I was concerned, but I'd learned that that was one battle I was just not going to win.

That first night, Claire's new house was a revelation. I'd seen her talents before, when she worked with my father renovating his grubby flats all over Dublin. That was before they became known as 'apartments'. But this time, in her own home, she had surpassed herself. She had turned a cramped and smelly redbrick into something open and spacious and, perhaps this is a strange thing to say, almost reverent in its clever use of light and natural materials. It made 'House of the Month' in the classiest of Ire-land's interior design magazines at the time, whose name I no longer remember. Claire's new home had the sort of hushed inter-ior I had rarely come across – at least, not in Dublin. The walls were all cream, the stair carpet a pale, muted colour, the tall win-dows filled with white, gauzy muslin. I remember that I admired the curve of the new brushed metal handle on her front door, the matching numbers. I'd never seen anything quite like it before, was startled at its brash modernity against the serene Victorian lines of a solid front door. It took me a moment or two to decide that I liked it, liked it a lot.

'It's new to this country,' she said. 'I've just finished writing an article on door furniture for the *Irish Times* property supplement.'

I grinned at her. Claire was always up to date. Beyond up to date, in fact. She created a need for fashionable accessories where none had existed before. I have to say I admired her for it.

'Georgie, you wouldn't believe the range, these days,' she said and she rolled her eyes up to heaven.

Something else I liked about her. She rarely took such things seriously – or, at least, did not take her expertise in such things too seriously. Claire was well aware of all the infidelities of fashion. But her sense of style, her up-to-dateness, her knowledge of what was trendy and what was not, was never a show-off thing, never that compulsive *Look at all the things I know* or even, *Look at all the things I **have*** that bedevilled many an evening for me, once Nora got into her stride. Luckily for me on that occasion, because Nora hadn't yet arrived, the door furniture conversation never got a chance to develop. Just as well, or we'd all have been catapulted into a full-blown treatise on chrome polish, wipe-down surfaces, watching paint dry.

And so the three of them will sit together this evening, in my notable absence, talking of other things. Something or someone will eventually break the spell. A phone call, perhaps, or an inappropriate observation from Nora. Perhaps a sharp reproof from Maggie, my most 'loyal opposition' as I once called her, given that she both supports me and challenges me on so many fronts at once. Who knows what the catalyst will be? What I do know is that tonight will be one of those times that is both an ending and a beginning. My absence will quickly become a presence, something to be confronted, its bones picked over, its carcass finally buried before the funeral party moves on.

Imagining them all tonight, Dublin seems light years away, almost as though my old life there has never existed. Or perhaps, *has* existed but in some hazy universe that keeps a parallel course with the one we call the real world. My connections to it have already begun to fade. And that is the feeling I get every time I come to Tuscany: that it is possible to walk out of your life and not miss it. To become a whole other person with different needs and attitudes and ambitions.

Like Claire from Clare, who blossomed in the most unexpected ways once she left both home and family behind. I've never told her this, but the first time I saw her, I was stunned. It was Freshers' Week in Trinity and we met at the English Society stand in Front Square. Over a quarter of a century ago. We were both about to become Junior Freshmen and I can still recall my own, studied nonchalance. But Claire's fear was so transparent that I took pity on her. With that glorious red hair, pale skin and wide blue eyes, she looked like a saint about to be martyred. I remember that the Secretary of the English Society couldn't keep his eyes off her. He was a nerdy guy, as young people today would say, but on that occasion, his jaw dropped so much I had to warn him against catching flies. Or wasps, or some such other nonsense.

Boudicca, Paul used to call her, as I remember. After the flame-haired warrior queen, he said. I looked her up, Boudicca, that is, once I heard him make the comparison between her and Claire. 'Tall and terrifying', according to the Greek historian Dio Cassius; 'a great mass of red hair fell over her shoulders'. I could never have called Claire 'terrifying', not in the warlike way that Cassius meant. I don't think that Claire has ever hurt a fly – well, perhaps once, but that was without meaning to. But she did arouse strong emotions in all who came across her. Sometimes envy, sometimes resentment, often admiration. She had a fine eye for individual style even then. She wore flowing dresses, mostly in shades of green, huge gilded bangles and torc-like necklaces. But I don't think she ever realized the full, silent charge of her impact. Or if she did, she had a wonderful knack of hiding it.

I've seen her on late nights, or very early mornings; sleepy or tipsy, withdrawn or confiding, and she's always the same. Serene, composed, even Madonna-like: the very opposite of what we perceive glamour to be.

She told me once about the research she had done, once her hair grew back wild and curly and a deeper shade of red, after her mother abandoned her. That was always Claire's word: abandoned. Her mother had not 'left' or 'run off' or even simply 'disappeared' – she had always 'abandoned' her husband and children and I think that Paul was the only one able to stop that hurting.

'Red hair and pale skin are a kind of protection,' she told me on that occasion. 'It was an advantage to women, thousands and thousands of years ago. It meant that our skin made vitamin D from sunlight, so that we didn't get rickets.'

I must have looked at her blankly. I didn't get the point of what she was trying to tell me.

'Rickets caused pelvic deformations,' she said, clearly warming to her theme. I suspected Paul's medical knowledge was behind this enthusiasm. 'It caused women to die in childbirth. So,' she grinned, 'my ancestors had an advantage and that's how I get to be here. Paul says it means we'll have lots and lots of babies.'

I didn't point out to her back then that I was there, too, without the crowning glory of red hair. Nor did I comment on her obvious desire for 'lots and lots of babies' – that was something else we didn't have in common.

'And the last bit of the jigsaw,' she said, and this is something that *did* strike me even at the time as being significant, although I didn't know why, couldn't have explained its resonance, 'red-haired women can endure more pain than anyone else, even more than red-haired men. What do you think of that?'

Poor Claire. Maybe that's why in more recent times she's

always chosen such unsuitable partners: because she can stand the pain. Or perhaps it's why the unsuitable ones have been drawn to her. Do your worst, her cells seem to say. I can take it.

It's strange, though. Claire has always had the sort of physical charm that women envy but that men seem to find intimidating. When we were young, I used to think that when boys looked at Claire, they had to have thought that nobody so lovely could possibly be available. Surely she'd already been swept off her feet: claimed by some *man*, while they were mere boys. Except for Paul, of course. He was brave enough to capture her. When all that ended, though, Claire seemed to go to ground. She stayed resolutely single, using her looks as a shield to repel all those who would dare to approach her. Meanwhile, the more ordinary-looking among us got dates, invitations, letters from love-struck youths.

Over the years, our little group has doled out too many evenings of comfort to Claire: too many to be good for her, I mean. Nevertheless, she's not blameless either. None of us is. How can we be? As my mother used to say, 'It takes two to tango.' And that was the sum total of her wisdom regarding the war between the sexes. I was to interpret it as best I saw fit. And I have done so, finding it as satisfying a way as any of accepting, and allocating, responsibility for the things I do and for the things done to me. And Claire was definitely responsible for the tension and bad feeling that fractured our group friendship, almost beyond repair, some ten or eleven years ago. But that's a whole other story.

I close the shutters in my bedroom now, but leave the windows open. That way, the night air can filter through to me, but the possibilities of bug infestations are reduced. Never one to take chances, I plug in my mosquito repellent, always mindful of my first joyful, heedless visit here about four years ago. Back then, I had thrown open the shutters of my rented villa in an exultation of welcome, dizzy on champagne and stars and velvety darkness. The following morning saw me in the local pharmacy, my arms bitten and swollen, my face unrecognizable. I had thrown back the sheet during the night, too, apparently leaving just my feet and shins covered. I will simply not go there on the ferocity and the number of bites that had left me, as the grave signorina with her white coat and antiseptic air told me, '*completamente avvelenata*'. Completely toxic. I remember thinking that there were probably quite a few people who would agree with that characterization, but I wasn't up to even a weak stab at humour.

I take off my makeup, tone and moisturize my face, brush my teeth with my new electric toothbrush. I undress in the huge bathroom, the tub already filled with warm, scented water, and I light the candles that I dotted around everywhere on my last visit. Just before I step in, my new mobile beeps. I scroll down through the text message and smile, surprised at the potency of long-distance love.

I know that a full bath is an irresponsible luxury in a land that is short of water. But who cares? I shall allow myself this, as often as I like, until he arrives. Tomorrow, the brisk regime of early walks and purposeful activity will begin.

For now, though, all I want is to float, quietly, on the small ocean of possibility that my life is about to become.

Tomorrow will bring what it will.

3. *Maggie*

Georgie and Claire and I used to call her Helly, back then: short for Helicopter. I'm talking about Nora, of course. She'd always had this amazing instinct for where and when the rest of us might be meeting. And she'd just turn up. One day, she was hovering at the margins of our little group and the next, there she was, installed at the centre of things. Although, to be fair, her presence among us was partly due to me, too.

Helly-Nora was three years older than the rest of us. At our age now, that kind of a gap means nothing. But back when we were eighteen, it was like an entire generation. When I met her first, I thought she was mature and a bit more serious than we were, and I liked that. I thought of her as a welcome change from the noisy fun and silliness of number 12, Rathmines Road.

Helly and I – sorry, Nora and I – ended up in the same French conversation class during our first term. We were thrown together by both of us arriving late. I'd been standing outside debating whether to go in at all. I was still nervous of the academics, and I felt a complete fool that I'd mixed up the venue. Nora was even more flustered than I was.

'Is this Mademoiselle Ondart's seminar?' She looked hot and damp, her forehead was wrinkled and perspiration was gathering in little beads across her upper lip. I remember noticing the faint shadow of a moustache and wondering why on earth she didn't bleach it.

'Yeah,' I said, and stubbed out my cigarette. 'But she's already started and I don't want to barge in. It's kinda rude, isn't it?'

Her anxiety moved up a step. I could see it in her face. 'Oh, but we can't *not* go in. Not when it's a conversation class. Because afterwards there's no way to catch up on what we've missed.'

I hadn't thought about that. Or if I had, I didn't care. I was never the most conscientious of students. I made sure I did just enough to get by. I liked Spanish and French well enough, but fashion was my passion back then. It still is. Not everything has changed. And music, of course. Those were the places where I really lived my life. The rest was just so much window-dressing as far as I was concerned. I got a real buzz out of making my own clothes and I even used to cut my own patterns. I loved the whole ritual of the tailor's chalk, the tissue paper, the clackety-clack of the Singer sewing machine, and all the while there'd be music belting away in the background.

Tamla Motown, now that was my kind of stuff. Stevie Wonder, Martha Reeves and the Vandellas, Otis Redding. Jimmy Ruffin crying over broken hearts, Diana Ross yearning after lost love, Marvin Gaye and Tammi Terrell singing their hearts out about high mountains and low valleys and rivers that weren't wide enough. About there being nothing like true love, baby – hours and hours of doom and betrayal and misery. My brother Paul never stopped teasing me about my taste in music. But I've often asked myself, over the years, if something inside me *knew*. I mean, if there was some instinct already there, at work, making sure that I was prepared for the life that ended up being mine. I like that kind of speculation, particularly at a time like this, when it doesn't matter any more.

My college years were not where I shone the brightest. I managed only a pass degree, and my parents were a bit sniffy about that, but it didn't bother me. On the day I met Nora, I couldn't have cared less about Mademoiselle Ondart and her corner on disapproval. You know the type. Tiny and neat and full of Parisian superiorities. But it was obvious that Nora felt differently. I would have been just as happy to go and have a fag and a coffee in the Buttery, but she was already walking towards the door of the seminar room. She was determined to have what she felt she was entitled to.

'Let's go in together,' she urged. 'I'll apologize for both of us. Okay?'

'Okay.' Whatever. I followed her inside and we took the first available chairs. Unfortunately, they were the ones closest to Mademoiselle herself, so we had to walk the whole length of the room under her irritated gaze. She was just getting into her stride, with her photocopies from *Le Monde*. She waved at us, her ringed and braceleted hand saying: 'Just get on with it, girls.'

Nora's spoken French wasn't bad and she told me after the seminar that she'd gone to France for a couple of months once she finished her Leaving Cert. Then she'd gone on to work in London. Both of these things seemed exotic to me at the time. I'd never lived anywhere else but Killiney.

'So, where did you work when you lived in London?' I was curious. Georgie and I were already thinking about the summer, doing a little bit of planning ahead. The idea of a few months in a big city like London appealed to us. That was assuming I passed my exams and didn't have to come home early to repeat. But I knew that failure wasn't an option. Not for me, particularly after the nuclear holocaust that had followed Paul's Pre-Med exams. Although my parents had made no secret of the fact that they were happy to have got both of us, Paul and me, to the stage where they no longer had any responsibility for us, they still insisted on academic success. You might say that they held the door open for us as soon as they decently could, but we went through it on their terms.

I don't think that Paul ever wanted to be a doctor, but it was one way of getting our parents' attention. I mean, he *really* needed them to notice him. And when he failed Pre-Med, he had more of their attention than he knew what to do with. Don't they say that for some people, negative attention is better than none at all? That's how Paul was back then, I'm convinced of it. As for me, I voted with my feet as soon as I was able. For as long as I can remember, I'd always wanted to be somewhere else, anywhere at all, as long as it was away from my parents, particularly my mother. I got very tired of always feeling in the way.

I was a serious disappointment to the old pair, I know that. I was a bit of a wild teenager, I did my fair share of illegal substances, developed a Dublin accent, all the better to piss them off, and I hung around for a while with the sort of people that they didn't like. I kept Georgie from them, too, as much as I could. They knew of her existence, all right; they approved of her and her family, and that was another reason for keeping them apart. Georgie was still living in Killiney back then. It was before her father's transformation from 'builder' into 'developer' and her family's move to Ballsbridge when she and I were both barely fifteen. She changed schools then and I missed her.

From the time Georgie left the neighbourhood, I deliberately lived a 'fuck you' lifestyle. It was one way of putting distance between me and my parents, their gin and tonics, their bridge club, their almighty golf. Looking back, I was probably a bit inconsistent – not to mention a complete nightmare by the time I reached eighteen. I was happy enough to have them pay my fees for Trinity and give me my monthly allowance, though. I figured, well, they have it. So I might as well spend it.

Anyway, I can remember that first conversation I had with Nora as though it was yesterday. I remember how I waited, dying to hear her reply and expecting to get loads of information about London. I wanted to hear about fashion, about places to see, things to do. But she just leafed through her notebook, as if she was looking for the right answer among all her neatly written tables of vocabulary and handy phrases.

'Oh, I just worked in an office,' she said. 'I did some temping. It wasn't terribly exciting, really.'

Now that was far too vague for me. 'But London – what about London?' I persisted. 'Is it a great city to live in?'

'Yeah,' she said. 'If you like big cities. I don't, not really.'

And that was the end of that. I got nothing else out of her, either, the next time I tried, so I got the message and gave up. It didn't take long for me to find out that what had seemed like Nora's grown-upness was, in fact, a sort of detached wariness that made her expect the worst from everyone. I don't know why, but I was drawn to her vulnerability. She seemed more honest, more connected to reality than the rest of us. She spoke her mind, sometimes without thinking. There was something childlike about her, and she was kind. In those early days, she was also lonely and latched on to me, and by extension to Georgie and Claire. We didn't mind, Claire and I, most of the time, but Georgie resented her from the word go.

And that's how Helly the Helicopter was born. Georgie christened her, said that Nora hovered about the three of us and made the space around us thrum. It was, she said, as though Nora sucked the oxygen from the air and the strength from our limbs. Eventually, the rest of us would give up, gasping, ashamed of ourselves, and invite her to wherever it was we happened to be going. There was an element of truth in all that Georgie said. But still. Nora needed us and neither Claire nor I had any intention of turning her away. Georgie had her own way in far too many other things for us to give in on that.

She – Georgie – and I had a falling out over Nora once. It was the first serious row we'd ever had, and we've been glued together ever since we were four. We had our whole lives mapped out when we were fourteen. Share a flat, make the most of college, of freedom. Have wild parties and wilder boyfriends and maybe, eventually, each settle down somewhere close to the other.

'What were you thinking about, for fuck's sake?' Georgie was incandescent.

It was her birthday, right in the dog days of January. Now, I hadn't quite invited Helly, not directly, but she had prised information out of me about what we three were up to at the weekend. I'd left the details as vague as I could and just said that Georgie would be the one doing the inviting. Her birthday, her guests, that kind of thing. But Helly turned up anyway, bringing a gift and flowers and wearing one of her brightest smiles.

I'd never seen Georgie so angry. I knew I needed to apologize, and fast. 'I'm sorry – but she did kinda invite herself. I just let slip that it was happening, right? We can't tell her to go.'

We were in Georgie's bedroom. She had just slammed the door on the party in the living room. Her eyes blazed. 'Like fuck we can't.'

I knew that she'd had a row with Danny – I'd heard her on the phone earlier – but she hadn't told me that. I had to pretend not to know. Instead, she was trying to make me believe that her rage was entirely due to Helly. I let her have her moment.

'I *told* you I didn't want her here. Christ knows, I put up with her every other time, but not tonight, please, just not tonight.'

Her temper reminded me of primary school, of the time when she'd got us both into trouble. We could only have been five or six at the time, just starting, I think, in Senior Infants. We were sat at the red table, and Mrs McCarthy had arranged eight of us small girls in a circle with piles of coloured art paper, scissors and gum placed in front of us. Melissa McKee had been put sitting between us and Georgie got really mad. She got up and marched across the classroom to where Mrs McCarthy was just starting to settle the next group of girls at the yellow table.

She tugged at the astonished teacher's sleeve. 'Can me and Maggie sit together?'

'Maggie and I,' corrected Mrs McCarthy automatically, before she realized what was happening. 'Georgina!' she said, when she'd recovered. 'Please do not leave your seat without permission. Now sit down and I'll be over to you in a moment, once everybody here has what they need.'

But Georgie stood her ground. As patiently as any adult, she repeated her request. This time she added a 'please'. Mrs McCarthy was matronly, slow to anger most days, but Georgie must have hit a nerve. 'Georgina,' she began. But she never got to finish.

'Maggie and me need to sit together because Melissa McKee . . . smells . . . of . . . wee.' Clear as a bell. She'd even paused between each of the final words, so that they sounded more dramatic.

There was silence, followed by some nervous titters from the yellow table. Then all hell broke loose. Mrs McCarthy shouted at Georgie, Melissa burst into tears and Georgie refused to sit down. The upshot was that we were both sent to the Principal's office – a bit unfairly, I've always thought, because I'd had no idea that Georgie was going to include me in her rant. Although we had both agreed the day before that Melissa McKee did, indeed, smell of wee.

I think we each had to write a letter of apology to Melissa. How cruel children can be to each other. And it was that cruelty I remembered as Georgie stood there in her bedroom, now an eighteen-year-old woman, but basically doing exactly the same thing all over again. The memory of Melissa's pain was keen and I was not going to humiliate Helly. She didn't deserve it. I banked on the fact that Georgie's angers were usually short-lived.

'Remember Melissa McKee?' I said to her. 'You got me a

week's double spellings for that caper. Remember? *And* extra tables! Now it's payback time, right?'

I watched as Georgie tried to puzzle it out. I let her. And I enjoyed the moment, I must admit. Her face cleared and then she cracked up. 'Melissa McKee! I haven't thought of her in years! She smelt of wee!'

Soon we were clutching each other, helpless with laughter. Claire knocked on the door and called out 'Hurry up, both of ye – people are arriving and I can hardly say ye're off havin' a row.'

Georgie wiped away the tears, still erupting into hysterics every time she thought of poor little Melissa.

'All right, just this once. The Helicopter stays. But no more Melissa McKee, okay?'

'You have my solemn word,' I told her. 'The debt is now paid.' Still giggling, we joined the party. And Georgie got over it.

That's how our friendship has always been, right from the very beginning. Barter, blackmail from time to time, a bit of cajoling when necessary – usually done by me. In return, I got the most generous friend, the most loyal, the fiercest defender of my corner that I have ever had. And given who I married, I've needed it. I have so many reasons to be thankful for Georgie's friendship.

It's strange, but there's one occasion that I keep coming back to and yet it wasn't all that important, not in the scheme of things. I mean, there are lots of more significant events that we've shared, she and I, if you were looking in from the outside. But this one time with Ray sums up the way Georgie looked out for me. It's what the Trinity lecturers would call 'emblematic', I think. Anyway, I was heavily pregnant with Gillian at the time and Eve was only thirteen months old. I was constantly tired. Maybe weary is a better word. Whatever. All I know is, I wasn't able to get up off the sofa. I felt as though my bones were melting and the only thing I wanted to do was sleep.

Ray was not the greatest of husbands when I was pregnant. To be honest, he wasn't the greatest of husbands when I *wasn't* pregnant, either, but it's amazing the things you can learn to live with when you have to. On the evening in question, I knew that Ray would be late home. He'd just been named 'Salesman of the Year' again, and there was, naturally, a celebration in the pub after work. Ray was one of those people who could sell sand to the Arabs, snow to the Eskimos. He was born to it. He'd rung me earlier in the day, cock-a-hoop, to tell me of his success. I was pleased for him, of course I was, but I was also uneasy. Ray was drinking up a storm in those days and with me pregnant, it was as though all the controls were off. And I no longer had the energy to fight him.

'Don't wait up, Doll,' he said to me over the phone. That was his nickname for me whenever he was feeling particularly pleased with things. Not necessarily with me, just with things in general. 'Have yourself an early night: expect me when you see me.'

I tried to get a word in, tried to plead with him to go easy. I wasn't asking for abstinence, or anything like that, just moderation. But he had already hung up. Ray always had the happy knack of knowing what I was going to say next.

I have no clear idea of what happened as the evening wore on. I only have what Ray told me afterwards, because Georgie never volunteered anything about it. According to him, and he told me this in a tone that was half-amazed, half-enraged, Georgie had been in Searson's with her cousin, Roberta – Bobbie – when Ray and his work buddies arrived at around six o'clock. At his insistence, she and Bobbie stayed to have a drink to celebrate his award and then they left to go to dinner. Georgie came back at around half-past ten, on her own. By that stage, my guess is that the party had thinned out a lot, but Ray would never admit that. He insisted that there were still four or five left from his department, that of course he couldn't leave until they did.

I said nothing. I just calculated the effect of four and a half hours of steady drinking on an empty stomach. Ray would have been feeling no pain by then, and the party would have been kept going by him. I've seen it all before, too many times. His rationalizations and I are old, if mistrustful, friends by now.

I never asked who the other 'four or five' were, either. That was Ray's careful way of not telling me that at least one of them was a woman. Whatever. According to himself, this is what happened next: the barman came over and tapped him on the shoulder.

'Phone call for you in the bar, sir.'

'Really?' said Ray. He said he was surprised, although he can't have been, not totally. Searson's was a well-known drinking-haunt of his. He probably stumbled out to the phone, although that's not how he tells it, and there stood Georgie. No phone call, just Georgie. I can imagine her expression, and I can also imagine my husband's. Apparently, she got right to the point.

'My car's outside the door,' said Georgie. 'I'm giving you a lift home.'

He said he told her he wasn't ready. Then, according to him, she said, 'Party's over, Ray. We're leaving now.' There must be a bit in the middle that he hasn't told me. Maybe he weighed up the options of throwing a strop in a public place against the impact of being seen leaving with a woman like Georgie. Maybe the barman refused to serve him. Whatever. The way Ray likes to tell it, he waved to the others and left. He might even have pretended to be amused. He gets like that when he's been drinking: he either feels amused by everything or belligerent about everything. One way or the other, I suspect he was so shocked that he did what he was told.

Do I imagine a barman grinning in the background? Work colleagues annoyed, or maybe relieved, that he left so abruptly and never went back? Maybe, maybe not. All I know is that I awoke to the sound of Ray's key in the front door – he took a moment or two to get in – and the sight of Georgie's tail-lights disappearing down the street just as I reached the porch.

I rang her the next day. The least I wanted to do was acknowledge what she had done. And, of course, I was curious. But she gave nothing away when I thanked her.

'Not at all,' she said, with the ease of a practised liar. 'I was going your way anyway and I could see that Ray needed a lift.'

We never mentioned it again. We didn't need to. I felt ashamed, grateful and sorrowful all at once. Georgie's ferocious personality made me wonder, not for the first time, if she would have made a better man of Ray than I could. But as I've said, such speculation doesn't really matter any more. What might or might not have happened is no longer of any relevance. And anyway, who has the responsibility of making a better man of Ray other than Ray himself?

But back to Nora. Without Georgie, Nora relaxed and could be good company. Her warmth and willingness to please made up for so many other things, as far as Claire and I were concerned. Once Georgie was on the scene, though, it was an entirely different matter. Nora coiled into herself, became clingy and needy, like a spoilt child. She would appear before us, lumbering into our personal space over and over again with that uncertain look across her eyes. It made her look hunted. And it was that way she had of expecting to be unhappy that used to make Georgie mad as hell. It brought out the worst in her and made her cruel or, at the very least, dismissive.

Claire would take her over then. If she hadn't, I don't think I would have, particularly once the birthday party incident had happened. I'd be able to feel my resistance weaken, but somehow I just couldn't get my mouth around the words. Anyway, I knew that Claire would do it for me. And by staying silent, I showed my loyalty to Georgie and that pleased her. Cowardly, I know, but there you have it. Or maybe not so cowardly, after all. We are bound so closely together, she and I, in an endless tit for tat of 'I look out for you, you look out for me.' I'm not complaining, far from it. It's something that has given me comfort, ever since I was old enough to recognize friendship for what it is.

Claire would stand up, all brisk and business-like, and say something like: 'Time we were going, lads: party time. Come on, Nora, we'll get the beer.' Then she'd wave towards Georgie and me. 'Ye two go on ahead. We'll catch up with ye later.'

And Helly would shuffle off gratefully after her. Georgie would eff and blind for a few minutes and then shrug it off. She knew, too, that Claire would take care of Helly and make sure she kept her well out of Georgie's orbit. She also knew that, although Claire might have been very gentle, she was still the most capable of all of us in getting money out of Nora for her round, or her share of the party-packs of beer. There is a fine thread of steel to Claire's spine: I should know. I've measured its strength. It wasn't until so many years later that I understood Nora's chronic shortage of money, and how she felt about it.

Anyway, I remember being aware even at the time we all knew each other first, that Nora was an odd mix of desperation and disapproval. She managed to make Claire and me feel sorry for her *and* want to please her at the same time. I've never worked out how she managed to do that. Knowing Nora was my first introduction to the power of the victim, the force of the outsider who is determined to become an insider.

In March of our first year at Trinity, Nora turned twenty-one. For months, she talked about nothing else – well, apart from her boyfriend Frank, of course, but we were already used to that. Georgie, Claire and I were on edge as we waited for the party invitation. I didn't know how we could bear her clone-like sisters and brothers for a whole night. We'd have had to make polite conversation over one glass of shandy. There was only one of

Nora's family, Eimear, with any sort of spark. I could see that she and Nora were alike in ways, but the younger girl seemed to have escaped all of her eldest sister's anxieties. She was bright and pretty and funny – and I have good reason to remember. All the others were so dull we used to wonder where Eimear had come from. It used to give rise to some fairly outrageous speculation, after a few glasses of Pedrotti. And if there was a party, Frank would be there, too, of course, banging on endlessly about his shoe-shop, as though any of us was interested in the benefits of 'wide-fitting, specialist leather' and how high heels were 'bad for the spine'.

I got stuck with him one night in O'Neill's. I had him on one side and Nora on the other. It was not a winning combination. We were on a night out. I wanted to be amused, not stuck between two lovebirds. And Frank may have turned out to be one of nature's gentlemen – but back in those days, he still hadn't grown a sense of humour. Georgie was quick enough to spot the dangers of how the seating was panning out, and she needed to go to the Ladies all of a sudden.

I had to listen, for what seemed like hours, to the damage I was doing to my body while wearing my favourite stilettos. I even got diagrams to prove it. Reduced circulation of the blood. Achilles heel. Crushed metatarsals. Did I know that seventy-five per cent of the body weight landed on one small part of the sole of the foot? Did I realize the impact of concrete, the aches and pains caused by bad posture, the increased likelihood of arthritic knees? Well, no, I hadn't known all of that, but I still wasn't giving up my high heels. Nora was glowing throughout this conversation, her feet looking the size of canal barges. I could feel my level of tolerant affection towards her begin to slip. It irritated me that she lurked so deeply in Frank's shadow. It was as though she disappeared in his company, that he was her eyes, her voice, her likes and dislikes. That night, she was wearing some ugly navy suede walking shoes that may have distributed her weight evenly, but they sure as hell did nothing for her legs. Finally, we agreed that the occasional wearing of high heels was just about okay, but by then I was nearly asleep. There are times when I have wished for Georgie's ease with rudeness. I'd love to have it, just for the odd occasion, but I can't seem to manage it. That's why the prospect of another night in Frank's company at Nora's twenty-first became almost too much to bear. But as the day of the birthday approached, Nora changed her mind.

'I've decided I'm not having a party for my twenty-first after all,' she announced one evening, while Claire was making a huge dish of lasagne. I always loved it when it was her turn to cook. I hated when it was Georgie's. I'd swear that she did her worst in the hope that she might not be asked again. No such luck, neither on her part nor on ours. We had to endure her burnt offerings twice a week. Our flat was nothing if not democratic in the preparation of food. Being broke was also a great incentive to get creative with soya meat substitute, cheap brands of pasta, and the stretching power of tins of flavoured tomatoes. And Claire was always inventive: she did things with herbs and fresh garlic and tiny portions of mozzarella cheese that brought us from the lows of student stodge all the way to the dizzy heights of the delicious. She made food that looked and tasted a lot better than it should. I learned a lot from Claire in the kitchen department. I think the only one of us who didn't was Georgie. And that was because she didn't want to.

'Oh?' said Claire now. She looked up from her cheese sauce, fixing Nora with that under-the-hair quizzical gaze that we had all come to know. 'No party at all, then?'

I asked 'Why?' almost at the same time, covering Georgie's sigh of relief.

Nora shrugged. I thought she was being far too casual, not like her usual self at all. I began to smell a rat. 'Mammy and

Daddy are taking all of us out to dinner in the Gresham. They thought it would be nicer for us to celebrate as a family.'

I said nothing. I could see Georgie working up to a response.

'That's a good idea,' she said quickly and with a little too much enthusiasm.

'That will be lovely,' said Claire, her warmth genuine. 'A really special night. And we can have dinner here, too, to celebrate. Just the four of us, some day after your birthday. Or before it, if you'd like?'

'Why not tonight?' said Georgie at once. 'I'll get us some wine and we'll give you your present and make an evening of it. Nothing like spontaneity! What do you say, Nora?'

I could see Claire stifle a smile. She and I were both able to read Georgie's mind on occasions like this. Maybe we'd picked up the talent from her. Nora had already more or less invited herself to dinner that Saturday and I could see how Georgie's train of thought was working. I'm stuck with her anyway, so why not make a virtue out of necessity? Besides, the present was in Claire's bedroom, waiting to be wrapped. The three of us had already clubbed together and bought her some cookery books she'd been hinting about for months. I think we always knew she'd be the first one of us to get married. Nora wanted a kitchen of her own more than any other woman I've ever known. I have often envied her that simplicity.

And on the night in question, celebrate is what we did. Lasagne, yet another screw-top bottle of grotty Pedrotti, some candles, a roughly wrapped set of cookery books and hey presto: the evening settled into a party. To be fair, Nora was fine – perky, even, and appreciative of her present in a way that I found touching. Even Georgie left her alone; her comments all evening were neutral, rather than provocative. I think the relief of having no party to attend had something to do with her benign approach. Looking back, Nora probably already knew what was going to happen at her birthday celebration the following weekend, and so she was more at ease. But she wasn't about to give anything away, not that night. And I don't blame her.

'Thank Christ for that,' groaned Georgie as the evening came to an end. We waved and closed the door behind Helly. Her father had come to collect her, as he often did. I never quite got that, that over-the-top kind of protectiveness. It's not as though her family had broken apart in the way Claire's had done, or even silently imploded, like mine and Georgie's. Georgie's parents, as well as my own, never bothered all that much to hide their hurry to be shut of their children. Or child, as in Georgie's case.

But Nora's family was different. They were almost too ordinary, too buttoned-down and respectable. Nothing had ever fallen apart there, so why the paranoia about the eldest daughter? We never understood it, and it was one more thing for Georgie to grumble about. Anyway, we gave Helly a good send-off. She was thrilled to bits with the whole evening. And I was glad to have had the chance to make up for my earlier lack of enthusiasm about Frank.

'No party,' said Claire with a grin, as Georgie leaned her shoulder against the front door. It always needed a firm shove. 'There you go, Georgie, no party.'

Georgie turned around, her face bright. She led the way back into the kitchen, calling out to us: 'We'll just have to have one of our own!' And she grabbed the bottle of Pedrotti, holding on to it as though it was her dancing partner. She waltzed around the table and then stopped abruptly. 'A party of our own, with people we *invite*! On home ground! With no hovering and no helicopters!' She poured us all another glass of red wine and we toasted each other. And Helly, too, at Claire's and my insistence.

I also remember that we did, indeed, throw an impromptu party. We held off on inviting people until a few days beforehand, in case the Gresham went on fire or war was declared or Helly's parents changed their mind at the last minute. It was a very good party, keeping up the reputation of number 12, Rathmines Road. At least, I think it was good: Claire and Georgie told me it was. My memory of it is different – hazy but different. Given what I think Ray got up to.

Never mind that. I can still remember the look of triumph on Nora's face when she marched into the Buttery early on the following Monday morning, where we were having what passed for breakfast. It was one of those small habits that had developed in the flat over the months, one to help us ease our way into the start of each new week. We had breakfast together in the Buttery, just Georgie, Claire and me, before our ten o'clock lecture. It all started because Georgie refused to do any housework at the weekends. It was a matter of principle with her. Weekends were for fun, she said, not wasted on domestic stuff like groceries or cleaning bathrooms or changing beds. Instead, we did each of those things on different days during the week. We shopped on a Monday afternoon, the three of us together, lugging bags of cheap fruit and vegetables from Moore Street all the way to Rathmines Road. I hated shopping day. Naturally, on Sundays, the cupboard was always bare. There would be hardly enough food to scrape together a dinner, and so breakfast on a Monday just didn't happen. The few slices of grey sliced pan curled together at the bottom of the bread bin tempted nobody. Nora always had breakfast at home, of course, but she'd sometimes arrive before we finished and join us for a cup of tea.

'Look!' she blurted now, and managed to knock into the table, slopping coffee into our saucers.

'Ah, Jesus, Nora!' Georgie said. 'Will you for f . . .' I gave her a look and she trailed off. Instead, she grabbed a tissue from her pocket and tried to soak up the mess. She was feeling a little rough around the edges, as the party had spilled over well into Sunday. I was still wrapped up in a miserable combination of hangover and disappointment. I'd got to sleep at four on Sunday morning after a crying fest that had left my eyes swollen and my face blotchy. I refused to move from my bed for the rest of the day. The upshot was that I couldn't sleep on Sunday night. I spent all of it reading, losing myself in *Middlemarch*. I've always loved the happy, romantic endings of Victorian novels. I would gladly have stayed in bed on Monday as well, but Georgie hauled me out. I was drained, exhausted. And it had nothing to do with George Eliot. But I do remember thinking, sourly, how appropriate it was that a woman had to pretend to be a man so that she could make a name for herself. Was there ever a time when they didn't make the rules?

'He's not worth it,' Georgie kept saying, wrenching back the curtains, pulling the duvet off my bed. Talk about a whirlwind. 'Ray's a shit, Maggie, and you know it.'

I did indeed know it, but in those days I just didn't seem able to do anything about it. I think by then I believed that Ray was all I deserved. We'd met just before Christmas, at the twenty-first birthday party of Jean, a cousin of mine. He'd swept me off my feet. He made straight for me, the minute I arrived at the party. Came right up to me, put his hand under my elbow and steered me out on to the tiny dance-floor.

'And tell me, who are *you*?' he said, as though I was the most interesting person in the room, as though he'd been waiting for me all his life. Up until then, all the really good-looking men had gone for Georgie, although she tells a different story. And she's right, in one way. I had no problem getting dates, as she kept on pointing out. The thing was, though, nothing ever lasted. Two, maybe three dates and that was it. I must have scared men off, or something. I don't know.

That night at Jean's party I was well ready for someone to fall for me. And Ray did. I have no doubt about it. He never left my side, he was eager to know all about me, he couldn't do enough for me. I never asked myself what might have happened, in more ways than one, had Georgie been there. Mind you, for some days afterwards, I wasn't sure what all that attention on Ray's part had actually been about. He promised to call and then he didn't. And then, finally, after about a week, he did. But only after Jean had jogged his memory, I'm sure of it, although she's never admitted it.

I think I have since worked it out that Ray is one of those men who gets completely involved with the moment, the present tense and whoever happens to be on his arm. When he was with me, he was really *with* me. But when he wasn't, he forgot. Simple as that. The next novelty took over. I remember in psychology learning about 'object permanence' and being so fascinated by the idea that it stuck with me. Babies of a certain age, it seems, show great interest in a toy, as long as they can see it or hold it. Take it away from them, hide it, make it disappear and so does their interest. Produce it again, and the interest rekindles. That's precisely how Ray has behaved over the years. And of course, when you add remorse and promises and fighting and making up into the equation, you end up with a very powerful mix. If I had known then what I know now, might it have made any difference to the choices I made? Maybe, maybe not. Youth, as they say, is wasted on the young.

And so when we met for the second time, Ray and I, he managed to take me over once again, despite all my best intentions to be cool and savvy and self-contained. Things were always so intense when we were together. I think I felt that he was mine, all mine, even though he might not have been worth the having, had I been in another frame of mind. But back then Georgie had Danny, Claire had Paul and even Helly had her Frank. I was tired of being without someone special in my life. I was growing tired of always being just Maggie, rather than part of a couple.

Anyway, on the occasion of our first Helly-less party in Rathmines some four months after we'd met, Ray left with someone else. At least, I think that's what he did, because he simply vanished into the night. He disappeared without trace only to reappear later, his face anguished, his eyes full of the tears of repentance. And so, the pattern was set. Lorraine, a friend of Claire's, had gone missing as well, according to Georgie. It wasn't all that difficult to put two and two together. Claire and Paul had gone to bed earlier, so she'd missed out on this bit of gossip. I hadn't the heart, just then, to fill in the gaps. Not yet. And that morning in the Buttery, Claire was looking bright and rested. And beautiful, of course. She was always the best behaved of the three of us at parties – except later on, when it came to men. Once Paul was no longer on the scene. But on that morning, Helly's face shone brighter even than hers.

'Look!' said Nora, for the second time. She sounded annoyed at our lack of reaction. And look we did. There, on the third finger of Helly's slightly pudgy left hand, was a ring, a diamond ring of respectable size and sparkle. I think that Georgie and I looked at it stupidly, not quite getting it. Claire copped on at once, as usual, saving all of us.

'Hel – Nora! Congratulations! Aren't you the dark horse! Tell us, please! Sit down, tell us everything!'

We already knew far too much about Frank, of course we did. More than we could possibly have wanted. 'Too much information' is what young people say. The phrase hadn't been invented back then. But I know what it means. Tales of 'my Frank' used to make Georgie groan, and she would leave the room once Nora began. As I've said, I've often longed for her ease with rudeness. But Nora was one of those people that I believe didn't notice any of the insults that headed in her direction. She was swaddled from head to toe in something that protected her. Maybe all that eagerness and all that pride about your own future has the ability to do that. I don't know. All I do know is that she never once noticed anything that could be called an offence. Victims can't afford to, I suppose.

Now she was smiling, her round face pink and glowing. 'Frank asked me to marry him on Saturday night!'

'And did you?' Georgie drawled.

I jumped in. 'That's great news, Nora! Congratulations! What a lovely ring!'

I stamped on Georgie's toe. It can't have hurt because she was wearing boots. But it did the trick. She sat up straighter, glared at me, and reached out her hand to hold Nora's. She did a half-decent imitation of enthusiasm. Nora's plain, open face was a picture of pure happiness. Why would anybody want to rain on that parade?

She was nodding away in delight. 'I didn't know, but Frank asked my father's permission last week. So Mammy and Daddy knew, of course, but I didn't. It was such a surprise!'

Claire was smiling broadly. 'And did he go down on one knee?'

Nora nodded again. 'Yes, and he gave me twelve long-stemmed red roses, too. And then we went to the Gresham and the meal was wonderful and we all stayed up late and I'm just so happy.'

I could see Georgie's expression: 'All the stereotypes in place, then.' I was thinking pretty much the same thing myself. I did have the grace to feel ashamed, though. And once the shame receded, I had the first stirrings of what I now know to be bitterness. Watching Nora glow like that made the ache I'd felt since Saturday night all the more intense. Ray was my first serious boyfriend and I suppose I didn't know what to expect, although something inside me warned me that so much pain wasn't normal. But then again, how do you know what's normal when you have no experience of normality? I should have listened to myself that day, though, listened to my own intuition. In all the time we had been together, Ray had not performed one single thoughtful or unselfish act. I mean, I see that now, but of course I didn't see it then. But part of me must have seen *something*, otherwise why the sudden lump in my throat, the sharp stab to the heart that made me realize that I would never be as happy as Nora, not as long as Ray was in my life?

'Sit down, Nora,' I said then. 'Would you like me to get you a cup of tea? A sticky bun to celebrate?'

'I'd love just a cup of tea, thanks.'

I stood up and took her hand and examined the ring all over again. 'It's a really beautiful ring, Nora, and Frank's a lucky man. I wish you both years and years of happiness.' And I walked off towards the self-service counters. I could feel Georgie's eyes on my back, but I didn't care. Tears stung me and I was glad of the chance to walk away.

And that was the end of Trinity for Nora, as I think we all suspected it would be. The wedding preparations, the house, the garden – she didn't have a minute, she said. She sat her exams in May, but then dropped out. Nothing that Georgie or Claire or I said was enough to make her change her mind. I think we were the ones who persuaded her to do her exams at least – her parents seemed not to care. I was surprised at that. I mean, they'd nearly suffocated her with protectiveness up until then. Georgie said that they were 'possessed of an unseemly eagerness' to have their daughter off their hands. She was reading George Gissing at the time, so Claire and I had to put up with a spate of stilted nineteenth-century language until she got it out of her system.

Frank wanted a woman at home, Helly told us. It was the right place to be, for a couple who planned on having dozens of children. Frank was older than she was, she kept telling us, and didn't want to wait.

'It's just,' she said, 'that we want to start a family straight away, once we're married. After all, Frank is thirty.'

'Does that mean,' asked Georgie, 'that you'll start trying now? After all, the wedding is only four months away. What difference would it make?'

Nora looked so upset that Claire and I had to turn away. We made sure to look busy with our rucksacks and packets of cigarettes. We rummaged around for matches and lighters. It was late May and we were sat together in O'Neill's, celebrating the last exam of first year.

'Of course not,' Nora said. She sounded indignant. 'Frank doesn't believe in sex before marriage.'

'And what about you?' asked Claire softly. 'What do you believe in?'

Helly blushed at Claire's question. She looked down at her bitten fingernails and twisted her engagement ring as she did so. I don't know why, but I felt sad for her just then. I felt as though there was something she wasn't telling, and I felt it strongly between us on that afternoon. But whatever it was, she was giving nothing away.

'Of course not,' she said again. But her lower lip trembled. 'I have more respect for myself than that.' And then she looked right at Claire.

Georgie and I glanced at one another but it was Claire who changed the subject. I thought Nora's words had stung. There was just the tiniest flicker across Claire's eyes to show that she had registered Nora's remark. Respect? I remember thinking. What has respect got to do with anything? She and Paul were still an item at that stage. They used to disappear into Claire's room on a Friday night and not come out till Sunday, most weekends. Well, apart from the occasional searches for food and bottles of wine. Georgie used to roll her eyes at the sounds of muffled laughter coming from the bedroom. We'd turn up the music when the laughter stopped and the cries became more, well . . . private. They really loved one another, those two. By that stage, too, Claire and I had become good friends. I'd stopped thinking of her as a threat. I was glad for Paul, too. I hadn't liked any of his previous girlfriends. Didn't think any of them were good enough.

I still don't know what possessed him to do what he did. All I know is, Claire was never the same afterwards. I still feel badly about that, that she felt she couldn't talk to me, because he was my big brother. She knew how close we were. She murmured something once about divided loyalties and families and blood being thicker than water. When I tried to say no, that that wasn't how it had to be between us, she silenced me with one of her clear, blue-eyed looks: half fire, half ice. On that afternoon in O'Neill's, she looked at Nora in the same way, but it was wasted on her. I admired Claire for her coolness. She no longer showed any trace of annoyance at the fact that someone who was supposed to be her friend had all but called her a slut.

'Well, as long as you're comfortable with whatever you've decided,' she said to Helly. 'Each to their own.' She drained her glass. 'And now it's your round, Georgie. Mine's a *glass* of Guinness, this time. Don't go wasting another pint on me.'

Claire and I spent one whole afternoon together the following September, a couple of weeks before Nora and Frank got married. It was unusual for there to be just the two of us, but Georgie was off doing her repeats. Failing her first-year exams had shocked her – shocked all of us. She was cranky and tired all the time, no fun at all. It was a relief when she headed off at half-past eight each morning. I was just back from London. I'd have stayed a lot longer only for Nora and Frank's wedding. I loved London, loved the feeling that nobody knew me there. Georgie liked it too, but not as much as I did. I think she was relieved to come back in August to study for her exams. In a funny way, I think she found that London was too big for her. Georgie has always liked to be the big fish in a small pond. That's not a criticism, by the way. That's just how she is and she's very good at it.

Me, I loved the spread-outness of the city, the different kinds of people, the whole feeling that London was kind of an extended village, made up of lots of smaller villages all strung together. I spent every free minute in Carnaby Street and Petticoat Lane, rummaging in the stalls for bargains. And I got them, too, by the ton. I couldn't believe the things I was able to pick up for half-nothing. Georgie and I stayed in a hostel in central London and our caretaker was a woman in her sixties. She used to sit in the evenings in her poky little office and knit and crochet, probably to pass the time. I got chatting to her one day and admired some of the stuff that she'd made. One thing led to another and she ended up lending me a sewing machine. Once Georgie left, I spent all my spare time in my room, altering my weekend bargains and having the time of my life.

During the day I did two jobs, one as a waitress in a restaurant called Galliano's, which was an upmarket caff with delusions of grandeur. Then I worked as a barmaid in the Frog and Nightgown in Crouch End. I've never understood the names that the English give their pubs. Anyway, I loathed both jobs with a passion. I hid it well, though, and earned a small fortune in tips. I think it was that summer that decided me, one way or the other, that earning my living would have to be somehow centred on clothes. I missed the range of markets when I came back to Dublin and almost got to resent Helly's wedding for pulling me back home before I was ready.

Anyway, the afternoon that Claire and I spent together was a typical one for early September. The weather is often better than in the summer. Or what's supposed to be summer in Ireland. We were lounging on the patio in hazy sunshine and she opened a bottle of wine. Claire had persuaded Georgie's dad to upgrade our flat. She'd even stayed in Dublin most of that summer to supervise the work. That was the start of Claire's passion for design and she was really good at it. She'd showered our landlord with plans and schemes and costings that surprised and impressed even us. She impressed him, too, and he offered her a job on the spot. He had lots of renovation projects going on all over Dublin. The man was loaded. He just couldn't seem to get it wrong, old man White. Everything he touched turned to gold. I remember how Claire had jumped at his offer, even though she'd seemed to be hell-bent earlier in the year on coming to London with Georgie and me. But whatever Georgie's dad lured her with had been too good, and so she stayed put, apart from the occasional long weekend with us, sneaking into our room in the hostel and sleeping on the floor. And of course, there was Paul, who stayed in Dublin that summer as well, another reason to stay close to home.

I remember thinking that maybe things weren't going too well between them and that Claire had stayed for the summer to put things right. Maybe she was trying to keep on fixing things. As you do. At least, that's what I believed at the time. There was no way I'd have asked her, though. We had an unspoken agreement that what happened between her and Paul was private, off limits. It would have made my life too difficult, had I been in the middle, as the sister and the friend. And, even though Paul and I had always shared most things, I would never have pried into his relationship with Claire, for the same reason. I think he understood that well enough.

But it meant that I missed him in a way I wasn't prepared to admit, not then. I remember thinking how much easier it would have been if he had fallen in love with somebody I could like that wasn't already my friend. My own problems with Ray complicated things even more. It was very hard watching the progress of the perfect relationship while I was often so unhappy with my own.

One practical benefit, though, for all of us in her staying in Dublin that summer was that we had a patio and a deck and a built-in barbecue long before other people like to think that they were invented.

'Well?' she was saying, as she tested the varnish on her well-manicured toenails. 'What do you make of Frank, then? Seriously, now. There's no Georgie here to be smart-arsed.'

I sipped while I pretended to consider my reply. 'Mmm,' I said. 'Well, Nora likes him and they suit each other, right? He's got the steady job, working in the family business and the pension is sorted. I think he'll do her just fine.' And I drained my glass.

Claire refilled it at once. 'Much activity between the sheets, do you think?' Her expression was demure, all downcast eyes and sweeping fringe – a carbon copy of the Princess Di look. Shy Di, as the papers loved calling her. But it was more than that. I remember feeling that there was a frailty to Claire that summer that hadn't been there before. And she'd had her hair cut, out of the blue. That was unusual in a household where everything was discussed, from men to money and what colour nail-varnish to wear. Georgie and I protested at the loss of all those voluptuous curls, but Claire had only shrugged.

'Time for a change, don't ye think?'

No, we didn't, and I'll bet Paul didn't, either. But I didn't dare ask.

Now I pretended to splutter at her curiosity about Helly and Frank's sex life. 'Claire! This is Nora we're talking about. Don't you remember that she and Frank don't believe in sex before marriage?'

Claire looked disbelieving.

'You don't remember? The day we finished our exams? She told us.' I decided I wouldn't mention 'respect' and how Claire herself had reacted to what Helly said. But I think she remembered. She went quiet.

'And you think it was the truth?'

'Absolutely,' I said. I visualized Frank, his thin wrists and thinner hair. 'Absolutely,' I said again, even more convinced. And then I felt ashamed of myself for thinking that sex should only be for the young and beautiful. Like us.

She ran her index finger down the stem of her glass and caught the few drops of Sauvignon Blanc that had escaped. When she spoke again, she seemed thoughtful. 'Oh, I don't know,' she said. 'I'm sure her little sojourn in London a few years back must have opened her eyes to a thing or two?'

I shook my head. 'No,' I said. 'There were no adventures. She didn't even like London. She told me so. She stayed at home with some aunt-in-law, or some shite like that, the whole time she was there. Helly's not one to take risks. I know her. Trust me.'

Claire sighed. 'Well, the only thing we can hope for is that Frank isn't another blunderer.' That was a great word of Claire's: blunderer. Her face brightened for a moment. 'Hey – didn't he say he'd fallen in love with Nora's ankles, when she went into the shop to buy shoes?'

I nodded. 'That's the official version.'

'Well, then, Maggie, me dear,' and she nodded and topped up our glasses again, 'he can't be all bad. A man who falls in love with a woman's ankles can't be all cardigan and slippers.'

Who knows? I hope she was right. Particularly when I think of Ray, who promised so much and delivered so little. Who let me down in all the ways that counted: fidelity, friendship, keeping his promises. By then, I could see Frank's devotion to Nora, and I was honest enough with myself, even at the time, to know that I envied it.

Last night I was rummaging through some old boxes that have sat at the bottom of my wardrobe for years and I came across the photos of Frank and Nora's wedding. Now I know that I've been crying at the drop of a hat these days, but those old photos finished me off. Twenty-five years. What struck me about them most was how *unprepared* we all looked. Not innocent exactly, nor even foolish: just completely unprepared for the fact that life is a string of random disasters and occasional happinesses held together by – if you're lucky – the cement of friendship and the glue of family. Back then, though, we all believed that there was a caring, moral order to the universe: you just had to find it. And being good, playing by the rules and treating everybody fairly meant that the caring universe came to you. You'd be saved from sickness, death, betrayal. Well, bollocks to all that. But it was that *belief* in love and justice and fair play that lit up all our young faces. Lit us up in dozens of faded photographs, all celebrating the bride and groom.

Nora and Frank's wedding reception was held in Portmarnock, in what was at the time one of the poshest venues on the Northside: the Country Club. Claire suffered the horrors as she read the menu. Prawn cocktail Marie Rose, roast turkey and honey-glazed ham, Black Forest gateau. And then the band. Oh my God, the band.

'Is this the *live* band?' Georgie whispered. 'How can you *tell*?'

Claire was speechless as the four young spangled men on stage murdered their instruments and shrilled us into silence with feedback. We all laughed like drains. I often think now that Frank and Nora's wedding may well have been the most unsophisticated of the three that took place within our small group: but it ended up being the most enduring marriage of all.

Ray and I were in the middle of a row that day. No surprises there, then. I had been embarrassed and upset at his . . . let's call it his over-friendly behaviour towards one of the bridesmaids. Nora's sister Eimear, for God's sake, not yet seventeen. How much of a cliché can one man bear to become? Afraid he would do a 'Godfather' on me, I followed him outside as he followed her and then he accused me of not trusting him. Heigh ho. I made that bed, yes indeed, and I've lain on it for over twenty years.

On her wedding day, Nora was the picture of innocence. Despite the makeup, her face still managed to look scrubbed and shiny. Her dress was white, of course. It was frothy, fussy, much too feminine for her clunky frame. I heard Claire sigh as we turned to watch Helly walk down the aisle on her father's arm. She nudged me and whispered: 'Wrong! All wrong! I steered her gently in the direction of the sleek, the tailored, the forgiving! And just *look* at what she chose: she looks like a slice of Pavlova.'

But despite her awkwardness, her crooked tiara and a wildly overgrown wedding bouquet, hopelessly out of keeping with her outfit, Nora looked the picture of pure and certain happiness. The photographs prove it. A honeymoon in Gran Canaria, a house in the suburbs and a pre-planned, already packaged Christmas in Tipperary with her in-laws. Georgie declared that Nora's citizenship of Stepford was now complete. And, of course, she returned from her honeymoon pregnant.

And what did this wedding do to the rest of us? Hard to pin it down, really. Except that I believe such a momentous step made all of us think. I mean about our relationships, our lives and what we wanted from them. I know I doubted that Ray and I could have a future. I felt a wave of certainty about our uncertainty together, right in the middle of the wedding ceremony as I watched the tenderness of Frank's expression when he put the ring on Helly's finger. We could hear how his voice shook and how he got some of the words mixed up. He joked afterwards that that was his way of getting out of the marriage if things didn't work out.

'Got the vows wrong, your Honour – contract can't be valid.'

He even raised the ghost of a smile on Helly's father's lips and that was some trick. I think we were all surprised at how witty his speech was that day. And he looked exactly like what he was. An ordinary man delighted that life had given him what he'd always wanted.

Paul and Claire, on the other hand, were on the verge of their split. I can still remember Claire's face at the end of the evening, when I ran into her in the Ladies. I had never seen her look like that.

'What is it?' I asked her. She was ashen. Our eyes met in the big mirror above the handbasin. She was very carefully repairing mascara.

'Nothing. I'm okay.'

'Claire! I'm your friend, for fuck's sake! Don't tell me there's nothing wrong! What's going on? Has something happened?'

She turned to me and said: 'I can't talk to you about this, Maggie, I just can't. So don't ask me.' And she leaned towards the mirror again.

Then I knew. 'It's Paul, isn't it? Something's happened between you and Paul. Tell me.'

She shook her head. 'Ask Paul to tell you. Blood's thicker than water.' She snapped closed her silk evening bag, the one I'd brought her back from London, and then she walked away.

The next part of the evening is a bit of a blur. Someone's uncle had been persuaded to sing, and once he got a hold of the microphone, there was no way he was letting go. I could hear the strains of *'An' goin' to a weddin' is the makin's of another . . . Oh dear me, how would it be if I died an aul' maid in the gaaaaaaarret?'* Nobody could stop him. Irish weddings in the eighties could be really tacky. And this was fast getting to be one of them. Nora's father tried to take the microphone away from Uncle whatever-his-name-was, but even he had no luck.

I couldn't see Claire in the crowd and had to listen to the bandleader call on Aunty Mary or Uncle Joe or whoever, to come on up and sing a song. And still the uncle on stage kept going '. . . *If I died an aul' maid in the gaaaaaaarret?'* I wanted to kick something.

'None of your business, Mags,' Paul said to me when I cornered him later on. I must admit that he looked only marginally less devastated than she did.

'But you *love* her,' I hissed in his ear. The band was deafening. 'I know you do. The two of you are great together. Why are you throwing it all away?'

He looked at me. 'It's over.' Then he shook his head. 'There are some things that can't be fixed, and there's no point in trying.'

Fixed? I remember asking myself. What could be broken between these two? They were the perfect couple. If it was us, me and Ray, *then* I could understand. I didn't know what kept me going back to him for more. The 'hook of hope', isn't that what the psychologists call it? The belief that *this* time, he means what he says.

I got no more out of Paul. Georgie and I talked about it afterwards. She could see how upset I was. And then even she dried up.

'Claire has asked me not to talk about it,' she said, when I asked her what was going on.

'Georgie, this is me, Maggie. Your best friend, remember? Or is there something here I'm missing?'

She shook her head and sighed. 'Of course not. Claire doesn't want the three of us to fall out over it.'

I looked at her. I was speechless.

She put her cup down. 'Truth?' she asked.

I nodded.

She leaned towards me and spoke quietly. 'Her heart is broken, Maggie. I don't think she can bear to talk about it. She refuses to tell me anything. We have to leave her alone. *You* have to leave her alone.'

And so I did. But that doesn't mean I got over it.

Nora and Frank's wedding was not 'the makin's of another', quite the opposite, in fact. While Helly lumbered off, snowed under with confetti and good wishes, Claire took herself home by taxi, so quietly that no one noticed she was gone. Except me. I saw her go. And she saw me, too. She looked back at me over her shoulder as she climbed into the back seat. There was sadness written all over her face and something else, too. Something I didn't recognize until years later. And by then, so many things were too late.

Shortly afterwards, I left. The heart had gone out of things for me. I couldn't find Ray, so I headed home on my own, my patience exhausted. True to form, he came crawling back the next day. He cried, his face white and remorseful. And I took him back, of course I did. It *would* be different, he promised. It *would*.

It would and it would and it would.

And Georgie?

She and Danny had danced all evening – but only the slow sets. They kept disappearing outside, and returning with shining eyes and broad grins. I knew what they were getting up to. Danny was a serious dope-head in those days. I suppose you could say he was serving his apprenticeship. I've never been sure why Georgie put up with that. She dabbled, but she never used like Danny did. I had the feeling even then that she was marking time with Danny. And that time was limited.

Less than two weeks later, term began. Into our second year, we were now Senior Freshmen. Georgie had passed her repeats with flying colours: she got herself a First. I was glad for her. Failure did not come easily to her. Her results were the excuse for some serious celebration. We still kept on the flat at number 12, but something among us had shifted. Weekends were different, Claire was different. Even Georgie was different. Her First seemed to fire up all her ambitions. She spent longer and longer days in the library. I was happy enough to take refuge in my sewing machine on the nights when she wasn't home. And there was always Ray. Astonishingly, I missed Helly during that second year. It's amazing the things familiarity will do to you.

I've put Nora's wedding photos, along with my own, back where they belong – at the top of the wardrobe this time, pushed towards the back behind the hat boxes. It really is the strangest thing, to see yourself from the point of view of the completely different person you can become over the years. When I see myself now, I no longer see myself, if you know what I mean. The young 'Maggie' and the forty-something Maggie are not even distantly related. 'Maggie' no longer exists.

At least she hasn't, up until now. Not for the longest time. But I can feel her presence. I'm beginning to welcome her back, the longer all of this goes on. Claire told me once about shedding her skin when she came to Dublin first, about the transformation of rural innocent into urban sophisticate. I like the image. Snaking along, leaving a life discarded. And I like that feeling of struggling out of a carapace, being born again as something new.

Breathing other air.

Wearing other skin.

4. *Georgie*

So. It is good to be home.

Everything around me here gives me pleasure. I don't know why I keep forgetting just how much. It's as though each visit is coloured like Tuscan pottery: vibrant and rich and completely right while in its own surroundings, but garish and tawdry under Irish skies. The time in between visits foments uncertainty, I have discovered. It's as though I suspect that with each return trip I'll be disappointed. That this time, the light will have dimmed, the glory dissipated. But once I get here, all that anxiety leaks away. My spirits begin to soar at the first sharp smell of cologne and black tobacco, at the wall of heat outside Peretola airport, even at the chaos of the car rental desks.

Yesterday, I didn't mind standing in line, waiting my turn. Instead, I people-watched. Under normal circumstances, I find rubbing elbows like this with the hoi-polloi distasteful. Maggie has called me an incurable snob. I make no apologies. But yesterday afternoon was – as were so many other things – definably different. Even though it was still months away from high season, the airport was swarming with anxious elderly Americans, imperious Brits, a motley crew of backpackers: a whole melting-pot of nationalities. As I've said, I am neither a patient nor an observant traveller, but for once the multitudes afforded me endless fascination. It was as though I were watching the world gain an added dimension, a consciousness of being poised on the cusp of

84

change. I realized even as I thought it how ridiculous that was: how insignificant, in the grand scheme of things, were the events of my personal universe. Nevertheless, I was seeing the people around me in sharp relief, their faces arresting, all the possible secrets of their small lives compelling in a way they had never seemed to be before. Even the woman at the Hertz desk, whose badge proclaimed her to be Patrizia, was of interest to me. No longer young, her makeup was heavy but impeccable, the eyes dark with defiantly spiky lashes. Her lips were outlined in what looked like black pencil, filled in with scarlet gloss. Just for a moment, I was reminded of Maggie. But Maggie would never wear such obvious, in-your-face lipliner – hers would be infinitely more subtle, a much better match. And neither would she wear such an expression of inhospitable boredom.

I greeted her – Patrizia, that is – pleasantly. My Italian isn't up to much, but I have to say I find Italians prefer the odd linguistic stumble to being shouted at. I have often watched their faces cloud over as yet another tourist behaves as though increasing the volume can make up for not speaking the language. So.

'Buona sera, signorina,' I said. And I slid my driver's licence towards her. 'Mi chiamo Georgina White.' Then I placed my passport in front of her, open at the photograph page. Ludicrous though that photo is, six years on. 'Ho prenotato un automóbile—'

But she wouldn't allow me go any further. 'For how many days?' she asked, her voice heavily accented, but the English fluid, confident. I detected more than a trace of weariness. Nevertheless, she had the grace to smile.

'Cinque . . . oh, sorry,' I said, in case she thought I was another objectionable tourist trying to score a point. I'd spent so long perfecting my spiel that just for an instant, it had seemed a shame to waste it. 'Five days,' I said. 'Initially.'

She nodded. She tapped on her keyboard. 'You wish extra insurance, or to add another driver?'

'No,' I said, all too used to the upselling that goes on on these occasions.

Just at that moment, my mobile beeped. I knew it had to be him. I made an apologetic gesture in Patrizia's direction, but she was no longer paying me any attention. I searched the small screen for the words I wanted to see. As usual, he did not disappoint. My response was brief, in the circumstances. He's used to that, too.

Patrizia tore off the multiple copies and ringed the places I had to sign with a thick black pen. Her gestures seemed aggressive. 'Here,' she said, stabbing at the places for my signature. 'And also here.' I took the pen she offered me and obeyed. Then she tore off the copy destined for the bottom of my handbag and smiled a brilliant, electric smile. 'Welcome to Firenze,' she said. 'Your car is in Bay 24, block C. Please check with this list.' And she handed me yet another sheet of paper. 'And this' – she jabbed with the black pen again – 'this is the number you call if you have problem.'

A problem or **problems**, I was tempted to say, but I didn't. Instead, I smiled back, but in a more restrained manner. After all, I am Irish. I didn't have the big hair, the glittering rings and bracelets, the high-voltage appearance – even in uniform – to go with such a Mediterranean smile. But she had disarmed me with her warmth. I felt swept up again into that maelstrom of affection and bafflement that has accompanied each of my visits to this extraordinary country.

To be fair, I think his text had something to do with it too: with that sense of welcome and homecoming that now submerged me.

'Thank you,' I said. I took the key and stuffed the paperwork into my handbag. 'Grazie,' I said, risking a farewell 'thank you'.

'A lei,' she replied. 'Buon viaggio.'

But I could see by her expression that she had already dismissed me, that she was girding herself to deal with the next, more problematic customer, who was already crowding me out of his way, his voice loud with complaint. Just at that moment, I knew how Patrizia felt. I knew it, because I have known it so many times myself. I have battled that same sense of dismay that accompanies the arrival of the client who refuses to be placated, whose satisfaction comes not from the item purchased, but rather from the transaction itself. And the more difficult that transaction, the more demanding, the more petulant they are permitted to be, the better and happier they feel. Finally, they go home triumphant and we resign ourselves to feeling our energy sapped and our cells clogged with resentment. We might have sold something and made a tidy profit, for sure, but it always feels as though we have been forced to buy into something that we didn't want. Such are the pitfalls of serving the public, the frustrations of relationships based on buying and selling.

So. Once I walked away clutching my car-key and my new sense of freedom, I felt filled with the recklessness that goes hand in hand with the casting off of polite responsibility.

I have to say that I struggled a little with my suitcase, my handbag and the various plastic bags from Dublin airport – filled with the Estée Lauder cleanser and moisturizer set that I hadn't been able to resist. And the bronzing powder. I had bought smoked salmon, too, and a couple of boxes of handmade chocolates on special offer. I no longer bring whiskey. Not since I discovered that Irish whiskey is cheaper in Italy anyway.

I mastered the intricacies of Peretola's car-hire system a couple of years back and I have never faltered since. Yesterday afternoon, once I sat behind the wheel of my Mercedes A140 – nothing wrong with a little luxury on such occasions, I've always felt – I was overcome with a rush of expectation and a sense of finality.

The drive from Florence to Volterra can be a challenging one, once I leave the motorway. But the car's progress up the steep climb was effortless. There was a mass of chalky dust thrown up by the tyres, unleashing the unmistakable smell of warmth, soon to be heat, and – I know it is a strange word to use – that scent of *foreignness* that makes me feel that I am truly here. Everything, even the dryness, seems thrilling in a new way every time I come back. And each time, I wonder why it is I have stayed away for so long, how it is I have been *able* to stay away. Everything is familiar but new. I love the way the olive trees glow silver in the sunshine, the way the vineyards stretch for miles, all the way to Volterra, it seems. The town rises in the distance, a sunny promise of shady, narrow streets, of morning coffee in the piazza, of tiny shops made for rummaging.

Yesterday evening, as I drove up the narrow, tree-lined driveway, I felt the ridiculous prickle of tears as I turned the last corner. I saw the faint tracery of shadows on the terracotta-coloured walls of the villa, the glint of sunshine on the unnaturally blue waters of the pool. It had seemed sensible, given the circumstances, to buy my own place here two years ago, rather than renting. My visits had become more frequent, rather than less, despite the old wisdom of not mixing business with pleasure. The new and exciting turn my life had taken made me feel it was time to set down new roots, to find new soil.

So. It was with no small sense of ceremony that I retrieved my key from the inside, zipped pocket of my handbag. Push, pull; pull, push: the opening of the heavy outside door acquired all the resonance of decisions made and implemented.

Once inside, the dim and musty air filled the hallway with such familiarity that it almost took my breath away. It was the smell of home. Home. Such an evocative word, so loaded with hope and expectation and belonging.

Well, here it is, for better or worse. And here am I.

The first thing I did when I got inside was to throw open all the windows. I love that routine of opening shutters, the way the metal bars whine just before the light floods in, reminding me to oil them into silence. But I already know that I never shall. Their creaks and gibbers have always been reminders of the silences I have left behind. I welcome them. And so, last night, once again, I decided that I'd leave them just as they are.

I remember the first day I saw this place, Paola's smiling face as she heaved open the front door, her friendly 'Buon giorno. Signora White?' Only she pronounced it *'Wyte'* with an emphasis on the 'y' and a complete inability to master its whispery 'h'. Never mind, she and I have had some fun since, with my lack of ability to count the syllables in some of the most extraordinarily lengthy Italian words that name the shortest of domestic objects. *Abbigliamento* for dress; *asciugamano* for towel. Paola introduced me to my personal favourite that day, too, over coffee: *sorseggiare* – to sip.

It was she who showed me around the villa late that afternoon, doing her duty gravely, thoroughly. She couldn't have known that I had already decided to buy, and her insistence on detail made me impatient. Not her fault, but nevertheless. At the end of the visit, we had a macchiato together in the gleaming kitchen. The smell of coffee was heady, almost intoxicating. She had prepared a plate of biscotti: thin slices of yellow brioche, some tiny, gleaming meringues, soft ovals of amaretti. A breath of warm wind made its way through the mosquito screen on the window. The mountains were visible through the wide metal grille, retreating from the ranks of olive groves. I wanted to live in this villa so badly it was a physical craving, as insistent as thirst or lust. We sat together at the small table, dipping the biscotti into the froth of our coffee and, woman to woman, with a bit of English here, a bit of Italian there, she told me that sometimes, there was a smell of damp in the kitchen; that sometimes, the plumbing in the bathroom was less than perfect. But by then, I didn't care. All it had taken for me to be sure was to take one step into the cool, tiled interior of the hallway. Something had shifted inside me and I was at peace. At peace and at home. *A casa.*

Paola had stood after a polite interval. She brought our cups to the clattery sink and rinsed them, with a thoroughness that spoke of something else. She had begun to look distracted, almost embarrassed. The air in the kitchen had become uneasy. I understood at once. I spoke without even thinking.

'Paola – le piace lavorare per me – qui – in casa?' I didn't care about whether my grammar was correct: all I wanted was to communicate that her job was still there, with me, soon to be the new owner.

Her smile was huge. 'Si, si, Signora Wyte, si, si!'

She said many other things too, but I heard only the occasional word like 'gentile' and 'piacere', but it didn't matter. Paola came with the house.

Once all the windows were open after my arrival last night, I set to unpacking with gusto. Paola used to insist on doing it for me at first, couldn't understand why I was so anxious to undertake one of the tasks that she regarded as hers. But she gave up insisting, eventually. 'Va bene, Signora, va bene,' she'd say in a tone of great weariness, shaking her head at the lunacies of foreigners.

But I enjoy unpacking. I enjoy the satisfaction afforded by all that hanging, folding, tidying; the making of home. Yesterday, in Paola's disapproving absence, I had fun, seeking out those places I had already prepared for toothbrush, makeup and perfume. Finally, I remembered to check the fridge and discovered that Paola, as good as her word, had stocked it just as I'd asked. Despite the unlived-in air of the white-tiled kitchen, everything was spotless. I've always noticed how Europeans – I mean real Europeans, not those of us who ended up with that designation by having our paltry little island towed by economic ropes towards the mainland – take their housekeeping really seriously. They understand scrubbing, scouring, dusting, polishing in the way our grandmothers used to do. We've lost that art, our generation, among so many others. Not that I long for its return. Well, perhaps I do, but only if I can pay others in order to indulge my appreciation of it. Nevertheless, I do notice that the Irish 'it'll do' approach to domestic cleaning does not exist outside of our own cabbage patch. Paola is what my mother might have called a 'little treasure'. The ancient skills of laundering and mending and fiercely economical grocery shopping are among her many talents. Not to mention cooking. The sort of cooking that takes hours in the kitchen, not the microwave moments that produce fodder little better than palatable. That's what my cooking was reduced to over the years: an indifferent response to the duty of filling plates for four, three times a day every day, three hundred and sixty-five days a year. I did the maths on that one during a particularly enraged period, but I've forgotten the result.

Anyway, this fridge was stuffed with what will now become the comforts of home: bresaola, pasta all' uovo, olives, rucola and a dizzying array of fruit. Standing in demure single file along the shelves of the fridge door are six bottles of Verdicchio. I made a present of some to Claire, after my last trip, but I know she still prefers Prosecco. I have to say I was a little disappointed the night we shared the bottle I'd brought back to her. I'd been filled with anticipation as she opened it, but it didn't taste quite as it does here. Something essential was missing.

'That's because it's a local wine,' was Claire's opinion. 'Best drunk in its own home, with heat and sun and proper food to show it off. Shouldn't force it to travel.'

I think she might be right. 'A bit like you used to feel?' I teased her. 'When you didn't want to leave home? And look at how you blossomed.'

'Ah,' she said. 'But I had all the right conditions.'

Once I'd finished my settling-in process, I poured a glass of nicely chilled Verdicchio and took myself out on to the small balcony off the main living room, the one that looks out over the southern part of Volterra. I sat, for perhaps two hours, or maybe three, looking around, listening to the stillness inside my own head. It felt good. I came in when I began to get drowsy and lay down on the bed that Paola had made up exactly to my instructions. I slept.

It was Paola's soft footstep outside the bedroom door that finally woke me this morning. Despite the leisurely bath, the travel weariness, the joy at being home, I still couldn't sleep last night. When I did drop off, I fell full-tilt into nightmare. It was a heart-pounding, body-sweating experience that stunned me into wakefulness and kept me on high alert until the small hours. I lay there, trying to control the fear, trying to understand the significance of what had happened in that dark universe of bad dreams. I was desperate to recall all the books I had once read about the interpretation of situations and symbols. I was determined to fight panic with philosophy. I was able to remember that appearing undressed in public in a dreamworld indicates a crushing sense of vulnerability; that falling means uncertainty and fear about what lies ahead – all pretty obvious stuff, I should think. Nevertheless, nothing worked, nothing calmed me. I am still no wiser this morning. Well, a little wiser, perhaps, about the dream's meaning with reference to the past, but what it might mean for the future continues to elude me.

I was in an aeroplane. So far so dull, you might say, given that that is how I'd spent most of the day. But, for some reason – one that was clear to me in the shadows of sleep, although I now no longer remember – we had stopped in mid-air, mid-flight, and were hovering above the blue sea below. The Captain's voice could be heard, tinnily, over the PA system. I can even remember his name; an ordinary name like John O'Reilly, something Irish and reassuring like that. He was telling us, in that overly-soothing voice that most of us know heralds disaster – particularly when you're a couple of miles away from solid ground – that he was having difficulty getting the stairs to the aircraft, and he asked for our patience while he and his crew resolved the problem.

Stairs to the aircraft? Thousands and thousands of feet above the sea? Fear slammed into my chest like a fist. How could all these other passengers just sit there, reading their papers, as though things like this happened every day? I remember that I left my seat and fled towards the cabin staff, aware that my breathing had quickened, that my palms had begun to sweat. The chief stewardess was standing at the now open cabin door, and she turned to greet me. Her ludicrous blonde beehive – a remnant of sixties' bad fashion – had come undone. Strands of dyed hair flung themselves wildly across her face, threatening to extinguish her features.

'Would you like to escape, Madam?' she asked me, smiling through the yellow mass. As though this were the most normal request in the world. Which I suppose it is, in the underworld of crashing aeroplanes and all the murky logic of the unconscious. I noticed that she was holding on to the stairs, keeping it in place with just one hand. 'Yes,' I said, although I knew that my voice was barely audible.

'Go ahead, then,' she said, as she nodded encouragement. She looked more like a kindergarten teacher urging her young charges towards the playground than a highly-trained professional intent on saving lives. 'You probably have a minute or two.'

I descended the stairs with leaden legs, focused on nothing other than my own survival. I didn't care about anyone else, couldn't care about anyone else. The stairs veered wildly from one

side to the other, metal clanging against metal, until I fell off, catapulted into the sea below. My yellow jacket kept me afloat and
then I wept with relief. I was alive. I had survived after all.

Then in that Technicolor slow-motion that only dreams have,
I watched as the plane broke in half and fell out of the sky,
descending gracefully towards the ocean below. I tried to swim
away from the wreckage, but I wasn't strong enough. I kept being
pulled back into its watery slipstream, back and back and back
until I was dragged below the glittering surface. I felt the water
course chokingly up my nose, down my throat, filling my mouth
with a cold saltiness. That's when I woke, gasping for air, weeping, sweating, my skin prickling with cold as I threw off the
thin coverlet I used more for the comfort of its weight than its
warmth.

Even if I assume that the aircraft symbolizes my old life breaking in two, how is it possible to drown in the safety of home?

I must have dozed off later in the morning, because the next
thing I knew I was listening to Paola make her way to the kitchen
to prepare coffee. Her footsteps were real, grounded, part of the
waking world. I felt grateful. I pulled the damp sheets off the bed
and made my way to the shower.

By early this afternoon, I'd begun to feel calmer. I started thinking about the letter I'd posted to Maggie at Frankfurt airport. I
tried to calculate when she might receive it. I want her to feel
secure. I'm not worried about the business end of things because
I am sure I left everything there in good order. Nevertheless,
dreams like last night's tend to take the ground from underneath
your feet, in more ways than one.

It's strange. Even though Maggie has never been here, it is her
presence I sense around me above anyone else's. Perhaps it's
because she is the one I feel most guilty about leaving behind. I
look around at all the small details of her thoughtfulness: scented

candles, tiny paintings brought from her travels, the throw from India that graces my sofa. I hoarded all her gifts over the last three years, never displaying any of them in Dublin. I wanted to keep them, to preserve their charms for just such an occasion as this. And then there's what I wear: from trousers to tops to suits to dresses – we designed and made them together, all of them. We tried and tested everything, to see what worked, what didn't. Maggie is, quite literally, stitched into the fabric of my life, and I into hers.

I came very close to telling her about my leaving, but it was the night she fell apart in Leitrim, the weekend she finally told Ray that she'd had enough. It was one of those moments when the truth was on the tip of my tongue but I couldn't bring myself to heap any further upset on her. She was already overloaded.

Was there ever a time when we were not so close, Maggie and I? Yes, of course, but not very often and never for very long. Doesn't that happen to everyone, that ebb and flow of friendship? I think we've done pretty well, all four of us, in fact, to have kept in touch as regularly as we have done over the past twenty-five years. I say four, but really Nora is a non-event as far as I'm concerned, and always has been. The rest of us have passed the years in ever-changing constellations of twos and threes, but for me, Maggie has always been the Pole star.

The one disconnected time I can remember is when Maggie went her own determined way after we left Trinity. She enrolled at the Grafton Academy and became immersed in the business of making patterns, stitching buttonholes, learning to use a sewing machine for God's sake – things she already knew backwards. I figured she'd become fed up with all those petty restrictions soon enough. Maggie didn't need craft: she was more than ready for art. But she was stubborn.

'It's my foundation, Georgie,' she said to me, on one of the many occasions when she refused to join me in running my boutique in Dalkey. 'I need to know that I *know* what I need before I do anything else. I'm the plodder, don't forget: I have to have something substantial behind me before I can go out on my own.'

I couldn't convince her and that frustrated me. From the Grafton Academy, she went to Brown Thomas and became a buyer. I thought I knew better than she did and waited until she became bored with it. But she didn't. Instead, she astonished me, astonished all of us. Within eighteen months, she had become their senior buyer, and I despaired of her ever coming to work for me.

'You're right to despair,' she said to me one night, over our customary bottle of wine. There was just the two of us. She was smiling. I'd noticed recently that she had become somehow smoother in her appearance: a glossier, more sophisticated version of herself. 'I'll never work *for* you. Maybe, if the circumstances were right, I might work *with* you. But that would take a lot of thrashing out.'

I remember I looked at her, embarrassed in her company for probably the first time in our lives. Because I had made a slip. I'd never meant to say 'work *for* me', had always meant 'with me', but perhaps Freud knew more than I've ever given him credit for.

And so, she made me wait. Or at least, that's what it felt like. In latter years, I think I can appreciate more that Maggie did what she had to do for herself – and that I didn't necessarily figure in all of her equations. That the decisions she made were not about me, but about her. Nevertheless, I had to wait out the Brown Thomas years, and finally the Karen years before I got what I wanted.

Karen was Maggie's cousin. She owned a boutique, and at the time that Maggie went into partnership with her, the business was ailing. The stock was tired and old; Karen hadn't the foresight to move with the times. Maggie transformed all of that. She brought all she had learned at Brown Thomas to her new venture, all her financial expertise, all that creativity ready to burst at the seams. I hounded her, I admit it. I needed her on board, couldn't expand my business without her. But being Maggie, she didn't make her move until she was ready. Finally, she called me.

'I'm really excited, Georgie,' she told me. 'I think that there is a chance for us to join forces now. I'm going to email you some designs and some customer requests and I want you to look at them. Then come and meet me.'

I couldn't wait. Maggie's call had made me feel, for the first time in years, challenged, enthused, excited even. Not a familiar feeling for me. I tend more towards the controlled.

'Everything okay?' I asked her, on the day I visited. She looked tired, and that made me anxious. I was afraid that it meant I mightn't get what I'd come for. It was one of those quiet October Mondays, late in the afternoon, at a time when only the most resolute of boutiques hopes for business. Maggie met me at the front of the shop, motioning towards Karen, who was clearing a rail just inside the door. She was folding garments with exquisite care, placing them into beds of tissue paper and cellophane.

'Be careful,' Maggie warned me. 'Mind the door. It tends to slam if you don't hold on to it. Should be fixed by the end of the week.'

I nodded at Karen. 'Hi, how's it going?'

She grinned at me, her large face broadening into a smile of welcome. 'Rushed off our feet.' And she gestured to the empty shop. 'But I'm not complaining. Christmas madness will happen soon enough.'

'We'll be in the back,' Maggie said, 'if the hordes arrive.'

Karen waved in our direction without even looking up. I followed Maggie into the small workroom that I knew she and Karen used for alterations – nothing structural, of course, only the usual changes to hemlines or sleeve lengths: anything else they sent out. Maggie would have known that they were far more valuable front of shop than practising their sewing skills in a cramped and ugly back room.

She opened the steel door into the small yard and lit a cigarette. She stood on the step, blowing smoke out into the evening air. Then she waved at it with her hand, sending it further out into the cold. This was years before the smoking ban, but even an inveterate smoker like Maggie knew that any potential customers wouldn't appreciate the smell of stale tobacco.

'Okay,' I said. 'What's the story?' I leaned down and pulled the drawings she had emailed me from my briefcase.

'Do you like them?' she asked.

'Only so much they kept me up all night,' I said. And she grinned. 'Is this it, Maggie? Are you telling me you're ready? Because these designs are sensational. They're exactly what my customers will buy and I already stock all the high-end accessories to go with them. Are you and Karen really ready?'

Her gaze was steady. 'I've already bought Karen out,' she said. 'It's my business, in every sense.'

I couldn't help it. I was stunned. Maggie showing this much foresight? Then I realized how much she must have learned by serving her apprenticeship with others. Wise woman: she had learned all she needed to know at someone else's expense.

'All Karen needs is a job,' she went on, 'and I've guaranteed she can have it, for as long as she wants. So that has to be part of any deal between the two of us – that's you and me. She's the best salesperson I've ever come across. Shite at accounts, mind you, but that's okay.'

We both laughed. And so, finally we became partners. But partners in a very different way from the one I had imagined. She invited *me* to join her. I didn't need to think about it. I sold up Dalkey and came to her and Karen's place in Ranelagh. She was a good negotiator, Maggie, and we hammered out an agreement that took care of us both. More than business, we were each aware of the potential catastrophe of fractured friendship.

'Let's avoid it at all costs,' she said to me. 'I'd rather we haggled now than fight in five years' time. Let's have it all out in the open, now, no holds barred.'

In the end, the negotiations went on for six hard weeks. We were both glad when they were over, and we treated ourselves to a weekend in Paris the day after we'd signed.

'Exclusivity will be our thing,' she said to me, as we sipped coffee at a pavement café on the Left Bank and watched the stylish and bohemian worlds strut their stuff before us. 'Doesn't matter how much it costs: women will always buy exclusivity. No discounts, no stuff brought in for "sales" – nothing like that. Top dollar all the way.'

That weekend I discovered that, in her own way, Maggie was every bit as ruthless as I was. She was an exciting person to work with, too. She'd lose herself, her brittleness, in the heady excitement of creativity. 'What about *this*?' she'd say, pinning a swathe of colour against a shape that was just not working for us; or she'd lift a hemline, drop a shoulder. Immediately, I'd see her design transformed.

I grew to understand a Maggie I didn't know I knew. I'd always loved her, now I came to respect her, her judgement, her considered approach to problems that might have seemed insuperable to others – even to me. It is a cliché to say it, I know, but we went from strength to strength.

It was as though separately, our minds worked well and productively, creatively. But together, we were more than the sum of our parts. Our skills seemed to explode when we joined forces. We had the wealthy women of Dublin and, latterly, Belfast and Cork, clamouring for our designs. We could charge what we liked. Nobody cared. Our 'ImagIna' label – a combination of both our names: 'Mag' for Margaret and 'Ina' for Georgina, a potent allusion, we felt, to both imagination and image – set the Irish fashion world alight. And if I exaggerate, well, I feel entitled to. They were heady days – of manic work, publicity, promotions – and sales beyond our wildest calculations.

We laughed, often, she and I, about the fact that the prices on our handwritten labels elicited not shock, but a kind of reverence, a respect that both of us found outlandish. We never pushed it too far: Maggie's careful market research saw to that. But we milked it. Oh yes, we milked it. And as for our final . . . well, let's call them 'collaborations', they were nothing short of startling.

I shall miss her, and I know she'll miss me, particularly at first. Forty years is a long time. But I'll make it up to her, one way and another. For the foreseeable future, though, we'll just have to be patient.

In the meantime, I shall keep writing to her, and tell her more and more as the need evolves. I trust her to keep my secret. That's one of the great things about Maggie's and my friendship. We have never needed to explain anything away.

We understand. We know how to wait.

And now my bath is ready. Right on time, my phone lights up, its vibrations pushing it across the table towards me. I flip back the cover, ready to smile.

But the words are not what I expect. They hint at probable delay, at potential trouble. It seems that things are not what they seem. The final line, of love and longing and poetry, is meant to soothe and reassure. But it does just the opposite. And I cannot call back. That has been agreed between us.

This is not something that warm water, scented candles and heady words can fix. But I must settle and wait. I have no control. I must be patient and see what tomorrow brings.

5. *Nora*

Frank says that from the first minute I walked into his shop, he knew that he was going to marry me.

It still gives me goose pimples, every time he reminds me of that. I had very slim ankles, he says, and he had always liked that in a woman. I looked at myself a bit differently after that. Me? Nora? With sexy ankles? I don't know, but I suppose I'd never thought much about my feet before. On the day we met, I was looking to buy a pair of flat navy shoes, more like walking shoes, really, that I needed to match my new blue jeans. In fact, I had just recently managed to fit into a pair of size sixteen denims, my first pair ever, and I wanted suede walking shoes that would also go with my new duffel coat. It was a bit like a uniform, Trinity rules for dressing that I never completely understood, if I'm honest. Or if I did, I never managed to pull it off, not in the way the other three did. Claire could fall out of bed, throw on a bin-liner and still look gorgeous. She was always elegant. It hasn't done her much good, though, has it, over the years?

Maggie had to work a bit harder than that. She used to make most of her own clothes back when I knew her first. She said she had to, that she was way too small for the fashionable stuff. If she wasn't making herself things from scratch, she'd be altering bits and pieces instead to make them suit her better. Cheap things that she'd rummage at market stalls to find, or that she'd buy from children's departments during the sales. She was always able to adapt anything to suit her, even though she was curvy. She'd look bang up to the minute and would do it so economically that I envied her.

And then there was Georgie. Well, Georgie had a style all of her own. Sometimes she'd go casual, sometimes tailored and old-fashioned, almost, but somehow she always got away with it. She had a passion for knitting that started some time towards the end of first year, just before I left Trinity. I suppose that's where her business idea came from later on, although the passion for knitting didn't last. At one stage, I used to think that Georgie might become a teacher, because she read so much. But she was much too selfish for a career like that. She cared about surface things far too much. Georgie was like one of those animals that change how they look so that they can fit in with their surroundings. Chameleons, I think they're called. Something like that, anyway.

'Can I help you?' Those were the first words that Frank ever spoke to me. The thing I noticed about him was how kind his eyes were, how they creased at the corners when he smiled. It was just a few months after I'd come back from London and nobody had smiled much at me there.

'Yes,' I said. And I remember thinking that this had to be a sign that things were going to start getting better for me. In fact, I'd found most of my first term at Trinity a very unfriendly time. I was older than all the other first years, and there was nobody there from my old school, either. All of them had gone to UCD, but Daddy had insisted that Trinity was a better choice for me. I wouldn't know anybody there, he said. Nobody would know our family if I went to Trinity, but they might if I went to UCD. Stillorgan was just that bit 'too close for comfort', was how he put it. The afternoon that I met Frank, someone who had promised to meet me for coffee hadn't turned up at the Buttery. I'd met her at an English lecture the day before. Blake baffled me. I understood nothing about the *Songs of Innocence and Experience* and I could see that she didn't either. I knew it by looking at her blank face and the way she held on to her pen. Her knuckles showed white and she didn't take one note. Neither did I. I hoped then that she was someone who needed a friend just as much as I did.

Miriam Fuller, that was her name. Isn't it funny that it has just come back to me now, after all these years? I can't remember the last time I thought about Miriam Fuller. That day, I'd sat at the table in the Buttery on my own and waited for her. I'm sure now that nobody paid much attention to me, but at the time I felt self-conscious. I sat there for an hour or more and then it dawned on me that she wasn't delayed. She wasn't coming at all. Once I realized it, I couldn't wait to get out. I'll never forget how upset I felt. I could feel my face grow red and couldn't get out the back door fast enough. I told Maggie about it a few weeks later and she was kind.

Mammy had given me some money that morning to buy my shoes and tights and other bits and pieces that I needed, so that's what I decided to do. Money was always so difficult with my parents, particularly since Eddie. I think that they were afraid to give me more than my bus fare after that. It made things hard for me because the girls always expected me to buy my round and help out with the parties that we held, maybe once every term. But I just didn't have it. I never had it. Not till Frank.

I was glad to make my escape from Trinity that day, the day Miriam Fuller never showed up, and I made my way towards Henry Street. I'd always liked the look of Fitzsimons's shoe shop, but I'd never bought anything there before. Mammy always said it was a bit dearer than the others, but you couldn't fault the quality. And that afternoon, I felt that I needed quality more than anything else. I wanted something solid and dependable that wouldn't let me down.

I pushed open the door of the shop and stepped inside. It was small and that surprised me. The window with its display of boots and shoes and even furry slippers had made me think that it would be much bigger, but it wasn't. In fact, there were only three chairs for customers and a cramped bit of corridor that led to the till. Most of the space was taken up with shelves piled high with cardboard boxes. I wondered how anybody could know what was in all of them. The smell of new leather was everywhere, and so was polish and something else that I couldn't name then, but now I know was aftershave.

The shop was quiet and empty, apart from one tall, thin man behind the till. He had a bundle of what looked like receipts and he was concentrating on totting things up. It wasn't a very busy time in the shoe business. A late, grey Monday evening in early November. Afterwards, Frank told me that it was too long after the summer sales for crowds and too soon for the Christmas rush. The man at the till, who of course turned out to be Frank, looked up from his papers the minute I closed the door behind me. He continued to look as I walked towards him, and then he took his glasses off with the one quick movement I have come to know so well. Frank has never liked it that he needs to wear glasses. I've never minded and have always found his short-sightedness charming. Now he grumbles that he's both short-sighted and long-sighted at the same time. He can't see the number on the bus and he can't read the small print, unless he holds the newspaper at arm's length. That day, though, he was able to see me well enough.

'May I try these on?' I pointed to the navy shoes I had just spotted. Suede, with one wide strap and a low, sturdy heel. In fact, I was pleased at how I sounded. I came across as formal and polite, and I made sure not to seem too friendly with a shopkeeper. My father, in his precise, legal way, had always been very strict on the difference between 'can' and 'may'. Right then, I was grateful to him.

'Certainly, miss,' Frank said, and I saw that his smile faded a little. He told me afterwards that he'd hoped I'd be a little bit more friendly, that I'd respond at once to how deeply, instantly, he had admired me.

But I felt the need to be careful. I remember stepping away from him, further than was strictly necessary, just to make a point of the distance that there should be between us. He backed off then, in every sense, and his face looked, I don't know, a bit fallen. He was so different from Eddie. Poles apart. The two of them couldn't have been more unalike. But still. I had learned that it paid to be careful.

The navy shoes on display were a six, but they were too big. Frank suggested a five, instead of a five and a half, because he said that good-quality walking shoes tended to be of a generous size. I wasn't sure, but I said I'd try them on anyway. I remember how eager he looked as he trotted off to the stores to find me a pair of size fives. I thought what an obliging man he was. He was gone a long time. Just my luck, I said to myself. He'll be out of fives. But in fact he came back with a whole pile of boxes in his hands. I was glad that he had thought to bring me lots of different styles to try on. I'd have hated to walk out of there without buying something, especially after all the trouble he'd gone to.

He sat on a low stool in front of me, shaped a little bit like a filled-in triangle with a sloping leather seat, and he pulled out the wads of tissue paper from one of the shoes. 'These are really good quality,' he said, 'and we stock a waterproof cleaner that keeps them looking good.'

'Oh, okay,' I said. I had forgotten that suede often got stained and soggy in the rain. Then he took my right foot in his hands and eased on the soft navy suede. He had the shoehorn ready, but he didn't need to use it.

'Is that comfortable?' he asked me after a bit.

'Yes,' I said. 'It feels fine.'

'Would you like to try the left one, then?'

I nodded. 'Thank you, yes.'

He did the same with the other shoe and this time, he had to use the shoehorn at the last minute. But his hands were gentle. He looked up at me apologetically.

'Most people have one foot slightly larger than the other,' he said. 'It's perfectly normal, nothing to worry about.'

I nodded. I found that those words said in such a kindly tone touched me and made my eyes fill with tears. I hadn't had kindness in such a long time. I had to stand up and walk away from him, down to the end of the shop, in case he noticed. I looked into the mirrors placed low on the floor that reflected only my feet and ankles. I could feel him looking at me still, but now it didn't make me uneasy any more. When I was able, I made my way back to my chair and sat down again. And then I smiled at him. It was the least I could do to thank him for his kindness.

'These are very comfortable,' I said. 'I like them a lot. I think I'll take them.' I felt pleased. A full size smaller than the last ones I had bought in London. Another good sign, maybe.

He nodded and looked satisfied. 'An excellent choice,' he said. He took the shoes up to the till and I followed him. Even then, I remember feeling a bit sad that buying the shoes had taken such a short time. I felt that I might like to linger for longer. The memory of his hand on the sole of my foot was a warm and comforting one.

'Is there anything else I can help you with?' he asked then.

I don't know, I must have looked a bit blank because the next words he spoke came out all in a rush.

'We've just got in a new range of Italian leather,' he said. 'Very fine, very feminine. I think the black or the navy court would suit you very well. That is, if you are looking for a slightly more dressy shoe.'

I remember wondering why he seemed so nervous. As a matter of fact, I *was* looking for something with a higher heel to wear with my new skirts. Fine quality wool skirts, or so my mother told me. Her voice had been very firm as she said it. She must have seen the disappointment on my face. Merino, I think she said they were, but I didn't care what they were made of. I didn't like them. They were dull and dark and safe. They didn't suit the Trinity uniform at all. But by then I had learned not to argue with her or with Daddy.

'Actually, yes,' I said. 'I do need a more formal pair as well.'

Then he relaxed and smiled again in the way he had when I'd entered the shop.

'You just sit yourself down there,' he said, pointing to the chair I had only just got up out of, 'and I'll show you what I've got.'

And that was it, really. I left the shop with two pairs of shoes, one flat, one dressy, and although I didn't know it at the time I had Frank's phone number in *both* shoe boxes. He told me afterwards that he'd always believed in taking no chances with the important things in life. He had been very discreet and very polite. He must have scribbled down his telephone number on a couple of bits of till roll while he searched for the size fives in the store room.

'Please don't take this amiss,' said the note. 'I really enjoyed meeting you and would value your company again. Forgive me if I offend. My number is 8335584. Respectfully yours, Frank Fitzsimons.'

Luckily, I took the shoes out of their boxes while I was still in my bedroom, on my own, otherwise I don't know what would have happened. I was surprised but not surprised at the same time. I folded both bits of paper and put them into my purse, where no one was likely to look. Then I took the two pairs of shoes down to the kitchen to show to Mammy.

I let a week go by and then I tried his number. He answered at once and I wondered if he'd been waiting by the phone all that time for me to call. I felt shy and anxious and a little bit foolish, too.

'Frank Fitzsimons?' I asked.

'That's right,' said a voice. It sounded hurried, as though he had been running somewhere and my call had stopped him in his tracks.

I didn't know what to say. I was about to hang up because I felt my cheeks starting to burn with embarrassment. How could you say, 'I'm the girl who bought two pairs of shoes from you last Monday afternoon, one navy, one black.' Then he might say, 'What time on Monday afternoon?' or 'What sort of shoes?' or something like that, and then what would I say? For all I knew, he might be in the habit of putting little notes into all his women customers' shoe boxes. In fact, he might even be another Eddie, only with a different way of getting close to me.

'I know who you are,' he said quickly. 'Please don't hang up. You bought one pair of suede walking shoes and one pair of Italian leather courts. I took the risk of putting my phone number in with your purchases.' There was a pause, but I didn't feel able to fill it.

'I hope I didn't offend,' he said. 'But I did want to meet you again.'

I really didn't know what to say. 'Well,' I said, and got no further after that. And then: 'Well,' again, with almost no change of tone.

'Please,' he said, 'please let me know your name.'

I hesitated for a minute. I was afraid that there might be no going back this time either. 'It's Nora,' I said. I wasn't sure about this conversation, wasn't sure about it at all, but at least he couldn't see my face over the phone. And I knew that I could hang up any time I wanted to and he'd never be able to find me. That was something to be grateful for.

'I'd like to meet you, Nora. It's a lovely name, by the way.'

'Thank you,' I said.

'Just meet me for an hour, after work, any time this week. You name the place. A cup of coffee, a drink – you decide.' His voice was nice, firm, and I could feel that he was smiling. I imagined I could see the creases at the corners of his eyes.

'Bewley's?' I said, naming the first place that came into my head.

There was another pause. 'I might not make it before Bewley's closes. The shop stays open until six.'

'Oh.' I hadn't thought of that. I felt foolish all over again. I should have thought of that.

'Perhaps the Earl Mooney?' he said. 'It's very central – top of North Earl Street, near O'Connell Street?'

A pub, I thought. And not a very nice one, late at night. In fact I had often seen old men staggering out after closing time, full of Guinness and bad temper. But it should be fine in the early evening.

'I know it,' I said. 'I think that would be all right.'

'Shall we say a quarter past six tomorrow then? Half-six, if you prefer. Sometimes I get delayed closing up and I wouldn't want you waiting for me.'

I could feel all my anxiety beginning to drain away. He sounded like a gentleman, a real old-fashioned gentleman. He reminded me of the polite lovers in Jane Austen's books. Men like Captain Wentworth. I'd fallen for Captain Wentworth straight away. I'd read all of Jane Austen's novels the summer after I did my Leaving Cert. I couldn't get enough of them. I read them at the same time as I began to realize that men in ordinary life – men like Eddie – didn't behave like Wentworth or Dashwood or even Bingham and Darcy. It was a funny coincidence, I've often thought since. Well, not funny really, more like strange. There I was as an eighteen-year-old girl running away across Europe with Eddie, at the same speed as disappointment and grief were making their way back towards me. I suppose the mercy of it is that I didn't know it at the time. I didn't know about unhappy endings back then.

'Yes, all right,' I said, 'half-six is fine but I'll have to go by eight o'clock at the latest.'

'That's perfectly all right,' he said. 'You already have my home number should you change your mind, and the shop number is in the phone book. Number eleven, Henry Street.'

'I won't change my mind,' I heard myself saying. And it was true. I knew by then that I wouldn't.

Frank was waiting for me as I came through the door of the pub. I had the impression of shiny wood and stained glass and huge open spaces. He came towards me at once, a newspaper tucked under his arm. I thought he wasn't as tall as he had seemed in the shoe shop, but maybe that was just the high ceilings of the Earl Mooney. High ceilings like that make everything look smaller.

'Nora,' he said, and took my hand. 'How nice to see you again.' He nodded towards a corner of the pub, but he didn't let go of my hand. 'There's a grand quiet table over here.'

We ordered coffee first and then he had a pint. I had a dry Martini and white lemonade. All too soon, it was eight o'clock. I didn't need to go, not really, but I wasn't going to tell him that, not on a first date. Frank listened to me that night. I think that that's what really made me like him. He still listens in the same manner, even after all these years. In fact, he listens in that intense way that people have when they want to understand what someone else is saying. You know that they're really interested. I don't mean 'listening' by just staying quiet and waiting for the chance to jump into the conversation and tell *their* story just as soon as there's a bit of a gap.

That night, I told him about Trinity, about the lonely feelings I had that I hadn't even admitted to myself. About being different and not fitting in; that kind of thing. I even told him about Miriam Fuller. That first evening was all about me, and that was something new in itself. When I finished he just nodded and then took my hand in both of his. I liked his warmth. It reminded me of how he'd held my foot, just before he eased on my new shoe.

'I'd like to see you again, Nora. As a matter of fact, I'd very much like to see you again.'

Frank said this as I stood up to go. He rose with me, and held my duffel coat while I struggled my way into it. I never did find it easy when someone else held my coat. My arms seemed to keep missing the sleeves and I'd jab at the air uselessly until whoever was holding the coat would bring the sleeves to me, rather than me to the sleeves. It was always embarrassing but I was never able to say no, thank you, I can do it myself. This time, though, it was a blessing in disguise. All that faffing about with the coat meant that I had my back to Frank when he said that he wanted to see me again, in that tone of voice that left no doubt but that he meant it. By the time I turned to face him, I think my colour had returned to normal.

'I'd like that,' I said. And I watched as his face lit up from the inside.

'Good, good,' he said. 'Perhaps you could give me your number and I'll call you tomorrow.'

I hesitated.

'Or perhaps the day after, if that suits you better,' he offered then.

'It's easier for me to call you,' I said, and watched as his face slumped again, the way it had that first day in the shop. 'I will call, I promise. It's just not so convenient for me to get calls at home.' I hoped that he'd accept that, that he wouldn't push me or ask any awkward questions.

He nodded and made no comment about the strangeness of

my home. What sort of family didn't allow its children to speak on the telephone? Ones like mine, I wanted to tell him, with hard rules and judgements and no forgiveness. Ones like mine.

He squeezed my hand. 'Then I'll wait until you do so. If it's easier, you could always call to the shop. Next time, I'd like very much to take you out to dinner, if you think you'd enjoy that.'

I smiled at him then. 'Could we go to the Sunflower?'

He laughed. 'We could indeed. Are you a fan of Chinese food, then?'

I nodded. I preferred Indian, but in those days Dublin didn't give us a lot of choice. And I could hardly offer to cook for him.

'Friday?' he said. He'd walked me to my bus stop and waited till my bus arrived.

'Yes, Friday would be lovely. Thank you.'

'Why don't we have a drink in the Gresham at eight and I'll book us a table in the Sunflower for afterwards?'

'Yes,' I said again, 'why not? Let's do that.'

'Good. I'll look forward to your call.'

We waved to each other as I got on the number 10 bus and I allowed the numbness to settle around me all the way home. A nice man, a gentle man, a man like Captain Wentworth. Not handsome, certainly, but then neither was I. He did have nice eyes, though, and a lovely smile. You can forgive a lot when that's the case. Not that I had anything to forgive. Quite the opposite.

Time would tell, as my mother used to say. Time would tell.

It took a few weeks before Frank understood that I had a real passion for cooking. By that time, we'd had dinner in all of the few decent restaurants and hotels that Dublin had to offer. Of course, it's all different now, but back then there were very few places to try. The Trocadero, Quo Vadis, Nico's; then there were the hotels, the Gresham, the Hibernian, the Shelbourne. And outside the city centre there was the Beaufield Mews, where you could have your dinner surrounded by lovely antique furniture and paintings. I have very fond memories of all of those places. Maybe there were one or two others, as well, but I don't remember them any more.

'Why don't we cook at my house?' Frank said to me one Wednesday when I dropped into the shop to see him. It was that quiet half-hour just before closing, or so we both hoped. Frank said it had been hectic all week. He had a young woman in to help him over the busy times, but she'd already gone home by the time I arrived. It was very near Christmas, I remember, and I think that people were worn out shopping by then. I had taken to dropping into the shop like this most weeks. That way, we were able to make our arrangements to meet in person without having to use the phone. If Frank found this strange, he never said. In fact, he never once pushed me to explain why phoning me at home kept on being such a problem.

But he must have seen something in my face or else something in the way I hesitated over his invitation, because he rushed to say: 'Only if you feel comfortable, that is. Only if you feel it's appropriate.' Just then, the door of the shop opened and a woman came in, dragging a screaming toddler by one arm. 'Excuse me, my dear,' he said and went to deal with his customer.

My dear, I remember thinking. He'd called me 'my dear'. I stood behind the till as I had done lots of other times, in case the phone rang or another customer came in while Frank was busy. I liked helping out there because it made me feel useful. I liked the fact that Frank needed me. That afternoon, I watched as he soothed the shrieking toddler and let him play with the machine that gave an accurate reading of the shoe sizes needed for children. Their feet grow so quickly, Frank had explained to me, and the bones can be deformed all too easily by ill-fitting footwear. The little boy was fascinated as he watched the X-ray of his feet and the mother was beaming.

I stood at the till, and thought about the other words Frank had said. 'Only if you feel it's appropriate.' Years and years later, when I saw the film *Thelma and Louise* and one of them, I think Thelma, says: 'I've had it up to my ass with "sedate",' I knew just what she meant. By then, I was growing very tired of all the things that were supposed to be correct. Sedate, correct, appropriate: they're the same thing, really. In fact, my father, with his legal language and legal judgements, was always going on about the things that were appropriate. Well, I thought, to blue blazes with that. This is a nice man. I'm going to cook dinner at Frank's house and nobody is going to stop me.

It was the first time since London that I'd decided to lie to my parents. I was twenty, after all, nearly twenty-one. It was high time I started to get a life of my own. I had started spending time with Maggie and Claire at the flat. Not Georgie, of course. Most of the time I spent there, I made sure that she wouldn't be around. It wasn't too difficult to work it out. Her lecture timetable was different from ours. I used to have fantasies about what it would be like to share with Claire and Maggie. I'd have loved to be in a flat with other girls. But Mammy and Daddy wouldn't hear of it. It was a firm 'no' every time I brought it up. So I stopped. But I hated missing out on so much.

And so, when the mother and toddler left the shop that afternoon, I said to Frank, 'I'd love to cook for us at the weekend. Tell me where you live.' I spoke quickly because I was afraid of giving myself the time to change my mind.

'Are you sure?' he asked, but I could see how his smile kept getting wider. I nodded, beginning to feel embarrassed. Had I been too forward? It was too late to pull back now. Besides, most of me didn't want to.

'Yes, I'm sure,' I said. I was glad that my tone sounded so positive. 'I'll even bring everything with me. All the ingredients.'

He shook his head and his face was alive with eagerness. 'Tell you what,' he said, 'I've an even better idea. Why don't we meet up on Friday? It's my last Friday off before Christmas. We can have the afternoon and then do the shopping together. My local supermarket is very good and it stays open till six in the evening. We can drive there and get everything we need.'

And that's what we did. Frank had a lovely house in Kincora Road in Clontarf. I took the number 30 bus from Marlborough street at two o'clock on the Friday afternoon and got off at Vernon Avenue, where Frank was waiting for me. We walked up the Avenue and turned right on to a lovely leafy street that was packed with neat red-brick houses. Frank's was five or six from the end of the road. The front door was painted blue and the gardens both back and front, as I soon discovered, were tidy and well looked after, with the last leaves of a Virginia creeper still blazing against one wall. Inside, the house was full of light and colour and there was a beautiful extended kitchen. I don't know why, but the house surprised me. I had never met a house-proud man before.

'My brother Ciarán does kitchens,' Frank explained as he showed me around. 'He says that a good kitchen is what will always sell a house.'

I remember that I looked at him in surprise. 'Oh – are you thinking of selling, then?'

He took my hand and squeezed it. 'I'm hoping I'll need something bigger some day.'

I didn't answer. I didn't need to. But I could feel myself begin to blush. Both of us knew what he had just said.

We went to the supermarket in Frank's Ford Fiesta. Nolan's, I think it was called. As we walked up and down the aisles together I thought: 'This feels so normal, so right.' Doing these simple things with him had begun to make me feel happy for the first time in nearly three years. And so that was the night that I told him about Megan.

We had just finished dinner and the table was full of little china bowls of leftovers – raita, Bombay pickle, poppadoms, that sort of thing. They were all things that wouldn't keep until the following day, so we hadn't bothered with the clingfilm. Frank had bought candles, too, and they lit up everything very prettily. I'd had at least one glass of wine more than I was used to, and it gave me the courage I needed.

'I need to tell you something, Frank,' I said. By that time in our relationship, he had kissed me a few times, but he had never pushed me any further than that. I had known him less than three months but I trusted him. I had learned by then that how long you knew someone was no measure of how much you could trust them. I thought of my parents, in fact, when I thought about trust. Earlier that afternoon, Frank and I had kissed and cuddled on his sofa with great tenderness, but I couldn't relax because my story was sitting there on the cushions between us, taking up space.

'I know,' he said quietly. 'I've felt something worrying you all day. Whatever it is, you can tell me. You can be sure of me, Nora. Nothing will change the way I feel about you.'

And so I told him about Eddie. About how we met at a Rugby Club dance the year I'd done my Leaving Cert and about how I'd fallen head over heels for him. I told Frank about how he'd persuaded me to run away to France with him. I told him everything, including how my parents had had to chase after us from Calais to Paris to Perpignan for more than three months and how they finally caught up with us at the Spanish border. But by then it was all too late. We'd run out of money – my savings, mostly – and I'd just found out that I was pregnant and there was no longer any 'us'. I know, I know, it is such a small story and such an ordinary one but I can't help that. I've always been ordinary and at least with Frank I was able to stop pretending I would ever be anything else. The end of my story is just as obvious, too.

Eddie disappeared into the night once my parents arrived and I never saw him again. In fact I have never seen him again, not from that day to this. He doesn't even know he has a daughter out there somewhere and I'd imagine he doesn't care either. He never came looking for me again, not even once.

'My parents sent me to London,' I said. 'I have an aunt there – well, she's not really family, she's a kind of aunt-in-law, I suppose, but she took me in.'

Frank's hand never moved from mine. He was every bit as still as the air in the room around us. 'Was she kind to you?'

I shrugged. 'Well, she wasn't unkind, I suppose. I did all the cooking and minded the children and I got board and lodgings in return. She was out at work during the day so we didn't really see much of one another.'

Frank smiled. 'So that's how you learned to be such a great cook. That's the best meal I've ever eaten.'

I remember how grateful I was to him for saying that. At least I'd taken something home from London with me, something that would be useful. 'Thank you.'

'Go on,' he said. 'Tell me the rest. If you were working that hard during the day, what did you do for company in the evenings and at weekends?'

Company. If only he knew. I had no use for company. If I'm honest I'd have to say that I was terrified of letting my daughter out of my sight even for an instant. I knew what was going to happen to her and to me. I already knew that I would lose her to strangers and never see her again and never hold her again. After they took her from me, I slept with one of her baby vests on my pillow. That way, I could smell her smell and pretend she was still with me. It was a smell made up of milk and talcum powder and baby sweetness. I'll never forget the panic when that smell began to fade. That was when I knew that she was gone for good.

I swallowed. I didn't want to cry, but I wanted to be sure that

I told him the truth as I remembered it. 'I used to go to bed early every night because I was so tired. And at the weekends I went to the park and the library a lot.'

'And your baby?' he said gently.

Then I cried. When he said 'your baby' I couldn't hold it in any longer. 'She was born in June last year. I tried to keep her, but I couldn't. I tried living in a bedsit for a while and getting a job and keeping things going, but I just couldn't do it.' I stopped, sobs where the words should be. Frank poured me a glass of water. I sipped for a bit and then I was able to continue.

'My parents insisted I had her adopted.' I remembered that awful day, my parents' stiff faces and how their disapproval of me was stitched into every inch of their bodies. And I remembered the way they'd both stayed away from me, at the other end of the room.

'What was her name?'

I looked at him, surprised that he didn't know, but of course he didn't. Nobody did. 'Megan,' I said. 'Her name is Megan and she has fair hair and blue eyes and I love her to bits.' I folded my arms on the table, put my head down and wept. I cried with loss and love and relief. Finally, I'd been able to tell someone who wouldn't look at me with appalled eyes and lips clamped shut into a tight, closed line. At last, here was someone who wouldn't look at me while their face filled up with rage and disappointment and bitterness.

I felt Frank's hand on my hair. 'Marry me, Nora,' he said. His voice was very tender. 'Marry me and let's go and find your little girl and make a family.'

I looked up at him in astonishment.

'I mean it,' he said, his face serious. 'We can find her and get her back. I'll do whatever it takes to get her back.'

Then I knew I loved him and that I would always love him

for saying that. I sat up and wiped my eyes with the backs of my hands. Frank handed me his napkin and I blew my nose.

'She's nearly eighteen months old, Frank, and she's living with a family somewhere in Wisconsin. The nuns arranged the adoption, but it was a private one without any papers. They said it was better that way because nobody would be able to interfere.'

I remembered their faces. They weren't cruel, those women, but watching one of them pick Megan up had made me feel like a wild animal. I wanted to throw myself at them, to scratch at their eyes and draw blood. 'We'd never find her, not without documents. And anyway, I couldn't rip her away from the only family she's ever known. How could I do that? Think how unhappy that would make her, even if we could ever *find* her.'

And then I started to cry again. Frank just went on stroking my hair. 'You don't need to decide tonight,' he said. 'We'll talk about it again, all of it. There's just one thing I would like you to decide, though, no matter what. Just between us. We don't need to tell anyone just yet, not until we're ready to. Will you marry me?'

I didn't need to think about it. 'Yes,' I said. 'Yes, I'll marry you.'

He stood then and pulled me to my feet. 'I wanted to marry you the first time you walked into my shop. I want to be with you. And we'll have children, as many as you want.' He wound his arms around me and I thought, not for the first time, how solid and substantial he felt to me, despite his lankiness. He kissed me and then he tried a joke. He could see how sorrowful I was, remembering it all over again. 'Now for some light relief. Those profiteroles look too good to leave till tomorrow. In fact, I could swear that they're winking at me.'

I laughed, grateful to him all over again. I remember how light my heart had begun to feel as we walked towards the kitchen. At last I allowed myself to believe that there might be a happy ending hesitating out there somewhere, waiting for me to come and get it.

After dessert, we sat on the sofa together for hours, Frank's arm around my shoulders, both of my hands holding on to his. We talked about where we'd live, how many children we'd have, how he'd always keep his promises.

And he has.

I know the others thought he was too old, too boring, too dull – more or less the same kind of things that they probably thought about me, particularly Georgie. Claire was kind when she found out we'd got engaged and so was Maggie. I remember being a bit surprised at Maggie. Of course, she always meant to be kind to me, but sometimes she was uneasy about it when Georgie was around. She thinks that I didn't notice, I'm sure, but I've always known that Maggie needed to be in Georgie's good books. That morning in the Buttery, I thought that Maggie was almost tearful when I showed her my ring. Georgie, though, was her usual spiteful self. The only thing she wanted to know was whether Frank and I were sleeping together. They knew nothing about Megan back then and they still know nothing. I'd promised my parents to tell nobody and I never broke my word, apart from Frank. And that was different because as far as I was concerned, that wasn't breaking my word, that was building our trust. Quite another thing altogether.

I've decided to tell the girls tonight, at Claire's party. Our twenty-fifth anniversary as girlfriends. It's a long time, with a lot of water under the bridge. I've decided to tell them now that Megan has come looking for me.

I think that a lot of secrets will be revealed this evening. I know that Maggie is building up to something, and Georgie was very evasive the last time we all met. As for Claire, I feel sorry for her sometimes, despite all her talents and her beauty. I think that she would have loved to be a mother. I may be wrong, but I think that's why she's had so many men. Sometimes, I've caught something in her eyes when she looks at our children. I don't mean just my children, I mean all eight of our children, Maggie's and Georgie's and mine. It's not anything that the others would know to look for, or even recognize if they saw it. It's the look of loss, the hurtful reminder that other people's children can be when you haven't got any of your own. It's how I used to look, I know, after I lost Megan. All my boys were wonderful, don't get me wrong. But there was still something missing. Even though my three are all grown up now, the sight of a pink dress or a doll, or some lace-edged baby sock still has the power to move me.

I watched a programme on television recently about earthquakes. The scientist described the conditions that forced the earth to violence and upheaval. He described the shock to the earth's core as *seismic*. Seismic. The minute I heard the word, I knew that *that* was the one I had been looking for, down all the years. I'd heard it before, of course, and knew what it meant. But I had only applied it to geological upheavals. Now I knew better. My loss of Megan was seismic. That's how I can recognize that kind of loss so clearly in Claire's blue eyes.

I know that she is going to be the most hurt by what I have to tell her this evening. Her gentleness has made me think about this a lot, but I can't help it. It's the others I need to tell, and she's part of the others. In fact, even if I don't tell her, even if I try to keep it from her, one of the others will tell her anyway. And the truth is, part of me wants to see her realize that all the gorgeousness in the world doesn't get you what you want. That sometimes just being plain and ordinary is good enough.

I've played by the rules all my life. I deserve my sons and now my daughter. Claire broke the rules. She broke all of them, so many times. Take that awful time with Ray. I'll never forget the night she told us. Such a terrible evening. Even for Georgie, the soup was foul and the bread stale. Her coq au vin tasted of nothing, nothing at all. Claire was distressed, and smoked her way through the whole evening. Maggie was harder on her than I've ever seen her before. But something about that evening stayed with me, and niggled at me over and over again. Whatever about Claire, I saw something in Georgie that night that I didn't realize at the time, but that I now believe was relief.

I wasn't able to say much back then, on the night of the terrible food and the even more terrible revelations, because Georgie wouldn't let me. And so I watched the others instead. That has always been my job in the group. To shut up and observe. Nobody's ever interested in what I see or what I think. But it's strange, the way life can sometimes turn things around to your advantage. I have become a really good observer over the years and that is precisely because no one else could be bothered with my 'take' on anything. Nora was always the dull one. Nora was the silent one. Nora was always the one who didn't matter. There was this belief that anything I saw, anything my intuition told me or anything I observed in others, was simply not worth listening to. And so I sat and gathered secrets.

And my secret from that night is, that even while Claire was confessing to her disgraceful affair with Ray, it was Georgie who looked like the guilty one. I saw that expression on her face when she joined us at the table, once those poor, sad little twins were finally in bed. I don't believe that Georgie has ever been a good mother, not in the true meaning of the word. She has always been too selfish.

Now, it has taken several years for this bit of hindsight to take shape. In fact, I'm not sure when it was that I realized what I saw on that difficult evening. It took a while to dawn on me that what I saw was Georgie's relief that she wasn't the one to have been caught. That time. Nothing to do with Ray, of course. That's not what I mean. But I'm sure there was someone else around. I'm positive she'd been unfaithful to Pete. The reason I'm so sure is because I saw it happen again, and perhaps even again. I am not so stupid as the others like to think I am. And this time, I had all the benefits of a ringside seat.

It is no more than three years ago. The reason I can be so certain of the timing is because it was Robbie's twenty-first birthday that June. I had bought a navy and white dress for the party and that's what I was wearing that Sunday a few weeks later when I saw Georgie. Frank and I had gone out to lunch in Castleknock. He had chosen the restaurant, he said, as a kind of double celebration. It would be our private party to celebrate our eldest son's coming of age and also to remember the first real date we had ever had. He'd booked us a table at a sophisticated Chinese restaurant and kept it as a surprise. When we arrived, he turned around to me and grinned.

'The best in the city, I'm told – and a very long way from the Sunflower in O'Connell Street.' And it was, oh my goodness, it was. The dim sum was, well, that doesn't matter for now. What matters is that I saw her. Georgie. My eyes were drawn to the imposing figure at the kerb, just outside the restaurant window. I saw a tall, fair-haired woman dressed in a white linen trouser-suit. At first, there was just something familiar about the way she stood. Her back was to me, and she was waiting to cross the road. I was admiring her figure and thinking how good this woman looked in white because it is a very difficult colour to wear, particularly if you are a blonde. Some subtle sequins marked the hem of the jacket and also the cuffs of the sleeves. I could see them glint in the sunlight from where I sat. That little sprinkling of sequins was Maggie's and Georgie's trademark for their summer collection that year.

Personally, I think that sequins are vulgar, no matter how tiny they are. I remember a blue top that I really liked with sequins sewn around the neckline. I bought it because I liked the shape and then spent a whole evening picking out the sequins and replacing them with small knots of embroidery. I was very satisfied with the results and in fact, I still have that top, years later. I still wear it on occasion. I've never understood this two-or-three-collections-of-clothes-a-year business, although Maggie and Georgie have done well out of it. I was just about to tap Frank on the arm, to say: 'Look at that woman. She's the image of Georgie, and I bet that's one of their suits that she's wearing.' The lights changed then and the woman turned her face. I saw that it was her.

I don't know why I was so shocked, except that the feeling brought me back to that awful evening around her table when Claire confessed to sleeping with Ray. It had been the same sort of internal explosion then as now. I can recognize bad behaviour when I see it. I was certain that this woman, who was now definitely Georgie, was up to no good.

'Are you ready to order, my dear?' Frank asked me, just as the last flash of trouser-leg disappeared across the road and down the opposite pavement. I was itching to turn my head to see where she went but I didn't dare.

'Yes,' I said. 'I'm going to have exactly what I ordered in the Sunflower all those years ago, but this time, the food will be real!'

We had a lovely afternoon, Frank and I. In fact, I almost forgot about Georgie. But once we drove out of the car park, and down the same direction as the woman in the suit, I couldn't help myself and I started to look out for her. There were rows and rows of houses and the occasional large pub. Then we passed a small shop that seemed to specialize in motorbikes. I looked at it closely as we drove by. I had plenty of time to look because the pedestrian lights changed to red as we came up to the crossing. It was one of those places where the shop was at ground level and had a small flat above it. I remember thinking that it probably smelt of grease and engine-oil. The door opened, and at just that instant, I caught a flash of white. Trouser-leg; linen; I'd bet my life on it and would have bet my life on it even then.

I knew then for certain that it *had* to be Georgie. I sat back, feeling as though I had been slapped. What on earth was she doing in a place like that? The door closed behind her and Frank and I drove off. I said nothing to Frank because my heart was pounding so much.

I did mention it to her once. I wanted to see her reaction. 'What a lovely suit, Georgie,' I said, feeling brave, the next time we met. We were all at Maggie's. Ray was away on business and we always had dinner at her house when Ray wasn't there even if it wasn't Maggie's turn. It was an unspoken rule, once what had happened between him and Claire happened. Although none of us ever talked about that. It was such a long time ago. But *I* know that their affair left its shadow. *I* know that things were never the same between us all afterwards. I'm not one of those people who shrug their shoulders at all sorts of bad behaviour. Some things are just plain wrong.

Anyway, the four of us met earlier than usual. It was one of those late July evenings when it's warm enough to sit outside on a patio or a deck. It was one of the few times when the air actually smells like summer. The sort of night that makes you go outside and enjoy it because you know it may not come again. That particular dinner happened to be the Friday after Frank and I had had lunch in Castleknock. I touched the hem of Georgie's jacket, and I swear that I could see her flinch. 'I haven't seen this before,' I said. 'Aren't the little sequins a lovely touch?'

She smiled at me then and examined the sleeves as though she was looking for something. Doing that allowed her to move away from me. It was only a step or two, but it was enough for me to notice.

'Thanks, Nora,' she said, 'it's one of a new line Maggie and I are developing. It's the first time I've worn it.'

'Really?' I asked. I remember thinking that the surprise in my voice was particularly well done. 'I thought I saw one just like it last weekend. And the woman looked very like you, too, from the back.'

Georgie looked amused. Her glance said: 'No one looks very like me, not even from the back. I'm a one-off.'

'Oh, yes?' she said then, in that polite, patronizing tone that she kept just for me. 'Where was that?'

'In Castleknock.'

I watched as her face closed. One eyelid blinked and I recognized that guilty tic from almost ten years earlier. I was satisfied then because I just *knew* that I was right.

She looked at me. Her mouth was still smiling, but her eyes looked paler.

'Castleknock?' she said with one of her little frowns as she pretended to concentrate. Then she shook her head. I felt its dismissal. 'Must have been somebody else.'

I said nothing.

Just then, Maggie called out that the gazpacho was served and would we all hurry up and come outside or the ice cubes would have melted.

Georgie threw me a glance over her shoulder as we went out on to the deck. I thought I saw a glimmer of respect in it and something else, too, that I can't put my finger on. That makes me feel uneasy. But I still can't pin it down. In fact, her look said that maybe I was not the fool she had taken me to be all these years. That was enough for me. I felt pleased. I rarely, no never, came away from any meeting with Georgie feeling that I might have won.

We had our meal and our wine and our nightcap, the same as we'd always done. But I thought I caught Georgie looking thoughtful on a couple of occasions throughout the evening. My new sense of having scored some point against her kept coming back to me. After more than twenty years, I felt that the balance of power might have shifted a little, and I'm honest enough to say that I liked that.

However, I'm also sufficiently old and wise to know that things with Georgie are never simple. Nor with Maggie. And certainly not with Claire. But I don't mind. I have Megan to be grateful for, all these years later. At least my secret carries no shadow of shame. I was only a youngster, a foolish eighteen-year-old child, when I made my mistake. I can now look forward, in every sense, because I have finally had my past come full circle.

Exactly one week ago today, I got her letter – Megan's, I mean. I'd been cleaning up leaves in the front garden. The sort of sludgy ones that hang around under the shrubs once autumn is done, but you can't see them until everything else is bare. That kind of straggly bareness that the frosts of late February bring. Frank had told me to leave them, that he would rake them up at the weekend, but all that morning I'd felt edgy. I couldn't settle to anything. I didn't know what was wrong with me. I decided that a blast of cold air and exercise might do me good. So I pulled on my woolly hat and my gardening gloves and stepped outside on to the grass.

'Morning, Mrs Fitzsimons.'

It was Tom, our postman. 'Good morning, Tom. Cold enough for you?'

'It sure is, Mrs Fitz. And they say there's worse to come. Forecast is for snow.' He smiled and showed me a bundle of letters. 'You've got quite a haul today. Will I leave them in the porch for you?'

I don't think I answered him. I hope he didn't feel that I was rude. But the truth is, I was staring so hard at the letters he held in his hand that it seemed to take away my power of speech. Right on the top of the bundle was a blue envelope. All I could see was the American stamps and the looped, curling handwriting. How could I have known? I don't know how, but I did. I remember peeling my gloves off slowly and then holding out my hands.

'I'll take them,' I said.

I went straight into the kitchen and switched on the kettle. I could feel the knot in my stomach begin to tighten. One bit of me wanted to call Frank, at once, to tell him to come home and be with me while I opened the letter. Another bit of me wanted to be on my own, to have a solitary, private meeting with my daughter's words. And that's the bit that won. I stood at the counter and made myself a cup of tea, very slowly, while the envelope rested on the breakfast bar just beyond my reach. I kept looking at it, trying to guess its contents, unable to stretch out my hand and grasp it. Blue and silent, it lay before me and bridged a gap of almost twenty-seven years. It was the only connection I had left between the young me and the me that now sat in a bright and safe suburban kitchen, surrounded by all the things that make up an ordinary life.

I cried when I read Megan's words. Who wouldn't? About how her Mom and Pop had supported her search for her birth mother; about how they had praised my unselfishness in giving up my baby to a better life; about how they hoped that they also might meet me, in time. And my beautiful daughter sent photographs of herself, too. Dozens of them. Her letter was so careful of me. She wrote that she was coming to Ireland anyway to 'check out Trinity' before spending a semester there in the autumn – or the 'fall' as she called it. She stressed that I was not to feel forced into a meeting before I was ready, that she would wait.

Before I was ready! Knowing she was here, even for the shortest time, how on earth could I walk up Grafton Street, or pass the front gate of Trinity or wander through Stephen's Green without watching for her face everywhere I went? Watching for *our* face, in fact. Of all my children, she is the one who resembles me the best.

I think that one of the things in her letter that moved me most of all was that her American family had decided to keep her name. That comforted me, the fact that she had always been herself, always Megan, always present in her name every time I have thought about her over twenty-seven years.

Frank's joy was indescribable. He grabbed my hands and I watched as his eyes filled. He kept saying my name over and over again. 'Nora, Nora, that's wonderful, simply wonderful.' His kind face and his tears and his search for the right words made me realize all over again what a good man I had married.

'We must bring her to Ireland,' he said, 'the boys have to get to know their sister. Let's do it soon, very soon – no, let's you and I go and see her first, or you meet her first and then we both will – and then after that, maybe she might like to come and stay . . .'

'Slow down,' I had to say to him. We were both laughing and crying by then. 'She's already coming to see us. She'll be in Ireland in a week's time!'

'A week?' He looked as excited as a child. 'Where will we take her? What can we do to make her feel welcome – she'll be staying with us, won't she?' He was pacing, lifting up her letter and putting it down again as though he was looking for something.

I had to shush him, to get him to calm down a little. Which he did, once he had the time to absorb the news. Every so often, he'd take my hand and murmur, 'It's wonderful, Nora, just wonderful. All our prayers have been answered.'

That night, we told Robbie and Chris and Matthew. I think they were more bewildered at first than anything else, especially Matthew.

'But why did you have to give her away? Why couldn't you have kept her?'

I found that I couldn't speak. I was glad that Frank did it for me.

'They were very different times, son,' he told him. His voice had gone all quiet as he answered Matthew's question. He looked over at me and I knew he was remembering that night in Clontarf when I had cooked for him. The night I had first told him about Megan. 'There is no shame about being a single mother now,' he said, 'but there was then. Nana and Grandad Murphy had some very fixed ideas, just like a lot of people.'

Robbie and Chris listened to Frank, too, the way they always did. I felt a lump in my throat as I watched all their faces.

'Your mother would have wished otherwise,' Frank went on. 'But it wasn't possible for her to keep Megan. She did what she believed to be best for her child, just as she has always done, for all her children. And now,' he said, with a great beaming smile and rubbing his hands together the way he always did when something delighted him, 'she gets her reward. And you get the sister you never knew you had.'

I know I felt anxious, as neither Chris nor Robbie had said anything up until then. It had never occurred to me that they might be jealous, but it was something I had to consider. I needn't have worried. Chris got up from the table and walked around to where I was sitting. He lifted me up in the most enormous bear-hug I have ever had. His voice was choked.

'You're the best Mum,' he said. 'Just the best. I can't wait to meet her.'

It was like he had taken the cork out of a bottle after shaking it. We all began to talk at once. There was laughter, and Chris, the gentlest of my three sons, even shed tears. The evening blurred into the fizziness of warmth and love and family.

Robbie went out and bought champagne. I thought he still looked pale when he came back. Perhaps, as the eldest, he was the most taken aback. Believing he was the first and then finding out he wasn't.

'Are you sure you're all right, love?' I asked him as he insisted on topping up my glass again. I was beginning to feel quite giddy.

He smiled. 'Of course. It's a huge surprise, but it's great news. Just great. I'm really looking forward to meeting Megan.' There was a little pause, and I let it hang, in case he wanted to ask me something, something delicate. I had not mentioned Eddie, did not want to mention the madness that youthful passion brings with it and the destruction it can wreak on so many lives.

But all he said was: 'What day did you say she'll be arriving in Dublin?'

'On Sunday,' I said, 'her flight gets in at about eight in the morning.' And then I remembered. 'Oh, Robbie – that's when you leave for Italy!' For a moment, I was horrified at myself. 'I forgot!'

He nodded. 'I know. I was just checking the dates. Don't worry, we'll work something out.'

I looked at him, knowing that my face was full of dismay. 'She'll only be here for less than a week. Oh, Robbie, you can't miss it! Can't you defer your scholarship, or something? Go next year instead?'

He squeezed my hand. 'We'll work something out, Mum. I promise. Enjoy it and stop worrying.' His voice had the same determined ring as his father's, the exact same tone as when Frank had decided something. I thought it wiser to say nothing more just then.

But I did worry, of course I worried. I was frantic. What would I do if he wasn't there? Right then, studying the finer points of architecture seemed to me to be nothing compared to rebuilding my family. Of course, I'd been proud of him when he won his scholarship, but this was different. This was something nobody could have predicted. I needed all my children with me, all of us pulling together on such a momentous occasion. But I trust Robbie to do the right thing. After all, he has had good example all his life.

We stayed up late, Frank and I, talking. Robbie went to bed

first, and I was worried about how shaken he looked, how tired. It was as though something seismic had happened to him, too – and I suppose it had. The return of a sister you never knew you had has to throw all sorts of certainties into turmoil, doesn't it?

'Stop worrying, Mum, I've told you,' he said again, as he kissed me goodnight. I didn't like the edge to his voice, but given the night that was in it, I let it go.

'Goodnight, son,' said Frank. 'Something to stop us all in our tracks, isn't it? God is good.'

But Robbie didn't answer. After he left the room, Frank told me to relax and enjoy my news. He patted my hands, the way he used to do, when we knew each other first and I was in need of so much reassurance. He insisted that, scholarship or no scholarship, Robbie would eventually do the right thing. He just needed time to come around to it.

And my friends – will they do the right thing?

It has been so very difficult, keeping this news from them all over the last week. But I have felt very cautious, even though my heart and soul knows that that letter *is* from Megan, my own flesh-and-blood daughter, and that she has sought me out and wants to meet me. But my old pessimism has crept in from time to time: what if she changes her mind at the last minute, gets cold feet, decides to leave well enough alone? What if her counsellor persuades her to wait a bit longer – and I wasn't so sure I was happy about her having a counsellor in the first place. Weren't her Mom and Pop enough to help her through this decision? And if anything *did* go wrong, how could I tell everyone my extraordinary news and then maybe have it snatched away from me all over again, making things worse than if it had never been in the first place?

I think that I only truly believed in the fact of Megan's arrival once we spoke on the phone for the first time last night, once I heard her decisiveness – and her curiosity – for myself. She will be in my home in three days' time. And that means that for me and my friendships, tonight is the night. Will they accept, Claire and Maggie and Georgie, that I had to keep secrets? Will they all celebrate wholeheartedly – for once – the fact that I, too, have a life, have had a life in which things happen?

Time will tell, as my mother used to say. Time will tell.

I've often wondered what that actually means. Maybe tonight we'll all find out.

6. *Georgie*

So. I still have some loose ends to tie up.

By the time Maggie receives the letter I posted at Frankfurt airport, she'll already have begun to put two and two together. I have long experience of her intuition. Sometimes, our ability to understand each other is nothing short of startling.

Frankfurt is a nightmare, by the way. It's the sort of airport that can't make up its mind whether it's a transit point for passengers or a clearing house for terrorists on active service. The checks take for ever: all around me people were complaining about the multiple searches, the ambiguous hand signals of the security staff, the bad signposting. I have to say that I had a moment of regret that I had opted to collect my luggage, rather than having it sent direct to Florence. For an instant, the risk of having my things go missing seemed preferable to the interminable waiting. After almost two hours, I snatched my bag off the carousel under the nervous, watchful eyes of armed policemen. Not to mention the barely restrained German Shepherds. By the time I'd made my way to the relative sanity of the VIP lounge, I'd decided never again. Not through Frankfurt.

Anyway, back to Maggie. I hope she knows that I would never let her down. We've been friends ever since our Junior Infants' teacher, Mrs Lee, put us sitting together that first morning. We have always been the 'grandes dames' of our group: ours is the friendship that will endure beyond all the others. What I love most about Maggie is her loyalty. I got her into trouble so many times when we were young, and yet she never complained, never minded taking the punishment meted out to both of us, even though she deserved none of it. When we were teenagers, we got cleverer at getting away with things. Maggie was blessed with an innocent face: I was not. Her wide-eyed look of dismay retrieved many a dodgy situation. I can remember, too, the way her energy would fill a room. She drew people to her, with that magical combination she has of warmth and lively good humour.

'We make a good team, you and I,' she used to say. And we did: there's no doubt about it. She attracted the boys, moths to her flame. Then I filtered them. I got rid of the creeps. The only time the system failed – one of our greater ironies – was with Ray. He approached her by stealth, when I wasn't around. By the time I met him, Maggie was already hooked. I've never felt his charm myself, but others have. She was snared quickly, too quickly: burnt by the combination of his dark good looks and his obvious need of her. The problem was that he needed other women, too, and Maggie has always been too forgiving. If anybody understands that, I do.

'He's a shit, Maggie, and you know it.' I remember one time wrenching the duvet off her bed, refusing to let her lie down under his bad behaviour. It was the morning after one of our many parties at number 12, Rathmines Road. I'd watched Ray the night before, as he'd sidled over towards Lorraine, a schoolfriend of Claire's who had managed to insinuate her way into our company. She was spilling out of her dress and Ray's eyes were alight with all that was promised by those full, high breasts, those long legs. He was like that, our Ray. He was never one for the understated. And while Maggie was someone whose appearance always made an impact, on that night no one could have held a candle to Lorraine.

Besides, Maggie and Claire were busy handing out plates and

cutlery and paper cups of red wine, so poor Ray felt abandoned, or so he later claimed. Nevertheless, I saw that he'd awaited an opportunity to make a beeline for Lorraine: he hadn't had the time to feel at a loose end. He lit her cigarette, listened to her in that grave, attentive way he'd managed to cultivate: head to one side, his gestures mirroring hers, flattering, gentlemanly, radiating – of all things – *kindness*. And then, wham! The trap was sprung, all steel and style and no substance. I watched them leave, too, Ray's hand under Lorraine's elbow to steady her as they walked out the front door of the flat. And the strange thing is, Maggie *knew* it: she knew that Ray was no good. He wasn't any good *for* her, he wasn't even good *to* her. But he kept her with him by a canny combination of neediness, repentance and empty promises. And she kept going back for more.

Even after that awful time with Claire, ten years ago now, Maggie still went back to him, still forgave him. That was the one and only time our group fell apart. I'm still not sure how we all came back from that. Perhaps we never have. Perhaps we just poured salt on to that too, ignoring the stain as it spread.

On the night in question, the night at my house, neither Maggie nor Claire had offered to bring anything to help me out, which should have been enough to warn me that something serious was afoot. But I was busy with other matters. My daughters, Carla and Lillian, rebellious nine-year-olds, were refusing to settle. They demanded to be let stay up later and they fought me with everything that lies in a twins' armoury. It was way past their bedtime and I was out of patience. All I wanted was to join the others downstairs. By the time I came back to the dining room, the twins were sobbing piteously in their beds, comforting each other in their own secret language of exclusion. But by then, I was too tired to care.

The soup bowls were still on the table, and the discarded remnants of bread. I was surprised: one or other of us usually cleared the débris, loaded the dishwasher, no matter whose house we were in. And Maggie was smoking like a train. I noticed, to my astonishment, that Claire was holding a cigarette too, shaking, between her long fingers. Claire hadn't smoked since she was a student; and even then, she had done it without conviction. I didn't bother to look at Nora. Whatever was of interest was happening right at that moment, between Claire and Maggie. Nora was merely the observer: that was and is her mission in life. I sat and poured myself a glass of wine and took a large sip before I broke the silence. 'What's up?' I asked.

'Ask Claire,' said Maggie. Her voice was tight. Even in the candlelight, her face looked crumpled, the skin around her eyes creased and papery.

'Okay,' I said, and turned towards Claire. I was struck, as always, by her loveliness. That halo of hair, the perfect skin, those luminous eyes. Whatever was churning inside her at that moment was not reflected in the perfection of her pre-Raphaelite face.

'So, Claire? What is it? What's going on?' I tried to keep my tone neutral.

She tapped her cigarette against the ashtray and I noticed that her whole body was trembling now. 'It's . . .' and she shook her head. 'I don't want to talk about it, please, not here. Not tonight.' She looked across the table at Maggie, her eyes all mute appeal.

'Well, I want to talk about it,' said Maggie. Her tone verged on the belligerent. That was not like Maggie, not like her at all. 'I'm among friends – at least, I always thought I was.' She crushed out her cigarette and immediately reached for another. Her long red fingernails gleamed in the candlelight. I took a deep breath and refilled all our glasses.

'Come on, Claire,' Maggie said. There was a note of false jollity in her voice, as though cajoling a truculent child with whom she was losing patience. 'How long has it been going on?'

I closed my eyes, briefly, and breathed quietly for a moment.

Ray. Maggie's husband, Ray: it had to be. In flagrante, again. But with *Claire* this time?

'There isn't anything . . . going on. There never *was* anything *going on.* It was just the one time, months ago, and it was a mistake. My mistake.' Now Claire's voice began to crack, stifling the sobs that were gathering at the base of her throat. 'I didn't tell you because . . . it was nothing, that's all. It was a stupid, selfish mistake and I didn't want to hurt you.'

Maggie put down her wine glass and glared at her. 'You sleep with my husband and you don't want to hurt me? What is it you were trying to do, then – become my friend for life?'

Claire winced and slumped back in her chair. I wanted to intervene, but I knew that I couldn't. She looked over at me and I could almost see what she was thinking, because I was thinking the same thing. Was the blame to be all hers: didn't Ray deserve even a little? And how could you tell one of your oldest and best friends that you were – what? – drunk and incapable when their errant husband found his way into your bed? That's how it had to have been: that, or something very like it. How else would Claire have become entangled with someone like Ray? I know Claire. She wouldn't have touched him with a bargepole. Talk about Beauty and the Beast.

I glanced over at Nora. Her mouth was opening and closing like a stranded fish. Just for that moment, I felt sorry for her. She was completely out of her depth: this was not something that kitchen towels and Saxa salt could help to mop up and discard in yesterday's newspaper.

Then I spoke. 'Are you sure it's over?' I directed my question at Claire, my tone harsher than I intended.

'It never began. It wasn't a relationship, it wasn't even an affair; nothing like that.' She looked at us pleadingly, weeping openly now. The tears made her look fragile, almost transparent: if anything, even more alluring. I sympathized wholeheartedly with Maggie. Such wounded beauty must have been really hard to take, given the circumstances. Claire's voice became quieter, more controlled. 'There was just the once, last Christmas. I'd had too much to drink and I was very upset . . . over . . . something.'

So. I was right after all, I remember thinking. Ray took advantage of her. Nevertheless, she'd been a foolish woman for letting him. I wondered would she ever be any different? Would she never learn how to keep men in their proper place: in a place defined by her, not one that allowed them to spill their messy lives all over hers, leaving a tsunami of grief and hurt and loss in their wake?

She bit her lip, shook her head. None of us asked her: what was the something that had you so distressed? What were you so upset about that you'd betray your friend, all your friends? She acknowledged our silent refusal to be curious and forgiving and swallowed that punishment, too. 'It doesn't matter what it was. But Ray was . . . kind. He comforted me.'

I'll bet he did, I thought, the little bastard. But I said nothing. Not yet.

'I told him that it had been a terrible mistake, that we shouldn't . . . that I didn't . . . couldn't . . .'

For one hysterical moment, I wanted to laugh out loud. How could Claire call Ray a worthless piece of shit that she wouldn't be seen dead with, and not insult his wife of all those patient years?

'I met him once, afterwards, just the once to tell him that . . . he said we needed to talk. I . . . told him I wouldn't see him again.'

'But not before you slept with him for the second time, isn't that right?' Maggie was standing by then, drawn up to her full height of five foot one. Luckily, Claire remained seated. And she didn't reply. I knew there was something she wasn't telling. After all, this was Maggie's moment. She'd earned it. She deserved it.

I was thinking: Ray just had to tell her, didn't he? Couldn't help himself. Had to give his wife chapter and verse, add insult to injury. I could imagine him whining and whingeing, confessing everything and begging forgiveness all at the same time. But also, in some obscure way, boasting, smiling smugly to himself. I'm so sorry, dear, a moment of sheer madness – but, gosh, see how attractive I am to women? I just can't help myself. Even your best friends can't resist me.

Just then, I noticed Nora was about to speak. Her face was prim, her mouth a fine, disapproving line: default mode, as I used to call it, despite protests from Claire and Maggie. I raised my hand. 'Don't, Nora. Don't say anything.' I could feel her look at me, feel the white heat of her resentment boring into the back of my head as I turned to face Maggie. But I didn't care. It was time I took charge. After all, it was my house. Somebody had to do something, to salvage whatever there was left to be salvaged. 'What do you want to do, Maggie?' I could see that she was about to crumble. But she didn't. I allowed her to interpret my question in any way she chose.

'I want to go home,' she managed finally. She stood up and spoke with dignity. 'I want to go home to my husband. And my family.' And then she walked, slowly and with great care, towards the dining-room door. 'Now, please – call me a taxi,' and she closed the door quietly behind her.

Remembering all of this, Maggie's exit, Nora's fussing, Claire's weeping, I can still feel the ache that filled the room that night, as each of us contemplated all the intertwining losses and griefs and half-truths that we would have to wade through in the coming months, perhaps years. We tried to tread cautiously at first, but nothing worked. It took two years – well, two years and three months, to be exact – for this rupture even to begin to be healed. And the really sad thing was, we all knew that Ray wasn't worth it. Ray was, and always has been, a serial adulterer. We knew it and guarded it and sat on such knowledge and never mentioned the war. What hurt Maggie most, I think, was the fact that now her husband's infidelities were out in the open, infiltrating that safe and comfortable existence that she loved to share with her friends. He had finally tainted the only part of her life that had ever been completely hers.

They made up eventually, Claire and Maggie, one night in my house when Nora was in Tipperary with her in-laws. I invited them both separately, so that neither knew the other would be there. I had them arrive at different times. When they met in my living room, they were both instantly angry at me, which was exactly what I had intended.

'Be as pissed off with me as you like,' I said to them. 'It's been over two years and things have . . . moved on.' I knew, because Maggie had told me, that Ray had recently moved on, too, into the territory of his latest secretary. 'So why shouldn't we move on, heal the breach? We need each other, you know we do.'

I uncorked the white wine that lay in the ice bucket on the coffee table. 'I'm going to see to the twins. I'll be back in half an hour. Just remember how miserable we all are without each other.' And I left. I meant it, too. I'd missed our evenings back then more than I'd thought I would, our phone conversations afterwards, the speculations, the gossip. Even leaving Nora out of the equation from my point of view, have you any idea how many possible combinations of friendship there are among three articulate, competitive, complex women? Enough to liven up most days of the week, that's for sure. And I still had each of them on the phone to me anyway, Maggie and Claire, almost daily. I was never sure how much information from one I was expected to feed back to the other. It had me exhausted.

So. The time came when I felt I had to do something, even if it backfired. And Nora's absences have often been times filled with opportunity for me, one way and another.

When I got back downstairs, the room was very still. The

twins had been angelic on that night, and we'd all taken turns reading aloud chapters from *The Big Friendly Giant.* Each of the girls was very proud of her ability to read. It was one of those glowing, quiet times that I'm glad we shared. I'd been able, too, to listen for raised voices, anger or slamming doors from the room below, but none of it had happened. Nevertheless, I knocked on the living-room door before I entered. Claire was hiccuping, the aftermath of what must have been a silent storm of sobbing. Maggie was holding her hand and stroked it, gently.

'Don't, Claire, don't break your heart over it. It's too—'

And then she stopped speaking. Fair enough. That was the deal that she and I had agreed on. The details would be between her and Claire. They were nobody else's business, certainly not mine. But I was relieved they had made up. It meant we could, maybe, patch things up and stitch our friendships back together again. Had Maggie and Claire remained estranged, I don't know what I would have done. I'd probably have fought her, my oldest friend, but I didn't want to. I was glad that night that I didn't have to.

Because Maggie and I rarely fight. Oh, she doesn't let me get away with things: she argues with me and challenges me and calls things as she sees them. But that's not fighting, not in my book. There are only two significant occasions of conflict that I can remember in the forty years we have been friends. Each occasion is very different from the other. The first makes me laugh. The second gives me pause for reflection. It still makes me wonder how well we can ever know someone else, how we always forget that they retain the capacity to surprise us and make us feel humble.

Anyway, the first time Maggie really stood up to me was about fourteen years in the brewing. It concerned a little girl called Melissa McKee – a child whom Maggie and I both knew while at primary school. As it happened, Melissa was put sitting between Maggie and me one day and I objected. The child wet her knickers constantly and even then, everything in me rebelled at the indignity of enduring that kind of unpleasantness: *any* kind of unpleasantness. Maggie was always the kinder of the two of us, that goes without saying. Nevertheless, my objections – vociferous and inappropriate – landed both of us in hot water and the Principal's office at the same time. She punished us with extra homework: spellings, I think. But it was no punishment for me. Books have been my refuge all my life. They gave me something to do to fill up the silences of my childhood home. Maggie minded, but she didn't kick up about it. At least not on that occasion. Our parents might have been summoned to the school as well, but I can no longer remember.

Years later, at some birthday party or other of mine, celebrated while we were all still at Trinity, I remember that I objected loudly to the presence of Nora, whom I emphatically had *not* invited. It was then that Maggie went in for the kill. She'd waited all that time, and now she was taking no prisoners. I wanted the Helicopter to go; Maggie was adamant that she should stay.

'Remember Melissa McKee?' she said to me. 'You got me extra spellings *and* tables for that caper. Now it's payback time.'

I was stunned. For a moment, all I could think was: who the *fuck* is Melissa McKee? It's *Nora Murphy* we're talking about here. Then I saw Maggie's grinning face, her slow nod, her 'come to me' hand gestures as she encouraged my memory, and I burst out laughing.

'Melissa McKee!' I said as I cracked up. 'She smelt of wee!'

And that was the end of occasion Number One. Occasion Number Two was more serious. It belonged to our teenage years. Or our Teenage Years, as our parents might have referred to them. With good reason. We were tearaways, Maggie and I. Given what adolescents get up to today, I suppose we weren't as bad as we might have been. Nevertheless, that didn't stop us trying. On this occasion, Maggie's demonstration of loyalty astounded me, even frightened me, I think, with its force and the depth of its implications. Don't the Chinese believe if someone saves your life, that you in turn become responsible for them, that you owe them for as long as you both shall live? Well, then.

We were about fifteen or so when my father abruptly told us – my mother and me, that is – that we were leaving Killiney. It probably came as no surprise to her, but I remember feeling a mixture of shock and disdain. He'd said this kind of thing before, a number of times, but nothing had ever happened. He talked about moving to a 'classier neighbourhood' in the same way that he'd mention politicians by their first names, boast about handshakes and deals done and money secreted in brown envelopes: all this when he thought I wasn't listening. Parents have no idea what their children hear while sitting at the top of the stairs, or peering through cracks in doorways while heated discussions ensue in bedrooms and kitchens and hallways: particularly in the days when phones were still located in the coldest, draughtiest places in the house. It is a lesson that has served me well with my own children. I have always remembered the acuteness of their capacity for hearing, along with their ability to make themselves invisible. Unhearing, unseeing, un-present, right in the midst of upheaval. And avidly taking everything in.

'The decision is made, Georgina,' my father told me, 'so there's no point in you going on about it.' At this stage, I had said nothing. I had decided to stay silent and furious. Nevertheless, it wouldn't have taken a genius to read my expression.

'Your mother and I have bought a house in Ballsbridge. As soon as the sale of this one is through, we're on our way.' His dismissiveness only served to feed my rage. I have never accepted anyone else's control over my life.

'You'll get used to it,' he said. 'It's not the dark side of the moon, you know. You can still see your friends.'

I looked over at my mother, the original Helicopter. She fought my father from time to time, but always gave in in the end. Her attitude was a partly combative, but mostly resigned martyrdom. Perhaps it came from being so much younger than he was. Such a relationship requires careful management, guile and insight – none of which my mother possessed. And so, my father was resplendent in his ownership of her. He had once boomed jovially to his cronies over drinks in our front room one Christmas how he had 'got' my mother 'while she was still young and pliable'. I can still feel how the sudden silence that resulted crawled all over my skin, making me want to slink away somewhere and cower in the darkness. But I stayed, hoping with a forlorn hope that this time, she would answer him and show some spirit. She did not. And he remained oblivious. The guests first looked down at their glasses and then at each other.

I can only have been about ten at that time, but I have never forgotten the feeling of vicarious humiliation. Before or since, I don't think I ever heard my mother express any opinion voluntarily – one that wasn't extracted as a result of my father's stern 'Well, Caroline? Is it or is it not so?' Just as he did now.

Her tone was weary. What little fight might have been left in her seemed to have disappeared. 'You'll settle, Georgina, you'll see. And you can always have your friends to stay.' Then she lit another cigarette and looked out of the window.

I left the sitting room in a rush, ran down the hallway and slammed the front door behind me as hard as I could. It was the most eloquent statement I could think of making in the midst of my impotence. I could feel the windows shake behind me. Maggie was waiting for me at the end of her street, ten minutes' walk away. She was sitting on one of the low whitewashed walls, swinging her legs. The O'Tooles' garden was always the neighbourhood meeting-point for us teenagers – something that made the new owners furious. They were not called O'Toole, but it didn't matter to us: that's how the corner house would always be known. That Saturday afternoon, we were the first to arrive, Maggie and I.

Without preamble, I said 'We're moving.' I was aware that my jaw was clenched.

Maggie looked at me, not understanding at first.

'We're moving to fucking Ballsbridge. They have the house up for sale.'

Her smile faded. She eased herself off the wall, stumbling in the process. Her backside grazed the pebble-dashing, dislodging flakes of paint. She brushed at the seat of her jeans, then wiped her hands on her denim-clad thighs before she spoke.

'When did they tell you?'

'Just now.' I remember angrily biting back tears, drawing blood in the process. I could taste its warm, coppery tinge on my tongue.

'When will you be going?' She was already pulling the packet of ten Carrolls out of her pocket. We were in the safe zone. Nobody from either house could see us, not even by telescope. Or radar. Or satellite. Thus we habitually reassured each other, fifteen-year-old technological sophisticates.

I shrugged. 'They didn't give me a date. I didn't ask. Whenever the house is sold, I suppose. I dunno – however long that takes.'

Then she smiled. 'Ballsbridge is not so far. I mean, it's not Cork, or anything. We can still meet at weekends. It doesn't have to change things.'

I felt grateful, hopeful almost. But I wasn't going to let her soothe my rage at my parents. I relished the purity of my wrath, my indignant response to injustice. 'It *will* change things, you know it will.'

'Not unless you let it,' Maggie said. 'Come on,' she urged, and made her way towards the green space. I followed, surprised at her matter-of-factness. We sat under the huge beech tree, the grass still warm and fragrant of late August. She pulled a cigarette out of her packet of ten, split the white paper cylinder up the centre and spilled commas of tobacco into the palm of her hand. Then she reached back into her jeans pocket and pulled out a tiny parcel of silver paper and a pack of Rizlas. I watched as she expertly rolled a joint. This, I knew, was Paul's doing. Four years older than us, already a student at Trinity. Maggie's big brother had always treated us as equals, taught us many things we were eager to know, and more than likely shouldn't have.

Then she lit up. I noticed that her fingernails were more bitten than usual, some of them topped with bloody streaks where she had nipped and nibbled at the flesh. The nails were so short they seemed to be growing inwards and downwards, embedding themselves back into the roots they had come from. It must have taken a huge effort of will to kill that habit. Maggie told me afterwards that she'd stopped biting her nails as soon as she left home: a conscious effort to show outwardly what her new freedom had brought her. Pride, self-esteem, relief. From what I can remember, at that time Paul was getting ready to repeat his exams and there was trouble in Maggie's household. Her parents had never tolerated failure of any kind.

'I wish they'd leave him alone,' she'd said to me earlier that week. Her distress was palpable. 'He's studying for *hours* every day. Nothing's *ever* enough for them.'

She adored her brother, and he her. For a moment, I wanted to ask how *she* was doing in the middle of all of that. But the enormity of my own loss took over and I let the moment pass.

Now she offered me the joint, holding her breath for the dope's maximum impact. I took it, although I didn't crave dope the way some of the others did. I've never liked the way I can't measure its effects. I've indulged, of course. What student didn't? But I've always preferred my substances legal and predictable.

There is no moral judgement in that: it's simply that you can't have a bad trip on a few glasses of wine. It's much easier to stay in control.

I took one drag and handed the joint back to her. 'I hate this,' I said. 'It'll mean new school, new neighbours, the lot.' As an only child, I believed that I had a greater right to complain than most. After all, I had no one to share things with in the furtive sanctuary of a bedroom, or over cups of tea in the empty kitchen of an even emptier house.

'What school will you be going to?' she asked after an interval. Maggie was ever the pragmatist. She accepted the realities of life in the way I never could. Accepted them, and then tried to fit her life around them without admitting defeat.

I shrugged, still angry. 'Dunno. They haven't told me yet.'

'We're not babies, Georgie. They can't stop us meeting, staying over and stuff. It doesn't have to change any of our plans, not unless you want it to.' There was the glint of challenge in Maggie's green eyes. My father's rise and rise in recent years, his designation as 'developer' rather than 'builder' had begun to drive a wedge between me and my old neighbours. He was seen variously as someone becoming too big for his boots, or getting above his station, or running away with himself – we Irish have countless phrases for people who dare to put their head above the appropriate socially defined parapet. Not that I had any respect for my father's dealings at that time. I didn't. Nevertheless, even then I was acutely aware of the mass of contradictions that seethed between those who grasped at prosperity and held on to it, and those who aspired to do so but failed. Hence the origins of begrudgery.

So. Maggie's tone made me angry. 'What the fuck do you mean "if I want to"?' What are you talking about?'

But she never got time to answer. We'd been so engrossed in our exchange that neither of us had noticed the Guard – or Bean Garda, as I think we still called them back in those days – who now materialized beside us. We both froze, Maggie with the joint halfway to her lips.

'I'll take that,' said the uniformed young woman, holding out her hand towards the joint. Talk about a smoking gun. Maggie handed it over without a word. 'What's your name?'

Maggie told her. 'And your address?' She wrote busily.

Then she looked at me. 'And you are?' she said, turning to a new page in her notebook.

'Georgina White,' I said, my heart hammering. Great, I was thinking. Perfect timing. Talk about giving my parents an excuse to ground me for life. Now the house move would be not just a financial, but a moral imperative in order to safeguard my well-being. I could have kicked myself.

'It's nuttin' to do wi' her,' Maggie said.

I looked at her in surprise. Her accent had fallen by about a dozen notches – it was pure Dublin. Even her stance was insolent, her normal posture replaced by an inner-city slouch.

'Oh?' the Garda raised her eyebrows, looking over at me, deeply suspicious. At the same time, I could see her hesitate. I could almost see her thinking: all that paperwork . . . She could hardly have ignored Maggie, caught as she was in flagrante. But I was a different matter.

'Yeah,' said Maggie, loudly, drawing the attention back to herself. She rummaged in her jeans pocket and handed over her silver-wrapped booty. 'She's a sap. She didn't even wanna try i'.'

The Guard looked from one of us to the other. 'Where do you live?' she asked me. I told her and she nodded. 'Is what Margaret says true?'

I could feel Maggie's glare. 'Yes,' I said, my accent pointedly different from hers. I felt shame descend like a shroud, spilling over my head, settling about my feet.

'Go home,' the Guard advised me.

'Yeah,' said Maggie. 'Go home. Ya sap.'

I turned and fled. I wept my way across the green, stumbled home blinded by tears of rage and guilt and self-pity. Maggie got into terrible trouble that night. She was brought to the Garda station, her parents were called, she was given an official warning. She felt, she said, the full weight, the full Majesty of the Law. Even then, she mocked herself, with Frank O'Connor for company. She had to report to the Junior Liaison Officer, she said, every week for six months. And she had to help out at the local youth club, something she took to with surprising alacrity.

'Some chance I have of getting up to any mischief,' she said, when school resumed a few days later. She said it with a weak grin. 'I'm grounded till I'm thirty – if I'm lucky. I'll see nothing but my bedroom, the cop shop and a ping-pong table built for two.'

There was an awkward silence between us for a moment. My freedom from punishment, from the consequences of my own behaviour, filled the spaces between us.

'I rang but your dad wouldn't let me talk to you,' I said. This was true. But I also knew that I could have called to the door if I hadn't been too cowardly to do so.

'See what I mean?' she said, lightly. 'Grounded and incommunicado.'

'Why did you do it?' I asked her.

She shrugged. 'What was the point of both of us ending up in the shite? Besides, this way, I figure you owe me.' She was laughing at me.

I felt the most tremendous burden lifting from around my heart. I grinned back at her, filling up with love. 'You can bet on it,' I said. 'For ever. I won't forget.'

And I meant it.

Later that year, I did move house and school, but Maggie and I never lost touch. I made the running. I felt it was the least I could do. My duty, my promise. Despite all the times I'd got her into trouble, when the tables were turned, her only instinct was to save my skin. And so, I feel responsible for her, for her wellbeing.

How could I feel otherwise?

7. *Claire*

It has just come to me that next December, I'll be the same age as my mother was when she abandoned us. I'll be forty-four years old. Another birthday on the horizon and that makes me wonder how many more I'll have. The thought depresses me. I don't like thinking that I have a sell-by date ticking away somewhere inside me like yet another biological time bomb that's waiting to explode.

It's strange, the way the four of us hardly ever talk about getting older. Sometimes I wonder if we've *ever* talked about the things that are important, particularly over the last few years. Well, Maggie and I have, of course. I trust her. But Georgie's grown too cynical of late and Nora – well, Nora's life is very different from mine. She means well, but she has become a little too smug for any of my confidences.

I'll never forget her compassion towards me. Maggie, that is. There are still days, all these years later, when I burn with shame over how I hurt her. I can plead all the reasons I like, make all the excuses I like, but what I did was still wrong. For once, I'm with Nora. And now my forty-fourth birthday is the final marker, I think. No more chances. That chapter of my life will finally be closed.

Ray, of course, will be forty-five on the same day. That's how everything started between us on that night. He insisted that he wanted us to celebrate our shared birthday together. I hate

December and have hated it in triplicate ever since I was twelve years of age. For being the month I was born, for being the month of Christmas, for being the month my mother abandoned us. And, later on, for being the month when John Lennon died, but that's a given.

I had just been to the magazine's annual Christmas party in the Conrad Hotel. It had been one of those awful nights of forced jollity when everyone had to turn up wearing their shiniest new outfit and their widest smile. I was not in the mood, particularly on that evening. But being the editor brought some social responsibilities with it, and the Christmas endurance test happened to be one of them. I did my duty, stayed till ten o'clock and then slipped away. By then, the party was beginning to get a bit raucous. It was time to go home and I hoped that nobody had noticed me leave. I made my way down the stairs. I've always avoided the lift on these occasions because I hate being forced to share a cramped space with someone who might be a little too full of Christmas spirit.

'Claire!'

I heard a man's voice, familiar, but out of context. I half-turned, expecting to see some journalist or other running after me and insisting that I come back and rejoin the party. Or worse, someone from the office with a complaint and enough alcohol on board to have the courage to voice it.

'I *thought* it was you!'

It took me a moment. 'Ray!' I was relieved.

'What are you doing in this neck of the woods?' He was beaming.

'Christmas party. Upstairs. But I'm sneaking away early.'

He leaned towards me, and his expression was conspiratorial. 'Good idea,' he said. 'I promise I won't tell. I'm sick of Christmas cheer myself and we've still got more than three weeks to go.'

I smiled at that. He gestured towards the bar. 'Listen, I'm just finishing up here. Let me grab my coat and I'll walk out with you.'

'No, please, it's . . .' But he was already gone. Part of me wanted to hurtle out the door, to rush off into the night and leave him standing there on his own. I really didn't want his company, anybody's company. Not on that night. I've wished so many times over the years that I'd obeyed that gut instinct.

He was back almost at once. So quickly, in fact, that I wondered whether he'd been drinking alone. He seemed steady enough, but I knew from Maggie even back then that Ray had started drinking a lot more than was good for him.

'Let's go somewhere a bit quieter,' he said then, and placed his hand under my elbow as he began to steer me out the door. I stopped at the top of the steps and turned to face him.

'It's Christmas, Ray, and it's ten o'clock at night. There *is* nowhere quieter. Anyhow, I'm tired. I don't mean to be rude, but all I want is a taxi to take me home.'

'Guaranteed. I'll put you into one myself. But first, a drink – just the one – given the time of year that's in it.'

I should have insisted. I should have pointed out all the contradictions he had already mentioned about the season and the burden of cheer it brought with it. But as I said, I was tired. Too tired even to argue. He brought us into a nearby pub that was much quieter than I expected. He winked at me.

'See? Leave it to Ray. You can usually get a seat in here,' he said. 'It's not trendy enough for the younger crowd and it's too trendy for the oldies. Come on, let me take your coat.'

I let him. I sat down.

'Back in a mo'.'

He disappeared at once towards the bar. I closed my eyes, trying to block out the events of the day. I wanted them to slip away from me. I went looking for forgetfulness in the dark. When I opened my eyes again, Ray was putting an ice bucket on the table. Inside, up to its neck in ice-cubes, was a bottle of champagne.

'Ray!' I said. 'What on earth are you doing!'

He eased the cork out of the bottle. The sound stilled the conversations at the bar for a moment and all heads turned in our direction. Then it started up again as though nothing much had happened.

He grinned. 'I think I remember that you and I have a significant date in common. Let's celebrate *that* instead of Christmas. Seems like much more fun.' He handed me a flute, half-filled with froth. 'Here's to birthdays. I'm a gentleman so I'll just mention that I'm thirty-five on Thursday next and I know that you are a good deal younger. Cheers.' And he raised his glass.

I had to laugh at that. The bitterness of the sound was audible even to me. 'Oh, yes – there's all of a year between us.'

'Come on,' he urged. 'Raise your glass. To shared birthdays.'

What can I say? I raised my glass. And I raised it again and again and again.

I don't want to remember all the gory details. And 'remember' is not an accurate word anyhow. What remains of that night is burned on to my hard disk. It plays and replays with an accuracy that I can only describe as forensic, every time I let my guard down. I don't need to try to recall all that happened. I need to make no effort at all. The details leap out of their own accord, each one tumbling after the other. A whole regiment of parachutists determined to capture enemy territory. They scorch their path into heart and soul as they go.

Yes, I was tired, yes, I was lonely, yes, I was despondent. Yes and yes and yes again. It should have made no difference. Maggie was my friend, is my friend, and she was entitled to better, far better, from me. For more than two years afterwards, she wouldn't speak to me. We four no longer met – at least, not as a group. Georgie and I used to, and I'd get a phone call from Nora fairly regularly. But I always dreaded her calls. I felt badly enough myself and Nora was too honest to pretend to feel other than she did, although she said her piece kindly enough. I avoided her because I needed no more reminders of the awfulness of what I had done.

Then, one evening, Georgie manoeuvred the two of us together – Maggie and me, that is. I'll always be grateful to her for that. I'm sure she did it more for Maggie's sake than for mine, but that doesn't matter. Either way, it was a kind and loyal thing to do and it remains one of the times that Georgie has surprised me the most. But, however grateful I might be to Georgie and the part she played, I still can't get over Maggie's generosity. Her tearful forgiveness was more than I deserved. Not only did she not judge me, she somehow found the will to be understanding. And afterwards, although I am still not quite sure how this happened, the four of us found a way back to our evenings again, and our friendships. I'm not saying that things were easy, or even as they had been before, but still, we were able to forge something out of the wreckage.

That night with Ray I was seduced by something so simple, so unexpected that I'm amazed more men don't know about it. It was kindness. No more and no less. Some time towards the end of the first bottle of champagne, I began to cry. I couldn't help myself. I've never been any good at drinking. It either makes me paranoid or it makes me weep. Sometimes the two happen together, and that is not a pretty sight. But these were tears that should have waited, as usual, until I was in my bath, surrounded by the comforts of warm water, the scent of bath-oil and the privacy of my own home. Ray seemed unsurprised and unmoved by my tears. I wondered afterwards if he was used to seeing women cry, but such an uneasy thought seemed to be at odds with his behaviour. He patted my hand and hunched towards me so that the people standing behind him couldn't see my distress. And no,

I wasn't crying over another man, at least not directly, not in the way that that implies.

'What is it, Claire?' His voice was quiet. It seemed full of concern. I know that Ray has been unfaithful to Maggie several times over the years. I even knew it then. But all I saw on that evening, at least up to that point, was friendship. And so I told him. About my treatments. My failures. My longings.

'I've given up on men,' I said, sobbing into the handkerchief he handed me. 'Really.' It was true. I'd been with John for just over a year, but we were never going to be long-term together and we both knew it. I hadn't even told him about the hospital treatments. I was terrified that he might take fright and bolt when I needed him most. Dishonest? That's for sure. Make a man a father and then abandon him? I admit it. It was not my finest hour.

For just that moment, it was a relief to talk to Ray, to talk to anyone who would listen without having to pretend any more. 'I don't expect a relationship. I'm not even looking for one. All I want is a baby. And after today, I can't even have that.'

Ray said nothing. He just looked at me and waited for me to stop crying. Finally, he said: 'What happened today?' But so quietly I could hardly hear him over the noise in the bar.

I wiped my eyes, blew my nose and tried to get control of myself. 'Six months ago,' I told him, 'I managed to persuade a doctor to give me fertility treatment. I've been trying to have a baby for three years and nothing's happened. I was desperate.'

Desperate? There isn't a word in the English language that can approach how I felt. The initial excitement, the anticipation behind the popping of every Clomid, the taking of my temperature, the mechanics of sex on the right day, at the right hour. I kept myself alive with the oxygen of promise: the promise of a baby, of *babies* even, if the treatment was successful. And they kept on telling me just how successful it could be. Statistics swam behind the rosy spectacles of this hopeful mother, of the many hopeful mothers that shared all those afternoons in plush, carpeted rooms as we sat waiting for consultants to tell us our fate. We'd leaf through magazines, making polite conversation, pretending that we felt normal. As though we weren't fuelled by an all-consuming rage that Mother Nature had abandoned us, had singled us out for a litany of losses before we had even begun. There was always the cruelty of hope to lure us on to the next stage. Beyond this medication, that medication and the other medication, there was always the tantalizing promise of IVF. We patients endured the constant drip-feed of optimism and expectation, the certainty of a take-home baby at the end of it all. Well, it hadn't happened. At least not to me.

Ray refilled my glass and I remember that I downed it in one gulp. 'I pretended to be married, but the doctor knew. Anyhow, we went ahead with the treatment but this is the last cycle she's prepared to prescribe. She told me so this afternoon.' I shrugged. 'So that's that.'

By then, I was feeling light-headed. It wasn't a pleasant feeling. It was like the night of my first party with Maggie and Georgie in our flat in Rathmines when the dope had made me sick. The memory of that, of my friends and how they had looked after me, on that occasion and on others, propelled me all at once into standing. I looked at Ray and I remember feeling amazed, confused, just for an instant. It was as though I was seeing him for the first time. He was unfamiliar and distant. What on earth was I doing? Telling this man things I hadn't even told my closest friends? What was I thinking? I finally began to feel the return of some sort of sanity, even though it was through a haze of champagne.

'I have to go,' I said. I remember that I stumbled, almost falling back into the chair again. I knew that my departure was abrupt, that my behaviour must appear to be very strange. But I couldn't wait. All I knew was that I needed to be gone. I needed to be home.

'Wait,' he said, flinging out one arm to catch me. 'You can't go home alone, not like this. Let me take you.'

'No,' I protested. 'I'll be all right. I'm going to get a taxi.'

'I'm coming with you,' he said. 'It's the party season. Taxis'll be thin on the ground at this hour. And you're a little . . . the worse for wear.'

The worse for wear. That brought me back – back to Paul, to the night we met. I didn't want to remember how I had lost him, how I had driven away the one man I did love and still do, for better and for worse.

Ray steadied me then and helped me into my coat. He put one arm around my shoulders and opened the door of the pub. Unfortunately, we got a taxi immediately. I say 'unfortunately' because maybe if I had had to stand and queue for longer in the freezing December air of Dublin, I might have sobered up more than I did. I'm not trying to make excuses. I did what I did and I am responsible for it and no one else is to blame. But it might have meant that I'd have resisted with more conviction when Ray pulled me towards him and kissed me. It might have meant that I'd have sent him packing instead of handing him my key when the taxi pulled up outside my house. It might have meant that I would not have allowed him to open my front door and bundle me inside.

What is there left to tell? How can I bear to remember the ordinary, sordid tale of betrayal that played itself out on my living-room sofa that night. How can I ever forget. Did I think of Maggie? No, I did not. I thought only of sperm and egg. I was driven by all the longings of thwarted motherhood. It was a madness, I no longer have any doubt about that. It was a compulsion, a yearning that refused to be denied. It has made me understand the force of addiction, that lunacy of desire that demands to be fulfilled or else it will kill you in the attempt. The end result, the possibility of a baby, was all I thought about, both that time and the next.

And that's what Maggie understood on that evening when Georgie finally brought us together after more than two years of silence. Years that had been filled by the yawning absences that betrayal brings in its wake. I think Maggie found all that grief easier to accept, finally, than love or lust. Maybe it didn't seem to be quite as big a betrayal in her eyes. At least, not on my part, anyhow. She never discussed what she felt about Ray, not with me. That night in Georgie's after we had spoken, she took my hand in hers. The gesture moved me so much that I broke down. So did she.

'I'm so sorry, Claire, so very sorry about everything. God, life is a real mess, sometimes. And yes, of course I want to forgive you.' She rummaged for tissues in her sleeve and handed me one. 'I knew nothing . . . I didn't realize . . . you'd been trying for so long. It never occurred to me. It's terrible, the whole thing is just terrible.'

I couldn't speak. I continued to sob as she stroked my hand. She never once mentioned the awful outcome that that evening might have had, never once alluded to how there might have been a child, her husband's child. I will never forget the depths of my own shame as she held both of my hands in hers.

'We'll talk about it again,' she sighed. 'Don't break your heart over it. We'll work our way through it somehow, you and I.'

And then Georgie came back into the room and we stopped our conversation. But we did meet again. I was glad to meet her on my own, happy that she had wanted to ask it of me. I felt that I owed her many things, among them the courtesy of a full explanation, long overdue.

There was more, much more that I still needed to tell her.

It's almost impossible to believe that the four of us have spent so many years orbiting each other's lives. Sometimes the gravitational forces pull us together, other times they force us apart. I suppose we've never been as close as the time when we were all students together. But in reality, that time lasted only a year. It's strange, it now seems to be much longer than that. Perhaps because we all lived that year with such intensity. Once the weddings started, though, the friendships all started to shift and change. At least, that's how I remember it.

Nora and Frank were the first of our group to get married. Pete and Georgie followed after a gap of some six years, after what I once described as a whirlwind romance, but Georgie disagreed with my characterization. In fact, she got very cross.

'It may be sudden, Claire, but this is nothing as trivial as romance. This is a *relationship*. It's time for me to settle down.'

I didn't comment. After all, how could I? I was the last person qualified to judge the love affairs of others, particularly those belonging to my friends. But I do remember wondering how she could be so calculating about it.

After the dizzy heights of Pete and Georgie, next came Maggie and Ray, just six months later. I've often felt sorry for Maggie on that score. But not as sorry as I used to feel for myself. All of these weddings in their different ways reinforced my singleness. I had to learn to be detached from them, to treat them almost as professional occasions. Nora and Frank's nuptials had already put paid to any future that Paul and I might have had – not that they were to blame, of course they weren't. The deed just happened to be done and dusted on their particular day. The weddings that came next simply repeated the point in case I hadn't got it the first time around.

If Nora and Frank were the very hallmarks of stability, then Pete and Georgie were the symbols of dynamism. Ireland was just beginning to emerge from the economic black hole of the eighties.

It was starting to be full of movers and shakers. Their reception in the Burlington Hotel was like a *Who's Who* of the famous and influential. I should know: I helped to organize it. I used to do things like that, occasionally, back in those days. I was the original Wedding Planner. I found that it went very nicely hand-in-hand with the business of my then magazine, *Irish-Style*.

Georgie and I worked well together, making sure that hers would be the society wedding of the year. And our success was recorded for all to see. I still have the four-page magazine spread to prove it. I made her a gift of a framed collage of the best photographs of the day and she still has it on her office wall. Or at least she did, the last time I looked.

On the day, it was fun to see how the newly rich and influential each kept an anxious eye on the other and on their own place in the pecking order. The seating plan was a complete nightmare, but we did it, Georgie and I. I developed a healthy respect for her ability to schmooze. There is no other way to describe the endless tact she showed where business connections were concerned. Bankers and builders – sorry, developers: our standing joke – rubbed shoulders with models and journalists and politicians and what Georgie called the 'fashionistas' of every possible shade.

On the day, the bride was magnificent. There is no other word for it. Her looks were never conventional and she knew she was not beautiful. So she went all out for regal. For a start, she wore no veil. She had her hair up, showing that lovely neck that I'd admired on the first day I saw her. Her only ornaments were an antique tiara, some long earrings and a string of pearls. She and Maggie designed and made her wedding dress, of course, which was in off-white and low-cut. It was tailored to the straight, strong lines that suited Georgie best and studded with seed pearls that caught the light from every possible angle. She didn't so much walk down the aisle as glide.

Ray was standing beside me in the church the day that

Georgie and Pete got married. I had decided not to bring a companion. I had got tired of the endless speculation around Claire and her unsuitable men. He turned to me as soon as the bride passed by our pew, with Maggie's small figure close behind.

'Isn't she a picture?' he grinned.

I hoped he meant Maggie.

Georgie's going-away outfit caused a bit of a stir among the women guests too, I was pleased to notice. It was a coat and dress, a subtle mix of ecru silk and linen, and it was infinitely more stylish than any of that season's offerings from Chanel. I could tell that that one outfit alone had just snared maybe another half-dozen potential customers. I rejoiced for both of them, for her and for Maggie. And her suitcase was filled with lots of other pieces besides. I know because Maggie and I had helped her pack. We had decided a long time back that the wedding might as well be a showcase for all of our different businesses.

'Why not?' Georgie had said. 'The three of us will never have such a captive audience again. And the aisle is every bit as good as the catwalk.'

Pete was solid and calm and tolerant on the day.

'This is Georgie's wedding,' he said to me with a smile, just a few days beforehand. 'I'm only here to get married.'

Georgie and Maggie had dressed him, too. Not to kill, but rather to highlight the bride. He was content with that and played his role of consort to the hilt. On a couple of occasions when Georgie seemed not to be getting her own way in the run-up to the big day, she snapped at him in my presence. Each time, he'd grin at me and say: 'Tell Her Majesty that I defer to her wishes.' Even then, I wondered at the wisdom of that. Too much deference cannot be good for a woman like Georgie.

Pete could work a room, though, every bit as well as Georgie could. I still believe that that wedding poured the foundations for the success that both of them began to enjoy just as soon as they were married. It seemed to me like an old-fashioned joining of empires, like the historical ones we used to read about in college. Georgie and Pete complemented each other. They were both talented, hard-working people, there is no doubt about that. But hey, the contacts help.

By the time Maggie and Ray's wedding day came along, only six months later, they were very much the also-rans. Don't get me wrong. The wedding was stylish because Maggie would have nothing less, and Georgie would have nothing less either, on her friend's behalf. But I felt that there was something tired about it. She, Maggie, that is, had wanted something small and intimate, a low-key affair, different in every way from Georgie's. I thought she had made a wise choice. There was no way she could ever hope to scale the heights that Georgie did. She simply didn't have the contacts. But its low-keyness spoke to me of something other than that. It was as though Maggie's heart wasn't in it. Although I tried to stay as neutral as I could during the months leading up to her big day, I couldn't help feeling uneasy. Her wedding had all the signs – subtle ones, but signs nonetheless, for those prepared to read them – of something she had got herself into and now she had to see it through.

I have often wondered, though, if that view is just something I have conveniently developed in retrospect. Something that might have more to do with guilt on my part, much more than I care to believe. The reasoning might go something like this: if they were such an ill-matched, ill-starred couple to begin with, then perhaps my own crime of betrayal mightn't be such an unforgivable one, after all. But it doesn't work for me. I can't let myself off the hook like that.

Georgie was to be Maggie's matron of honour – a term both of them hated with a passion. However, six weeks before the wedding, Georgie discovered that she was pregnant. She was livid. She was also, to use Maggie's phrase, as sick as a parrot, and there was absolutely no way that she was up to the duties of maid, matron, whatever she wanted to call it. Maggie was her usual, up-front, no-nonsense self when she arranged to meet me for coffee.

'You know that Georgie and I have been friends since we were kids,' she said, spooning the froth off her cappuccino into her mouth. I often wondered how she managed to eat and drink with such gusto as she did, and still keep the scarlet gloss of her lips looking perfect. I wear lipstick only rarely, and when I do, I seem to manage to eat it away almost instantly.

'We've promised each other ever since we were fourteen that we'd be each other's bridesmaids.' Maggie paused and I remembered how well she'd fulfilled that role at Georgie's own wedding. Georgie, the sisterless sophisticate. Maggie was wonderful on that day. She was playful, unobtrusive and managed to be everywhere she was needed – by Georgie's side, or playing with the little flower-girls, or helping the photographer capture the eager guests. It had felt to me as though there were two of her.

'Well, Georgie can't keep that promise now, even though she'd love to. It's driving her nuts that she can't.' She looked straight at me. Even then, I didn't know what was coming. 'And if she can't, the one person I'd love to have as my bridesmaid is you.'

I looked at her stupidly. 'Me?' Memories of Paul flooded, of that awful summer, of all the things that Maggie didn't know and might never know, unless I had the courage some day to tell her.

'Yeah,' she said, grinning at my surprise. She lit a cigarette and blew the smoke over her shoulder, away from me. 'You. Who else?' She made it sound like the most natural thing in the world. My eyes filled. I wanted to ask her, but she got there before me.

'Paul is still in Australia. He's not going to be able to make it home. Ray and I are going out to see them – we're meeting up in Singapore. If I thought he'd be here, I wouldn't ask you. It wouldn't be fair.'

Dear Maggie. I wanted to lean forwards and hug her. She had

such a knack of getting things out in the open, of being natural and easy with others around her. Instead of hugging her, though, I squeezed her hand. I see now that it was a gesture that was eerily prophetic of Georgie's living room, years into the future. But by then, so many things had been destroyed or damaged beyond repair. On this day, though, they were all still intact, all full of hope and promise and the certainties of friendships built to last. 'I'd love to be your bridesmaid,' I said, finally. 'I can't think of anything I'd like more.'

And she grinned, raising both of her thumbs in jubilation. She and I worked well together, too, during those last, hectic six weeks. I was anxious to do everything right and she was just as anxious to show me that I was not second-best and so we had a winning combination. On the day, Ray's behaviour was impeccable. He was handsome, courteous to all the guests and very attentive to Maggie. In fact, he had eyes only for her. She basked like a girl in his smiles and I was glad. Glad and relieved. I remember thinking even then, as I stood beside them at the altar, that maybe they had a chance, never mind Lorraine, never mind all the times he had strayed as a single man in the past. Maybe all of that would now be over, once he tied the knot.

I couldn't help remembering, though, the day he'd gone missing at Nora's wedding. That was the day he'd pulled the bridesmaid, no less, who happened to be the bride's sister. I wanted Maggie's love, loyalty and both her and Ray's hopes for a future together to win the day for both of them. I will always regret the part I may have played in any of the disillusionment that came next. But there is nothing that can be done now, at least not about that.

We saw Maggie and Ray off in a hail of confetti and rice. The taxi waited to bring them to Dublin airport and then to Australia for six weeks. To Australia and to Paul. He came back to Dublin only the once, for their father's funeral. I hadn't the courage to meet him so I invented a business trip to Dijon and fled. Maggie did not press me to stay. Her leaving now for Australia was not a happy moment. Too many memories collided. I counted the minutes until I could leave the hotel with decency.

I remember that as we all stood and waved outside the front door of the hotel, Georgie puked into a plastic bag she'd kept beside her – discreetly of course – all through the reception. I was grateful for the distraction. Pete was beaming, full of tenderness and delight at the thought of being a dad. He could talk about nothing else that day. But I could sense Georgie's rage. This was an occasion when she must have wanted to share centre stage, she and her oldest friend. Instead, here she was, hawking ignominiously into a sick sack. I have to confess that something about that amused me, despite my heartache. I got a sense of satisfaction that had its origins in that famous night some seven years previously. I remembered lurching home on my own and throwing up on the grass in Rathfarnham the time when she and Maggie – but particularly she – had been so knowing and all grown up, the night when the three of us had met in O'Neill's as brand-new students.

From where I stood, it was good to see Georgie, for the first time ever, no longer in control. For maybe the only time in her life, there were forces outside her influence that made her incapable of making anything different from what it already was. She just had to accept that this was how it was going to be and get on with it.

'This is shit, Claire, really shit,' she said, wiping away the tears that had escaped as she threw up. 'Look at me. How is it possible to feel so bad?' She was gripped by another wave of nausea. Her eyes looked navy, her face white and strained. She retched into the basin before her.

I tried to soothe her. I sat with her on a low upholstered stool in the ladies' room while other guests came in and out and looked over at us, full of curiosity. Maggie and Ray had left maybe twenty minutes earlier, and what Georgie had held together till then, she now let fall apart with no apology. I admired her and felt sorry for her on that night. One of the things I have always liked about Georgie is her protectiveness, her ability to look after Maggie and her willingness to do so. I've always been drawn to loyalty.

'I worry about her, Claire, I really do,' she said now. She dry-heaved once again, and I handed her a tissue. 'I don't trust Ray. He's not good for her. I'm afraid that it's all going to come unstuck.'

After that, she wasn't able to say anything more. I left her and went off to go and buy her a bottle of water at the bar. Pete was hovering outside and had been for some time. He and I agreed that it was time for Georgie to go home, to go to bed and go to sleep. I bought the water and went back to the Ladies to help her to the car. But by then she was already asleep, resting on her forearms, the top of her head reflected in the large mirrors above the basins. I didn't want to disturb her, but I knew that I had to. As I touched her on the shoulder, she jerked awake. In that instant, the one that exists between sleep and waking, I saw her face register confusion, uncertainty and pain.

I remember it as the only time I have ever known Georgie to display vulnerability.

I also treasure it as the one constant reminder I have of her selflessness in friendship.

Remembering Maggie's wedding makes me recall that other occasion, after my fiasco with Ray, when Maggie and I met on our own to talk. It was late one evening in March, a few weeks after Georgie had managed to get the two of us together in her living room. We were very careful about choosing where we should go. Maggie's house was impossible and I know that we both felt mine was tainted after what had happened there between Ray and me. And so Maggie chose Nico's, an old-fashioned Italian restaurant in the city centre. It was a comforting place. I had always thought of it as a bit shabby, but it had earned its reputation for good food and good wine several years back and had no need to impress anybody. I think we both liked the fact that it wasn't pretending to be anything it was not. Maggie and I still felt awkward in each other's presence – how could we not? – but we were both working hard at making that disappear.

I remember thinking on that evening that we were living one of those strange coincidences that Maggie can have known nothing about. Two years and four months had passed since my non-affair with Ray; fifteen years and four months had passed since my last painful conversation with Paul. They were both dates I would never forget.

He and I had met in the Gresham Hotel, where we were unlikely to run into anyone we knew. It was maybe a year after Nora's wedding, but I hadn't even begun to get over him. Maggie intervened for me. She begged him to meet me, just to talk. And Paul agreed to meet. He arrived shortly after I did and he was dressed in a suit and tie. I found that strange at the time. The minute I saw him, I was reminded of all the formality of a funeral and my chest tightened. I recall very little else. I'm sure our meeting went on for longer than I can remember, but most of it is a white-out.

He was pale as he came up to me and took my hand. He leaned towards me and kissed my cheek.

I squeezed his hand but there was no answering pressure. My courage failed me. I had hoped, of course I had, but something in me had known that this was how it was going to be. I slumped on to the sofa beside him. I had to force myself not to put my arms around him, not to pull his dark head towards me and hold him close the way I had done for so long.

I have often thought since that day that I should have fought harder for us. I have felt that maybe I was too docile, too accepting of his certainty that things were over between us. But how can you force someone to love you? How can you force them to feel something that they say they can no longer feel?

And how can you stop being to blame for something for which you are the only one to blame?

'I've tried, Claire, but I just can't put it behind me.' Paul spoke so quietly I could hardly hear him. 'It goes to the core of everything I believe a relationship should be. It's not only the baby that died. It's our trust.'

I remember how I winced at the word 'baby', and how much more I wince at it now. And of course I heard 'the baby that *you killed*'. A six-week pregnancy? Was there no room at all for a little more forgiveness?

I sat there numbly, not being able to speak.

Eventually, I summoned up the courage. I had nothing left to lose.

'I'll do anything, Paul, anything at all. Any penance you want. I love you. I don't want to lose you. I don't want to lose *us*.'

At that, he stood up abruptly. I could see that he was choked, that his eyes were wet.

'It's too late, Claire. I'm sorry – sorrier than you will ever know. You've already lost me. We've lost each other. I have to go.'

And that was that. I didn't blame him. I had done all that he said, and more. I sat for a while longer in the hotel lobby, watching happy couples come and go. Watching mothers and happy toddlers. As you do, as you can't help doing in these circumstances. I know that I sat for a long time wondering if there was any easy way to kill myself. Like Hamlet, I wanted my 'too, too solid flesh to melt'. But unfortunately, it wouldn't. It stayed stubborn and real and all too frozen. I made my way home to the flat, drank a full bottle of white wine and woke, shivering, to a filthy hangover that at least gave me some other focus for my pain.

I never saw him on my own again. I think we both avoided the places we knew the other might be, and so we rarely ran into each other. I know that Maggie was very careful. She never invited her brother back to the flat. Instead, she went to him. It must have been very hard on her, but she never said. I learned that as soon as Paul graduated, he went to Australia. Maggie told me that there were far more opportunities there for young doctors than there were in Ireland, something I had no difficulty in believing.

It was a casual acquaintance, some months later, who told me that he had gone to specialize in obstetrics. We were standing outside Bewley's in Grafton Street at the time that she told me. When she saw my reaction, Geraldine was immediately concerned.

'Claire? Are you okay? Did I say something wrong?'

I shook my head. I felt dizzy, my legs went weak, my throat filled with nausea. Time had not healed this sense of loss. Hadn't even begun to. 'No, no – of course not. I haven't been feeling well, that's all. Must be some sort of bug.'

She insisted on bringing me into the café, sitting me down, getting me a glass of water. I just wished that she would leave. I wanted to be on my own. It was a cruel reversal of the night that Paul and I had met. Then, my feeling unwell had been the means of bringing us together. Now, it was the sign that all the things I had done had driven us apart. His choice of obstetrics opened up all of those wounds, all over again. I still think about him. And that night with Maggie in the restaurant, I felt tortured by guilt, old and new. Her husband and her brother, I kept thinking. Her brother and her husband.

We ordered food and the waiter poured our wine. Maggie looked at me across the candlelit table. I could see that her expression was still guarded.

'I'm glad we can try and put it behind us, Claire. It hurt, I won't deny it, and some days it still hurts. But Ray was responsible too, it wasn't all you. And that's been part of the problem, having to admit that to myself. But I've missed you and the group. Life's too tough to spend it without your friends.' She raised her glass. 'Here's to Georgie. For once, being a bossy-boots brought about the right result.'

I smiled and repeated her toast, grateful all over again for friendship, particularly at a time like this. 'To Georgie.' We sipped in silence for a few moments.

'You wanted to tell me something else, didn't you?'

I was grateful for her directness. Maggie has always had that ability – to get right to the heart of the matter.

I drew breath and prepared myself. 'Yes. About Paul and me.'

She looked surprised. 'Paul?'

'Yes. Why we split up.'

She frowned. I thought she looked uncomfortable and wondered why. I had a moment of panic. Perhaps this wasn't a good idea. Perhaps this was me being selfish again. Maybe I wanted to have her hear my confession to make *me* feel better. Never mind about her.

'You don't have to tell me anything about that, Claire. It's all a very long time ago. What? Fifteen, sixteen years?'

I looked at her. 'Yes. I want to tell you what happened. I know you didn't understand and I wouldn't talk to you at the time. I'd like to now. If that's okay.'

She poured herself a glass of water. 'Sure,' she said. 'If it helps.'

'I need you to know because it's all connected. Back then, and now.' She looked wary again. Maybe she was afraid I was going to talk about Ray.

'I loved Paul. I've never stopped loving him. He wasn't the one who broke us up. It was me.' I could feel my eyes begin to fill. Whoever talked about time being a great healer was full of crap. Old hurts still hurt if their cause lives on.

The waiter placed our starters in front of us. He moved swiftly, quietly, around the table. Perhaps he sensed something.

'You remember Nora's wedding? Stupid question. But you know what I mean.'

'Of course I do. I knew something had happened between the two of you that night.'

I could feel my hands begin to tremble. I put down my cutlery. I wasn't able to hold my knife and fork any more.

'I had an abortion, Maggie. I didn't tell Paul until afterwards. He couldn't forgive me.'

'Ah.' Her eyes were filled with sadness. For me. And for her brother, too, I'd imagine. Perhaps even for herself. 'I'm sorry, Claire, I really am. That must have been awful for you.' She paused for a moment and something seemed to strike her. Maggie was always good at stitching things together, at reaching conclusions without needing to have everything spelt out. 'Are you telling me that you believe that's why you've never been able to become pregnant? Since, I mean.'

I nodded and bit the inside of my lip. It was a trick I had learned, one that stopped me crying. It gave me a different sort of pain to think about. 'Yes, but that's not . . . that's only part of it. I need you to understand.'

Poor Maggie. I knew that our split, Paul's and mine, had upset her deeply. She used to joke back then about us being sisters-in-law. She had been thrilled that Paul was finally with someone she could like. They'd always been close and I'd felt badly that she blamed *him* for our not being together, and not me. But I can't have felt badly enough to summon up the courage to tell her when it might have made a difference, can I? I regretted that and even as I was speaking, I was regretting being the source of yet more upset. But it was too late now to turn back. Too late in too many ways.

'It wasn't that Paul couldn't forgive me for the abortion. What he couldn't forgive was that I didn't trust him enough to tell him. That I went and did it on my own, without him. I broke him, Maggie. Not the other way around.'

Maggie lifted her napkin to her mouth. 'I'm so sorry, Claire. About all of it. I really am. I can't imagine how it was for you.'

I saw Maggie stuck for words for perhaps the first time ever. But I was driven to keep talking, to reveal my other, awful secret. That particular newsreel plays frequently in my internal cinema. A bit jerky in places, but it still tells its story with far too much clarity. Sometimes black and white, sometimes Technicolor, but always from start to finish. I have discovered that there is no detail too painful to omit. First, there was the panic of pregnancy after the only serious row Paul and I had ever had. It was about us going to London for the summer, or not going, in his case. I accused him of not loving me enough, not wanting to be with me enough.

'Claire.' I can still hear him groan. 'I failed two fuckin' exams. I have to repeat. I have to *study*. I can't go to London. I need to be here.'

I don't know why I kept pushing it. Did I think he was getting tired of me, of us? That he might leave me? I don't know. Maybe. Was I trying to test him, to see if he really loved me? Maybe that, too. One way or the other, though, I had my finger on the self-destruct button.

'You can study in London every bit as well as you can study here. Three months apart is just too *long*.'

All I wanted was for him to ask me to stay. But he wouldn't. He always said he'd never try to stop me doing the things I wanted to do. He said that I had a life of my own and he respected my independence. Right then, I didn't want my independence respected. I wanted him to need me, to put his arms around me and want to keep me with him. But then, of course, I was the needy one.

'That's not true and you know it.' I remembered how he ran his hands through his hair, a familiar gesture that immediately caused my heart to contract. 'I'd have to get a full-time job. Living in London costs a shitload of money. Don't you realize that?'

'You're working here,' I pointed out. Digging, always digging.

'*Part*-time,' he shouted, losing his temper.

There was more. Much more. Things were said that couldn't be taken back. He shouted at me over my 'abandonment routine'. About my driving a wedge between us. About my not trusting his love. And he was right. About all of it. I slammed out of his flat, shaking. I didn't want him to see me cry. Two days later, I discovered I was pregnant. Blame hormones, blame my mother for leaving me, blame blind, stupid panic: I booked a clinic, spun my father a yarn about needing extra money for rent, and did what thousands of Irish women had done before me and are still doing. I took the boat.

Here's where the images judder a bit. The coldness of the clinic. The kindness of the counsellor at my 'it's not too late to change your mind' interview. Standard procedure beforehand, I believe. Not just because I was Irish and Catholic and terrified out of my mind. And where were my friends in all of this? In ignorance, which was exactly where I wanted them to be.

How could I trust that none of my three friends would let something slip by accident? My reasons for keeping Paul in the same ignorance were more complex. Perhaps a mix of I'm leaving you before you decide to leave me; a potent memory of a woman trapped with children in a life she didn't want, humming 'Lucy in the Sky with Diamonds' as she scrubbed the kitchen tiles.

And so I signed the clinic's form, got into bed and waited. I was determined not to see myself there, not to take in any of my surroundings, not the pale green of the room, not the starch in the sheets, not the Irish accents of the nurses. None of it. I decided not to speak to any of the other women. Most of us avoided eye-contact, anyhow. I don't know which was greater: the sense of fear or the sense of loss. I didn't want to share anybody else's grief because I already had enough of my own. And of course it was safer that way because somebody would be sure to know me. Somebody would know my home place. And then somebody would tell.

When it was over, I made the journey home, bleeding my way through seventeen underground stops, three changes of line and all the chaos of Euston station.

Paul had been haunting Rathmines Road in my absence, according to Georgie. She was curious about what was going on and made no effort to hide it. I'd hoped to come back to an empty flat, but the gods were not on my side. She'd made coffee and offered to make me a cup.

'Kettle's boiled,' she said. 'I'm heading out in a minute. Danny's waiting for me. Sure you don't want one?'

I shook my head, not trusting to speech just at that moment. The smell of her cigarette smoke was making me feel sick. It reminded me of most of the women at the clinic, dragging madly on last cigarettes before they faced their particular firing squads.

I was glad that Georgie was on her way out. I didn't want a conversation just then. 'Have you and Paul fallen out?' she demanded. 'And where did you get to, anyway? Sneaking away like that and not telling. He hasn't been off the phone for three days.'

I put my bag down in the corner. There was no point in trying to hide it. 'I went to Ennistymon. My dad wasn't well,' I lied.

She lost interest. Didn't even ask if my father had recovered.

That's Georgie for you. Maggie had stayed over at Ray's for the weekend, so no more explanations were necessary just then. Once Georgie left, I filled the machine with blood-stained underwear, washing away the evidence like the Lady Macbeth of Rathmines. Then I lay down on the sofa and cried. I was home only a couple of hours when the phone rang.

'Claire.' I could hear the relief in Paul's voice. 'I miss you. This is stupid.'

He came over. We made up. Until he wanted to take me to bed. And then I had to tell him. I watched him fall apart as he put my words together and tried to make sense of them. He reminded me of my father after my mother abandoned us. His face contorted grey with grief, he wept so hoarsely he frightened me.

'How could you?' he said. 'How could you not trust me enough to tell me?'

I'm going to draw a veil over the rest of it, over all that summer when we tried to fix what I had broken. Instead, I ended up fixing flats: painting, decorating, designing tranquil garden spaces that became the polar opposite of the churning emptiness inside me. Georgie's father was generous with my wages, and I was able to pay my father back in record time. I did not want him to be responsible in any way for how I'd spent his money. Not that I'd ever have told him. But it wasn't about how he would feel, anyhow. It was about me, and the way I felt. I didn't want to live with the thought that I had sabotaged his generosity.

Each time Paul and I met over the next couple of months, the sense of desperation between us grew. Before that, bed had been our playground. I have never again found that intimacy, that fun, that pleasure that Paul and I shared, although I have looked for it ever since, in far too many beds. 'Wanton', he used to call me, sinking his hands into my hair, which he loved. He said it with admiration, with no hint of the moral judgement that usually goes with it. He liked the fact that it played with 'wantin''. He loved words. He could have been a writer, if he'd chosen, rather than a doctor. He was good at putting things together, making language sing. We used to play word games, too. Once, I gave him a present of a game of Scrabble, and we devised our own private rules for playing. 'Abandoned' was another favourite of his. He'd use it as a deliberate joke about my mother, turning the word around, finding joy in it, testing my growing sense of humour. Growing under his hands.

But after London, bed was no longer a place to play. The last time we made love, he cried. He must have known it was the last time. I didn't. I still kept hoping. I still believed that if I could manage enough love for both of us, he would find his own way back to me. Finally, on the day of Nora's wedding, he told me. That he still loved me, but something fundamental had gone for good. It was watching Frank and Nora together that had made him realize. And broken trust, he said, was something that could not be fixed. He would not spend his life looking over his shoulder.

Old hurt, new hurt. It's all the same. And in life's ironic little fashion, I brought it on myself. A self-fulfilling prophecy of loss and abandonment and lovelessness. That's me.

Maggie was pale in the candlelight.

'I wanted you to know the whole story,' I said. 'I started trying to have a baby when I was thirty. I knew by then that marriage wasn't going to happen for me – and I didn't want it. If I couldn't have Paul, then I didn't want anyone.'

She spoke softly. 'And you've carried that on your own for five years. Why didn't you say something to one of us, even if not to me? Sorry, that's a stupid thing to say. But we might have been able to . . . I don't know, comfort you.' Comfort Paul, too. But she didn't say that.

I smiled. 'It was easier to pretend. I hadn't been able to tell you about the abortion at the time, and then, well, months and years went by and it seemed better, easier for everyone not to. And it's the same with the infertility treatment. Think how difficult it would have been for all of you. You'd have tried to protect me. You might have felt guilty about your own children or felt sorry for me. I didn't want that.'

I could see Maggie thinking. Considering it in the generous, careful way she has always had, trying to match the possible with the actual. 'What about now?' she asked eventually. 'You're only thirty-five. There must be other doctors, other treatments.' She did not even mention the cruel irony of her brother's choice. Her brother with four children and a Tasmanian wife. Her nieces, her nephews. My loss, my losses. Our pasta remained uneaten. The waiter, deferential, concerned, approached us.

'Is everything all right, *signore*?'

Maggie looked at him as though she had no idea how he got there. 'What?' she said, her face blank.

'The food, *signora*. Is everything to your liking?'

'Yes, yes, thank you. Everything is fine.'

He nodded gravely, topped up our wine glasses and left. I could almost see him shaking his head to himself.

'Oh, I haven't given up hope,' I told her. 'But right now, I'm on a break – if that's the right term. I haven't been with anyone since John and I split up last year. I'm trying to take stock. I don't know how much more of the hope and despair treadmill I can take.' I paused. I didn't want to bring Ray into the conversation again and I didn't want to make excuses. 'The time with Ray was just after the first gynaecologist told me "no more treatments". To say I was devastated would be an understatement. That's the last bit of the jigsaw, Maggie. The bit I didn't have time to tell you in Georgie's last week.'

How glib that all sounded. It struck me afterwards that each of Ray's infidelities must have been like a small death for Maggie, too. I had never found, even for myself, words that would contain the violence of hope and the bitterness of failure that I had gone through every month for more than five years. Why should Maggie's pain not be similar to mine? The only difference was the cause.

I remember about three years ago reading a short story by Guy de Maupassant called 'Useless Beauty' and being shocked by the title into recognizing myself. That's how I felt. That's what I was. And to hear others comment on how lovely I looked seemed to me to twist the knife all the more. The gods enjoy these jokes. I'm convinced of it.

Maggie was looking at me as she sipped her wine. Her expression was one I couldn't read. I thought I saw compassion there, just like the night in Georgie's, but there was something else, too. I was not proud of myself or my sometimes tawdry tale. I felt that despite her forgiveness, her understanding both of my abortion and my longing for a baby, something in our friendship had shifted. After this, it would either be better or worse. But it could never be the same.

'I don't know what to say to you, Claire. This is just so difficult. I'm glad that you've told me, but sometimes . . .' She didn't finish and I didn't press her. 'Let's talk about it again.' And she squeezed my hand. 'But for now, let's eat. I'm hungry.'

She said it with just the ghost of a smile. Maggie's appetite was legendary. She loved food, loved wine, had no time for stalks of celery or lettuce leaves masquerading as a meal. Oh, she was disciplined most of the time – otherwise her famous curves might have lost the run of themselves. 'More gone west than Mae West,' she used to say. But when food was part of the celebration, Maggie indulged. Buy now, pay later, she used to say. I loved her appetite for life. It endured, despite all of the reasons that it might not. And so we ate, and tried to talk about other things. We even delighted the waiter by ordering a tiramisù to share. I think we were astonished that we were able to ride the waves of normality, although we were both conscious of the undertow.

I wonder if I will ever be able to bring myself to talk about it to the others. Nora would be of the opinion, I am sure, that my barrenness is a judgement from God because of my sexual immorality. I remember the time, just before she got married, when she accused me of having no respect for myself because I was sleeping with Paul. Her words had stung me. And their shadow haunted me, later that summer, made me feel like a sinner, made me believe that the abortion was punishment for my wrongdoing. That's how I felt anyhow. It's why I cut my hair off again, although not as dramatically as the first time.

How could I possibly tell someone like Nora, someone so moral and upright, someone whose life has followed a clear, straight ascent, that things are not so tidy for all of us? Abortion and Nora? Not even in the same sentence.

And Georgie? I don't think the abortion would faze her, but my longing to be a mother would. I think she'd see it as a reproach to her. It was no secret among us all that Georgie had never found motherhood easy. I remember how much she had once upset me by referring to her twins, Carla and Lillian, as her 'mistake'. They were about three at the time. Even more shocking was her expression as she said it. She meant it.

'Don't look at me like that,' she said. 'You have no idea what having children can do to your life.'

No, I thought. I don't. I'd only just started down the long road of trying to find out. But I wasn't going to tell her that. Not after an admission like the one she'd just made. And that's how Georgie has got away with so much, over the years. We don't challenge her enough.

I feel that in many ways, Nora may be the most honest of all of us. She endures Georgie's scorn in a way that I'm not able to. Nor is Maggie. There are too many old loyalties there, too many years between them for Maggie to tell Georgie that there might be some things she doesn't like about her. But Nora is firm in her views, even firmer in her disapproval of Georgie. And she's prepared to show it. I admire her for that. In ways, I wish I was more like her.

Whatever else we say about Nora – and we say a lot – her credentials as a mother are faultless. Maggie and I are both agreed on this. Nora and Frank are capable, devoted, excellent parents. Watching them makes me feel that the old-fashioned ways *work*. Not a popular view these days, but Frank and Nora's definition of themselves as traditional, solid, no-nonsense Father and Mother has produced the most stable family unit I've ever known. Frank brought home the bacon and Nora cooked it. That's how things were, that's how they were supposed to be in the self-contained universe of Noras and Franks. We've often wondered how 'a dry old stick' – Georgie's term – like Frank managed to father three handsome, articulate and clever sons. If Nora wished for a daughter, she has never said.

Her sons are her delight, she tells us, 'my boys' who make her life worth living. Robbie must be nearly twenty-five now – he was just a new baby the night the four of us made our pact. Now he's an architect, all six-foot four of him, with a winning combination of all his mother's and father's best features. Some sort of happy genetic accident must have gone on there. More his father's physique than his mother's, he's slim and dark and gorgeous. Only one of those qualities, it has to be said, was inherited from his father. DNA randomness has to account for the dark and gorgeous. He does, however, have Nora's brown eyes and sallow skin.

The second boy, Chris, is at Trinity and he is studying, I believe, to be a social worker.

'I'm just so proud of him,' Nora gushed at us when he'd told her of his choice. 'All my boys are so good, so unselfish.'

I thought Georgie might throw up at that. And on that occasion, okay, I can't say I blamed her.

Matthew, 'my baby' as Nora calls him, to his face and to his obvious embarrassment, is still at secondary school. Once he finishes his Leaving Cert next June, Nora has declared her job to be done. She's already talking about going back to work.

'Back?' scoffed Georgie. 'What does she mean, "back"? Madame Stepford has never worked a day in her life.' I have to admit, I can't see it either. Frank is fifty-five now and looking forward to an early retirement. Matthew will be taking over the business. I can see Frank wanting more time with Nora, not less. Anyhow, all of them together, all five of them as a unit, make me believe in family again.

Maggie has not been so lucky, of course, and continues not to be lucky. I can hardly complain about Ray's infidelities without seeming hypocritical, but the strain of all those years of hope and disappointment is definitely showing. She talks to Georgie a lot more than she does to me, for obvious reasons. And that's fine by me. Her kids are good, though. Eve and Gillian are both now at UCD and Kevin is the same age as Nora's Matthew, just about to be unleashed on the world. He's quiet, from what I can see, and shy. The girls are bundles of energy, just like Maggie used to be.

And then there's Georgie's daughters, Carla and Lillian. Their mother's 'mistake'. Lovely girls, I've always been very fond of them, but I get the sense that they gave up on their mother years ago. Pete's the anchor parent there, no doubt about it. A good man, dependable and caring. Faithful. I have never voiced this, not to anyone, but Georgie's marriage surprised me. She dumped Danny the year we left Trinity; now that was a good move. There's only so much cocaine a body can endure – Danny's, I mean, not Georgie's. He stuffed a fortune up his nostrils, that lad. But they had been together for four years. I think Georgie did love him.

Less than a year later, though, she called to tell me that she and Pete were engaged.

'I wanted to tell you first, Claire. After all, you were the one who introduced us!'

I was indeed. I remembered the night well. I knew that Georgie was looking to expand her business and I knew that she was hoping Maggie would join her. I had first come across Pete when the board of *Irish-Style* was hoping to float some new ventures. Pete had done the business and I hosted a small party at home afterwards to celebrate the magazine's new and improved financial status.

Naturally, I invited Georgie. I thought that she and Pete might be able to work something out for Georgie's boutique, 'Oui Two'. I liked him, and I encouraged his interest in Georgie. When I say I *liked* him, it was just that. I didn't find him particularly attractive, but I knew that both he and Georgie were at a loose end, romantically speaking, and thought they might share a few pleasant dinners. That's all. I certainly didn't expect anything more to develop between them. And not at the speed with which it did. When I voiced my surprise, and I wish I'd been able to hide it better, she was trenchant in her defence of their engagement. This was serious stuff, she kept telling me. Never mind the romance. Even then, her attitude unnerved me. I thought that, perhaps, the lady doth protest too much.

I often wondered if she had chosen Pete so that she might shine more brightly. Or maybe she was still on the rebound from all that drug-fuelled ecstasy with Danny. Who knows? She never talks about Pete, and I wonder if things there can be what they seem to be – ordinary and uneventful and lasting.

So there you have it. The Gospel according to Claire. Mind you, I've got some things spectacularly wrong in my time, and no doubt I will do so again. No matter what, the four of us women still get a buzz out of each other's company, and that can't be bad after twenty-five years. We'll all gather again this evening, this time around my table, and we'll celebrate a whole quarter-century of friendship. I know that while the routine of the evening might be predictable, it will be neither quiet nor dull.

I think I'll settle for that.

8. *Georgie*

So. Two days have now passed since the taxi driver hoped my day wouldn't be 'too sad'. Two days since the check-in clerk hoped I'd have 'a nice life' – or at least, that's what I heard her say.

Last night, I had a call on my mobile – one that broke the rules, but nevertheless. It reassured me, after a fashion. He can be very determined, this lover of mine, very firm in his views. Yes, there is a problem; yes, there may be a delay. But it changes nothing. Early or late, he will be here. I must be patient. I must wait. There are things, he said, that even I cannot control. Would I trust him? Yes, after all we have been through, I will trust him. I have no alternative.

And so, after my bath, I slept long and peacefully and awoke feeling refreshed. I spent this morning with Paola, shopping. We filled the large freezer in what used to be the stables. We also bought things like torches and candles to have to hand for when the power cuts happen, as they will: or so she assures me.

I couldn't help remembering Maggie's power cut in her new cottage in Leitrim on the weekend we spent there back in January. I came very close on the Saturday night to telling her how things in my life were poised for change, but something kept holding me back. Maybe it was that old debt to her that I was still conscious of. I continue to be aware of all that I owe her for her teenage loyalty, and for so many other times in between. I didn't want her knowledge of my new life to bring her punishment. And I suspected that it might.

Instead, I marvelled to myself at the similar trajectories of both of our lives – something of which Maggie is still unconscious. But there are some . . . circumstances around that modest cottage in Leitrim that she has just bought, I am sure of it. They will bear fruit at some stage in the near future. As for me, in my less-than-modest villa, I don't think that I have left too much to chance. But time will tell, as Nora used to say – probably still does. Time will tell.

Paola asked me yesterday over lunch, almost shyly, how long '*il signore*' intended to stay this time. I looked at her in surprise. I'd forgotten that she didn't know. 'For ever,' I said lightly, with a smile. '*Per sempre.*' I think she was satisfied with that. She never pries, never shows inappropriate curiosity. Nevertheless, I have told her that when '*il signore*' does arrive, we shall fend for ourselves for the first week or so. I suspect that she might have gathered that already.

I wondered this morning what her private thoughts must be. I received at least half a dozen text messages while we were shopping together, and each of them delighted me. I feel free enough here not to pretend; there is no need to control my responses. Nevertheless, Paola smiled at each insistent beep. I answered a clutch of messages when we stopped for lunch, not able to hold off any longer. I excused my lack of politeness: I assume the etiquette of texting is similar in Italy to what exists in Ireland. In other words, when you are at lunch in somebody else's company: don't.

But she waved her hand in the air. It was a gesture that was both conspiratorial and dismissive of my worries. I've managed to tell her in my halting Italian that, once next week is over, I shall contact her to establish whatever new arrangements will suit us best. In the meantime, naturally, I have reassured her that her wages will continue to be paid. Her gratitude when I told her that was touching.

For ever. *Per sempre*. That is what I was mulling over two nights ago as I made dinner for the last time in my suburban Dublin home: the meaning of 'for ever' and the fragility of all the promises that we make. I used to think in absolutes: this is good, this is bad, this is true, this false. Years ago, while I still clung to the belief that things could work out differently, I used to yearn for enough faith to believe that now might be bad, but tomorrow would be better. Part of me would long to have the solidity of black and white certainties back again, the comfort of the things that hold fast. But the fact was that my life was already being lived amid the murkiness of shades of grey. I just didn't realize it. It felt as though my only constant was friendship. It, after a fashion, lasts, although its contours shift and change. All the rest is smoke and mirrors. Nothing is for ever.

'What's for dinner, hon? I'm starving.' Pete's question the other evening startled me back from questions of faith and friendship to the fact that I had been pushing a lumpy white sauce around the pan for some time without noticing. I loathe cooking, always have done. The tyranny of the evening meal is something I have always resented.

I stopped stirring and turned to look at him. Tall, still slim despite the tendency towards a beer belly, which he works very hard at keeping in check, and grey-haired in a distinguished, academic sort of way. *Thou art Peter and upon this rock.* The thought came unbidden and startled me. He began to chop parsley for the sauce, taking over as he so often did. Solid, decent, dependable Peter. Rocklike in his husbandly devotion and his delighted fatherhood. I had the grace to feel sad just then. Not guilty any more, just sad.

'We're having some salmon and the roasted vegetables left over from yesterday,' I said. The girls love roasted vegetables.

Lillian does all the preparation and chopping and is delighted to take over the kitchen from her mother. Her mother never demurs. 'Will you mash the potatoes?' I continued poking at the lumps in the sauce, but to no effect. They refused to soften.

Pete put both hands on my shoulders and his thumbs worked their way into the bones at the back of my neck. I stopped resisting almost at once and he took the whisk from me. He began folding the parsley into the bubbling whiteness. I watched as he worked his magic. He rescued the sauce, smoothed and refined it, just as he had been able to rescue so many other things in the early years.

'Get Carla or Lillian to set the table,' he said. 'I'll mash the spuds in a minute.' He gestured towards one of the kitchen chairs. 'Why don't you sit down? There's a glass or two of that nice Chilean left over from yesterday. It's in the fridge.'

I retired from the fray. Lillian agreed to set the table and provide dessert, if Carla loaded and unloaded the dishwasher. A born negotiator, I've always thought. And a young woman who loved cooking. I've never got that, as the young people say. Never understood it. Nora was the only other domestically obsessed woman I've ever known – and I have no idea how the gene of cooking and kitchen competence ended up in Lillian's DNA. It didn't come from me.

I watched the twins last night. I stored up pictures, multi-coloured memories for later.

'You okay, Mum?' asked Carla. Pete and Lillian were clearing the table after we'd finished our main course. I looked at her soft, open face, dark eyes, long hair caught up into an untidy, fetching bun. I've always felt that bit closer to Carla than to her sister – maybe that's because she was born first. The twenty minutes that elapsed between her and Lillian's more difficult birth forged something different between us, something strong and clear, bright as precious metal.

'I'm fine, just fine.' I stroked a strand of escaping hair and tucked it behind her ear. 'All okay with you?'

She nodded. 'Yeah. We looked at some more flats today. There was one that Lillian really liked. I'm not so sure. But she said I could have the bigger bedroom with the en-suite, so I'm tempted.'

I smiled at her. 'Why her sudden generosity?'

''Cos it's cheaper than the one I like, and on a direct bus route to UCD. But I'm holding out for a while. She's not the only good negotiator in this family.' And she winked.

I looked at her in surprise. Carla has always had that ability – to say or do something that takes me aback, that shows how she learns and absorbs things all the time. But she does it quietly, without any of Lillian's showiness. I had to laugh at her expression and said something like 'That's my girl!' but I was thinking, again, how superfluous I now was to her life, to all their lives. Or maybe that was just my own rationalization, something I wanted to believe. Who knows? Who cares? I am past agonizing. All I know is that somehow, almost without my noticing, my fractious twins have become eighteen-year-old women, feisty, self-assured and full – as Maggie used to say – of piss and vinegar.

'Ta da!' Lillian emerged from the kitchen with her customary fanfare. She balanced a tray above her right shoulder with four dessert bowls and an enormous pavlova. The cake had sparklers positioned at each corner, spitting tongues of tiny fire. She laid it all on the table in front of me. 'Just to wish you bon voyage, Mama,' she said, pronouncing it as 'Ma-*maw*', 'and to say how terribly we'll all miss you, yet again.' Her tone was artificial, waspish.

That startled me. I thought I caught something fleeting in her expression, but it was gone, whatever it was, just as soon as I saw it.

'Now, Lillian,' drawled Pete, 'you know that sarcasm is the lowest form of wit.'

She looked at her father, all wide-eyed and innocent. 'But Papaw, you know that we can't manage without her.'

'Horseshit,' he said. His amiable expression never altered. 'You've been managing without both of us for years. You guys have now reached the stage of being able to buy and sell both of your parents.'

Carla and Lillian grinned across the table at each other. Once again, I saw that twin-style complicity, that steel-like closeness that, as children, had even manifested itself in the creation of their own obscure, private language.

'And have been wrapping us around their little fingers for eighteen years,' I said. 'You'd better be able to manage, come to think of it – now that you've decided to leave the bosom of your family.'

Lillian spooned dessert into bowls, making sure the portions were scrupulously equal. It was a hangover from childhood, this insistence on fairness. As toddlers, the twins used to squabble over cake and dessert, each sharp-eyed as they regarded the portion destined for the other. Nothing would convince them that one had not been short-changed, the other favoured. So I devised a simple system: one cut, the other chose. Thus a talent for precision was born, and in the event that mistakes were made in the cutting, the other twin had the advantage of choosing the larger portion. End of problem.

Carla popped a large strawberry into her mouth. 'Time to move on, Mother. You always said the day would come.' Her words were muffled and made her pronouncement sound distorted.

'Don't speak with your mouth full,' Pete said.

Carla stuck her tongue out at him, a gesture from childhood

that had always got her into trouble. But this time, neither of us rose to the bait.

Lillian turned to her sister. 'You can speak any way you like, once we move to Donnybrook.'

Carla inclined her head, the gesture a noncommittal one. I felt a surge of admiration for her silent assertiveness, her unwillingness to give way under pressure.

'I thought moving out of home meant putting away the things of childhood – not continuing to blow raspberries, or in this case strawberries,' Pete observed.

Carla hooted. 'No way, Dad, no way. Moving out means paying for our own right to be permanently silly.'

Lillian's mobile rang then and she left the table with an apologetic wave. Carla looked at her watch. 'Oops,' she said, and gathered the bowls off the table. 'I'll just finish with the dishwasher and then I'm off to the cinema. Mike'll be here at seven.'

We sat, Pete and I, in the silent aftermath of their departure.

'They're wonderful,' he said. 'At least we did a good job there.'

I stood up. We had had this sort of conversation before and I didn't want another one, not tonight. 'Not now, Pete, please,' I said. 'I've got to go and pack.'

'Then when,' he said. But it was no longer a question. He got up and left the table.

I looked around the dining room, at the surroundings that had been familiar to me for so many years. We'd moved into this house when the twins were three, anxious to send them to the highly regarded local primary school. Our rise had been dramatic, Pete's and mine: from obscure but hard-working young couple in the suburbs to the sudden wealth and cachet of Rathgar. Detached house, large gardens, domestic staff. Granted, my father – my parents – had played a not insignificant role in our advancement, but our arrival had every bit as much to do with us as with them. Pete's success as an investment banker was 'stellar', according to his associates, and the blossoming of my couture business with Maggie was no less spectacular. When I look back, I see an eternal triangle of influences and I wonder whether age has distorted the balance. What makes a life, anyway? How do you establish who gives what, who takes what? The other evening, as I looked around what had once been my home, everything had acquired an eerie strangeness, as though all that comfortable familiarity had mutated into something else. Now the table, the chairs, the curtains, even, had become arid and shadowy and looked as though they were about to crumble into cobwebby dust, just like Miss Havisham's gown.

I made my way upstairs and pulled my suitcase out of the wardrobe. I had already sent some boxes on ahead by post, so all I needed to pack were the usual essentials that accompanied any normal, four-day business trip. Nothing to arouse question or suspicion. But I'd have to say that Pete is not a suspicious man, never was.

I stayed up late, finishing emails and tidying up the ordinary business bits and pieces that hectic days leave no time for. The house was in darkness by the time I was ready to go to bed.

Then, I did something I haven't done in years. I went into Carla and Lillian's room. Despite our four large en-suite bedrooms, the twins have always chosen to share. Neither one could bear to be without the other. I found that a great comfort, last night. I knew that each would fill any temporary gap that might arise in the life of the other. They were both fast asleep in their single beds, each with one hand under her cheek and as always, facing towards her sister. I bent down and kissed Lillian and then Carla, very gently on the forehead, just on that spot near the temple where they had loved to be stroked as babies. I could feel emotion begin to gather at the base of my throat and had to pull myself away. Not for the first time, I gazed in wonder at these two adults who seemed to be my children but who were, in fact, separate individuals, perhaps even two strangers who had – or hadn't any longer – something to do with me. The point was that they now had a choice. Their welfare, their existence, their safety, even, no longer depended on me, or on anyone else. My job was done.

The last time I looked at the clock it was after one. I climbed into bed beside Pete, whose breathing was easy and regular. It occurred to me that he might have been feigning oblivion, but that is something else I shall never know. I settled down – or at least tried to – falling into that kind of uneasy, thinnish sleep that you get when you know you've only got three or four hours.

And now here I am, with the events of the last few days behind me. Few days, few hours, few decades. What does it matter? The past fades very quickly and the future is uncertain.

What matters for now is now.

Paola is sweeping the balcony by the time I get back from my walk. It rained last night, and the soil now has a pleasant smell, sweet and heavy like fruit just about to turn. I need these solitary walks, find that they help to clear my head, fire me up for whatever demands the day will bring. I felt on edge earlier this morning and I knew that I would not be able to settle until I had done some normal things, routine things, something that involved physical movement. As a result, I pushed myself hard along the hilly roads, quickening my pace, lengthening my stride so that my muscles are now aching, my knees protesting.

I have been consumed with curiosity all morning, wondering how things ended up the other night at Claire's. Pete is predictable, of course: he'll have called her and Maggie and Nora once he gets my email. They'll all have agonized together about my absence. They'll have tried my mobile, too, not once but several times, each of them needing to be convinced individually that the number was already disconnected. And they'll also discover that my email address is no longer extant. Their messages will bounce off a satellite and land back in their inboxes, the technological equivalent of Elvis's 'Return to Sender'. It's a curious feeling, to be cut loose like this, particularly when so much of my recent life has depended completely upon communications. I had toyed with the idea of keeping on the old mobile phoneline and checking messages from time to time, but I decided that that might have the potential to suck me back in again to all the things that I need to leave behind. I am not stupid. I am aware that anyone who tries hard enough will be able to discover where I am. I have left things in place for Pete, no loose ends. My email will help him find them sooner rather than later. And once his anger subsides, he'll realize that he no longer wants me back. I know this already. It will take *him* some time to realize that he knows it, too. My friends will each deal with my absence in their own way. And I have plans for my daughters. My letters await them. I know them well enough to know that, in time, they will forgive me.

Forward. That's where my focus needs to be: moving forward. No time for sentimentality, for spurious regrets, for what ifs and maybes. I've had all of those, for far too long now.

And once *he* arrives, the last vestiges of my old life will have finally disappeared. Except for Maggie, of course. She is the one exception I am prepared to make for now, until the dust settles. Meanwhile, I rejoice in the newness of everything here, its obvious and shiny sense of difference.

Paola is calling. The gardener must have arrived. It's time to begin the transformation of the dusty bowl that is my garden into an oasis of blooms and tranquillity. You have taught me well, Claire. This is something I will dedicate to you, my way of remembering.

That leaves only Nora. Ah, Nora. Despite myself, I shall remember you, too.

Without even needing to try.

9. *Claire*

I can't believe it.

Pete's voice on the phone was brittle, all his words stretched tight and thin. I thought that he might burst into tears at any moment.

'What do you mean, gone?' I asked. Do you know, I could feel feel even my hands begin to twitch, as though I was physically searching for connections, for some sort of logic. It was like rummaging around in a drawer full of odd socks. I knew that there had to be a match in there somewhere. I just had to find it.

'She's gone, Claire. She's left us. For good, it seems to me.'

Stupidly, I glanced at Georgie's place at my table, searching for any clue that might appear there. I almost expected her to materialize, looking like her usual self. Imposing, striking, making the occasional sardonic comment. Nora and Maggie had already begun to stare in my direction, their animated conversation stilled as abruptly as if someone had just pulled a plug. Even though I had taken the phone out of the living room, I came back to stand in the doorway once I heard Pete's words. I didn't want to be on my own when he let loose whatever missile from the wide blue yonder he was still trying to control. I could sense that it was already growing larger, speeding in my direction, leaving a thin white trail in its wake. My voice sounded shocked, even to me, ringing hollow and shallow in my ears. For that first split second, I'd thought he meant that Georgie was dead. Some dreadful calamity, some freak of nature.

Once he said 'left', I began to calm down.

Nora was sitting right at the edge of her chair. Even while I was speaking to Pete – or rather, while he was speaking to me – I was aware that she was already enjoying the electric spark of the storm that she'd sensed was crackling above all our heads.

'She left some . . . things for me to find,' Pete said, his voice beginning to settle a little. 'The invitation to your house tonight, with your phone number underlined in red. Some bank statements, one showing details of money withdrawn three weeks ago. The deeds of the house. And some other things, personal stuff between the two of us, that make me feel she's not coming back.'

My mind was hurtling off in several directions at once.

'I have to confess,' he went on, 'I never realized that Georgie had so much money.' And he started to laugh. A mirthless sound, if ever I heard one.

'Hang on a second – she and I spoke on the phone yesterday afternoon. When did you see her last?' I still couldn't take it in.

'Last night,' he said. 'We had dinner together, the four of us. I went to bed around midnight and when I woke this morning, she'd gone. But there was nothing strange about that. It wasn't until I got an email from her this evening that I found all the stuff she'd left for me.' There was a pause. 'She's obviously not with you, then.'

'She was supposed to be. She even rang me yesterday to confirm the time. We've had tonight arranged for ages. I can't believe this, Pete. You're saying you knew she was going away?'

'Yeah. Just her usual business trip. She's always gone by five. I don't even hear her leave any more.'

Something he'd said earlier was nagging at me. 'Did you say she'd taken money with her?'

'Yeah,' he said. 'Quite a lot of money.'

'May I ask how much, Pete?' It was a dreadful, intrusive question but my thoughts were beginning to catch up with something. They were still tripping and falling over each other, but making progress towards a conclusion that was out there somewhere, waiting to be reached. I was sure of it. And anyhow, he didn't seem to mind. He sighed in a way that seemed to say: what difference does it make now?

'I haven't added it up yet,' he said. He seemed to consider for a moment. 'Not all of it, anyway. There's one account here for eighty-five thousand,' he said. 'Sterling. And that's just the one she cleared out a few weeks ago. There are others – all in euro, all closed at different times over the last year. At a very rough guess, it's well in excess of half a million.'

'Half a million,' I repeated. I saw Maggie sit up straighter. Her lips looked a sudden, startled scarlet in her pale face. Yes, I thought, *you* know something that the rest of us don't. *That's* what has been struggling to come to the surface of my mind for the past few minutes. That's the matching sock, the second shoe that has just fallen with a bang. Now I wanted to get off the phone, to know whatever it was that Maggie knew. And I had a very unaccustomed feeling, too, beginning to grow in the pit of my stomach. Relief, happiness, even, that this time, I wasn't the one causing all the grief. I brought myself back to Pete's voice with difficulty.

'I've never even seen that sterling account before,' he was saying. 'It's addressed to her at the boutique. Maybe Maggie knows something?'

'I'll ask her. And we'll get back to you. Or do you want to come over? We're all here. What I mean is,' I said, appalled at my slip, 'Maggie and Nora have just arrived.'

There was a pause. 'No. No, thanks. I think I'll stay here, just in case. The girls . . .'

'Of course,' I said.

'And there may be other stuff lying around for me to find. I'd prefer to find it before they do.'

'Of course,' I said again. And then he hung up.

Nora's eyes were wide with anticipation. She was enjoying this, I could see. 'What's happening?'

'It looks as though Georgie has done a runner.'

Maggie was getting whiter by the moment. She couldn't work her mouth properly, as though her lips had seized. 'What exactly did Pete say?'

I told her. She put her head in her hands. 'Jesus Christ,' she said. Then 'Oh, Jesus Christ,' again. She looked up. 'Is he coming over?' She couldn't keep the alarm out of her voice.

'No,' I said. 'But you'd better tell us what you know.'

Maggie shifted in her chair. She looked agitated. But it was more than that, too. I thought she looked forlorn.

'I don't *know* anything – not in the sense you mean. But I have suspected something – and I don't even know what it is – for the past while now.'

'Like what?' Nora was beginning to get impatient. She was twisting her rings again, the way she always did whenever something upset or excited her.

'She was very . . . ordered over the past few months. 'Course, Georgie has always been very organized but this was like she was . . . tying up loose ends, or whatever. I mean, she even changed our business accounts to "pay either", things like that, when they used to be "pay both". She said it would make things easier, that we wouldn't both have to sign for stuff if things were very busy, or if one of us was away.'

Maggie hadn't even reached for her cigarettes yet. This must be much worse than I thought. She took a large gulp of her gin and tonic instead.

'She brought me with her to Italy the last time, too, and introduced me to Roberto and all the other suppliers. I mean, she used to do that negotiating stuff herself. It used to bore me, and anyway, she was much better at it than I was. But she said it was high time I came to grips with all aspects of the business. I never asked why. I just enjoyed seeing Rome and Milan again.'

I waited for her to go on, but she seemed to have dried up. So I prompted her.

'Half a million, Maggie. Was the business doing that well?'

She shook her head. ''Course not. We'd never have that sort of money liquid.' She began to look uncomfortable. Now she reached for her packet of cigarettes and her lighter.

'Give, Maggie,' I said. 'Give.'

Nora

I always knew she was capable of something like this. I just knew it. Deserting her husband and her family like that and running off without a word. There's probably some man in the frame, too, and it wouldn't surprise me in the least if she has more than one on the go. And what about all that money! Where did she get all that money?

If I'm honest, I'd have to confess that I feel really angry as well. She has managed to steal the limelight once again and this time, she's not even in the same room as me. She has taken over the whole evening without even sitting in her usual chair. I thought this was going to be my night, that I would get my chance at long last to talk about Megan and to show them all the photographs I have in my handbag. But no. As usual, it will just have to wait and I'll end up being last, again.

Maggie is looking scared, though. I'd bet my life that she knows more than she's telling. I wonder if now would be the time to let these two know about the afternoon I saw Georgie in

Castleknock? When I'm sure she disappeared into that bike place with a young man?

Maggie has stood up and grabbed her cigarettes and lighter off the coffee table. She makes her way towards the door, but Claire calls after her.

'Come back, Maggie. Special dispensation for tonight.' She pulls a delicate ceramic bowl off the fireplace. 'You can even have an ashtray. Don't worry, it's sturdier than it looks.' Maggie sits down again. I can see by her that her mind is racing. Claire takes the bottle of Prosecco out of the ice bucket. 'I think we should start to drink up, lads, before the wine gets warm again in all this commotion. Even the ice has melted.'

Maggie takes her glass and begins to sip at the Prosecco but her face looks distracted, almost as if she doesn't know what she is doing. Her eyes are wide, her painted mouth is trembling and her fingers with those awful scarlet nails have begun to shake. It reminds me of that other evening in Georgie's so many years ago when Maggie wanted to kill Claire over Ray. And here we are again and there's still the drama, still the crisis, but as usual, it is all revolving around somebody else.

'This has to stay between us,' Maggie says.

The room goes very quiet. Claire halts in the middle of pouring her own glass of wine. I was about to sip at mine, but I stop. I see the glance that passes between the two of them. Immediately, I know what it means. Nobody ever told me what happened after the Ray disaster, but then, after a gap of almost two and a half years, our group evenings started up again and Claire and Maggie were back on speaking terms.

I am not stupid. I have caught many glances like this among the other three over the years and they think that I don't see or don't understand. That flash between Claire and Maggie a second ago means that it is now Claire's turn to forgive Maggie for something she knew or did or knows or has just suddenly guessed.

Maggie already has the look of someone who has put two and two together. Claire nods. I can see that the bargain has now been sealed between them.

Then Maggie turns to me. 'Nora?' she says. They are both waiting, both looking over at me for my answer. I hesitate. This is a rare moment for me. I've experienced it only once before, the time I let Georgie know that I had seen her in Castleknock, dressed to the nines in her fancy linen suit and up to no good. I enjoy the moment for as long as I can. It makes me understand a little bit more about how people feel about power. It must become addictive. In that instant, I understand Georgie more than I ever have before. I nod. 'Yes,' I say. 'I'll keep it between us. As long as it's nothing illegal, of course.'

'Right,' says Maggie. She takes a deep breath. 'Georgie and I started to expand the business about six years ago. We wanted to buy floor-space in two established boutiques, one in Belfast and the other in Cork. You remember that, don't you?'

Both Claire and I just nod.

'We borrowed a hundred grand from the bank as working capital, and as usual, we nearly had to sign away our children's lives to get it. Georgie was really pissed off at the time, but there was nothing we could do about it.'

She stubs out her cigarette and I can see that she immediately wants to light another one. It really is a disgusting habit.

'Around the same time, she got interested in buying stocks and shares on the internet. I don't know who was advising her and I never asked. All she'd say was that it was some broker she'd met. Anyway, she started making money. Not a lot at first, but she never lost out on any of her deals. She always knew the best times to buy and sell, it was like an instinct with her.'

I think to myself instinct my eye. That was no instinct but some broker or financial whizz-kid who warmed her bed and gave her advice as payment. One of those men in fancy suits, I have no doubt about it. I can see Claire look at Maggie in astonishment.

Maggie pulls her lighter towards her. 'Now here's where it might start to get a bit dodgy.'

Claire looks over at me. I decide to stay silent. If I'm honest, I'd have to say that curiosity is now getting the better of me. I just want her to get on with it. I'm dying to find out what happens next.

'Georgie asked me if I'd like her to invest some money for me. I said "yes". I'd been looking to buy a cottage somewhere in the country, for weekends, just. I needed some place I can call my own. Somewhere I can be by myself . . .'

Yes, yes, I think, starting to get impatient. Let's not go down the road of tiresome Ray any more. Just keep going and tell us what happened.

'I gave her ten thousand euro altogether, over the last four years. Not all at once, 'course – in dribs and drabs. Most of it was the money my dad left me. Lucky money.' She shrugged. 'Georgie called me one night to tell me that she'd had a tip. She couldn't tell me any more than that, except that she was going to buy shares in some mining company in Alaska, or somewhere like that. She was very sure they were about to go through the roof, that some announcement was pending.'

Claire refills our glasses. 'A tip, Maggie. Or insider trading?' her voice is very quiet.

Maggie looks up at her. 'I don't know, Claire, and that's the truth. She called them our "collaborations". All I know is that Georgie managed the transactions – said she was building me a nice little portfolio. She'd call me from time to time, give me only a little while to make up my mind whether to buy or sell.' Maggie pauses. Her expression is filled with admiration. I don't feel so sure.

'She was never wrong. That one time, the time of the Alaska mining company? It took a while, but our shares quadrupled in value. She rang me one morning and told me she was going to offload the lot, told me what I was likely to get. I agreed, told her to go ahead and sell. That wasn't the only time. There was a computer games company, too, that she said all the analysts got spectacularly wrong. Nintendo – I'll never forget it. We bought low, then whatever game they produced went through the roof and we made a fortune. Well, a fortune for me. The upshot of it all was that within three years, our bank loan was paid off.'

She hesitates again and the effect is dramatic. Claire and I wait. I become conscious of the fact that I can't leave my engagement ring alone.

'And as well as that, as well as not having a business loan to pay back any more, I now have fifty grand in the building society and I've just bought a cottage in Leitrim.'

Her words are tripping over themselves. She simply cannot say them fast enough.

I gasp. I cannot help myself. 'But is that legal?'

Maggie grins. 'Yeah, Nora, it's all legal. Georgie left me in the happy position that I never did anything wrong and she didn't get caught – that's if there was ever anything to get caught *for*. Maybe she sailed a bit close to the wind, and maybe I should have asked more questions, but I didn't.' She shrugged. 'I bought and sold in small amounts, comparatively speaking and I was always very, very careful. But she must've gone for the kill every time.' She laughs. 'Half a million cash for Georgie. Well, I'll raise my glass to that.'

And she does. And so, eventually, do we.

Claire

Well. I don't know what to say. I'm flabbergasted.

If I thought that the evening was over after Maggie's revelation – and Pete's – I had another think coming. A lot of things have become clear to me tonight, so much so that I wonder how I haven't put them all together before this. Once they are assembled, they make perfect sense. They bring clarity and completeness to a picture that, up until tonight, I didn't realize had so many bits missing. It's like the way I felt that first day when I met Georgie in Front Square and she made things shimmer into focus for me. Except that now there are four of us, each with a different corner of the jigsaw.

I noticed that Nora was looking agitated, once Maggie confessed to her cottage in Leitrim and a nest-egg in the bank. I wondered why. She and Frank have never been short of money; their latest acquisition is a time-share in the Canaries. We all spent a good deal of time looking at her photographs, the last time we met. And a beautiful apartment it is, too. Quite a departure from Nora's normal frilly tastes.

I decided that more wine was called for. One glass above and beyond what she's used to, and Nora opens up like a steamed mussel. It was one of the many things about her that used to make Georgie mad as hell.

Used to make? Isn't it strange, how we become accustomed to the changes in our lives, how rapidly the past begins to fade? Right until that moment, I would never have believed it so easy to speak of someone with all the force of Georgie's presence in the past tense.

One good thing about Nora is that she only ever goes the extra mile in our company. That way, her Prosecco-fuelled indiscretions rarely cause any damage. I refilled her glass. To my surprise, she didn't protest, but took it from me wordlessly. Okay, I thought, something serious is going on here, too, not just Georgie's absence. Maggie noticed it as well.

'Nora?' she said. 'You're very quiet. Is everything okay? I mean, everything else, apart from Georgie?'

Nora's glance was fierce. She has never cared much for Georgie. And that's probably the biggest understatement I have ever made. Sometimes I've wondered what has kept her coming back for more. Maggie and I are fond of her and have protected her from the excesses of Georgie's tongue as much as we can. No matter what, though, Nora has always preferred to be *with* our group friendship rather than without it.

Before she answered Maggie's question, she knocked back her wine and held out her glass for yet more. Curiouser and curiouser. I reached for the bottle. Its levels were dropping fast. I wondered which of them, Maggie or Nora, would end up staying the night. Maybe both, I thought. A double whammy. Spare room and sofa. That made me pause for thought. I really didn't want Maggie on my sofa, the shameful scene of my tryst with her husband. Better get food going fast and line everyone's stomach.

'I have a life, too, you know,' Nora was saying. 'Not everything has to be *always* about Georgie. Or, in fact, about the two of you.'

Maggie and I knew better than to respond. Not yet, at least. We were both so restrained that we didn't even look at one another. I was afraid I might laugh, in that wholly inappropriate way that you do when you've just seen someone take a tumble on the ice, or fall downstairs, or make a fool of themselves in public.

Nora began to rummage in her handbag. 'You've always thought me a bit dull and boring, all of you, but especially Georgie.'

I could see Maggie was about to say something to that one, but Nora held up her hand. It was such an unlikely, imperious gesture that I was lost for words. But for the hairstyle, Nora at that moment was the closest match I've ever seen for Margaret Thatcher. I imagined her pointing a finger towards each of us and intoning, 'Out, out, out.' Instead, she sat up straight, her knees drawn primly together. In her lap lay an envelope, its contents bulking out so that the flap was pushed open. I caught a glimpse of red, but nothing more.

'At least you two were kind to me, and the three of us always got on well together, once *she* wasn't around. But I was never able to tell you what had happened before we all met. I was going to, tonight. And then, as usual, Georgie makes herself the centre of attention.'

Poor Nora, I thought. What she was saying was true. Georgie always dominated our gatherings. I handed around a plate of mini vol-au-vents, filled with slivers of smoked salmon and cream cheese. Not terribly substantial, but better than nothing. At least they'd be something of a distraction at what appeared to be yet another crucial stage of this extraordinary evening. I felt that for once, I was the one with the uneventful life.

Nora's tone was as close to bitter as I'd ever heard it. I knew that my silence was the wisest course just now and so I left the potential for speech to Maggie. While Nora might be angry at *her* for always colluding with Georgie, at least she didn't disapprove of her in the same way that she disapproved of me. It may have happened a quarter century ago, but I have never forgiven Nora for calling me a slut. I may well have been that since, in her terms, but back then I slept with one man. The man I have happened to love for the whole of my adult life. So I said nothing and waited for Maggie to take her cue.

'What is it, Nora?' her tone was kindly, but not patronizing. 'What was it that happened to you before you knew us? And there's no Georgie here, now. You can tell us.'

I admired her tact. I remembered the first night we'd met, how I watched the door of O'Neill's, waiting for the two of them to arrive together. I was fearful that they would always be two against one. Maggie warned me of the boundaries, on that occasion, telling me of how she and Georgie had been friends since they were four. In her eyes, Georgie would always be number one. I wondered what she was thinking now.

Nora reached into the envelope and pulled out a photograph of a laughing young woman in a red dress. That much I could see. She handed it to Maggie, who studied it for a moment and then raised one hand to her lips. Her mouth fell open. All in all, she was the classic cinematic gesture of amazement, almost a cliché. I didn't need her to say anything, didn't need either of them to explain. I had already begun to guess, seeing Maggie's response and Nora's expression of proud ownership. I waited my turn and Maggie handed me the photo without a word.

It was obvious. Nora's best features are her sallow skin and her dark eyes. She used to tan very nicely at the first hint of sun. I used to envy her that, among other things – like her three sons, for starters. Anyhow, with my colouring, the most I could achieve was a sprinkling of freckles across my nose. When Nora did become tanned, her brown eyes became lustrous and almost compensated for the chunkiness of her figure. The young woman in this photograph might have been Nora, a quarter of a century ago – but with a very different look on her face. She was the spit of her three brothers. When I say she might have been Nora, it was almost true, except for her unmistakable air of North American confidence. Maggie got up and put her arms around Nora and rocked her.

'Nora, Nora, Nora, why on earth didn't you tell us?'

Nora hugged her back. Tears coursed down her cheeks, making silvery tracks in her over-powdered makeup. 'I couldn't. First I'd been made promise not to, and then it was too late.'

I felt a mix of emotions as I held the photograph in my hands. Grief for my own lost motherhood, envy at the fact of somebody else being so richly rewarded, once again, where I had been deprived. But there was more. I felt sorrow too, for all the gaps and glitches in our knowledge of one another. Regret for all the

missed chances for being kind. I swallowed. This was one opportunity I decided I would not miss, one time when I could do
something generous for someone else. This wasn't my moment,
nor Maggie's, not even Georgie's. Right now belonged to Nora.

I sat down beside her on the sofa and took her hand. Her face
was shiny with crying. 'Nora,' I said, 'what a beautiful young
woman your daughter is. Tell us. Tell your friends everything,
right from the very beginning.'

And she did.

The irony was not lost on any of us that tonight, schemed for
and planned for and oh so carefully orchestrated by Georgie over
what had to have been a long period of time, became, in all the
ways that counted, a night that belonged to Nora.

What was it I had said about predictable? My friends never
cease to amaze me.

Pete called back, sometime between the prolonged starters and
the abrupt main course. I put Maggie on to him. We could hear
only her part of the conversation, naturally, but Nora and I could
deduce how carefully she was treading, yet how honest she was
attempting to be.

'I'm not going to lie to you, Pete. I'll tell you what I know –
and even some of the things that I might suspect. But Georgie is
my friend and my first loyalty is to her.' We waited to see how
that would go down. Predictably, I thought. Pete's a good man
and he's no fool.

'I appreciate that, Pete, and I'll help you as much as I can.'
Another pause.

'My guess would be Italy, but you never can tell . . . could tell
with Georgie. I swear I have no hard information on where she's
gone, just that one gut instinct. This is as much a surprise to me
as it is to you.'

There was a long gap, with lots of 'mms' and 'yeahs' from Maggie.

'Yeah, the business *is* doing great. I've no problem showing you the books if you want to see them. But not half-a-million-cash-each-great. No way.'

Here Maggie's tone became more guarded. 'All I know is, she became a dab hand at buying and selling shares. No, not through a broker, at least that's what she told me. Over the internet. Yeah. That's what she said.'

She gestured for another cigarette and, to my surprise, Nora leapt up and brought her one, and her lighter. She even lit it for her.

'Any personal post was her own, Pete. I never saw her open it, there was never anything for me even to catch a glimpse of. Anything that had to do with her, rather than the business, went straight into her briefcase. No, of course I never asked. Jesus, it was none of my business.'

I could feel that the conversation was winding to a close – or this instalment of it, anyhow. I suspected that there would be many more.

Maggie came back and joined us. She shook her head. 'Poor guy,' she said. 'I think the shock is just about wearing off now and he's livid. Absolutely livid. But I really don't think I can be of any more help to him.'

'Come on, lads,' I said. 'Let's sit over to the table and eat something. We can carry on our conversation over dinner.'

The table seemed empty, as though more than one of us was missing. On a couple of occasions, I could have sworn I saw a shimmer around the empty chair. I thought of Banquo's ghost and the hair stood up on the back of my neck. I hustled us all back to the living room as soon as I could and set the coffee and petits fours on the low lacquered tables I had brought back from China.

Nora dived at the petits fours and immediately made appreciative noises. 'Did you make these?' she asked.

I smiled. Ever the housewife, even in the midst of betrayal. Georgie would have enjoyed that. 'I did indeed. Everything home-made in honour of the celebration that was in it – or supposed to be in it.'

'They're good,' she said. I noticed how relaxed she looked – not just because of the extra wine but because something seemed different about her. If I were fanciful, I'd say that she looked taller, her shoulders straighter now that an old burden had been cast aside. And maybe the fact of Georgie's absence had something to do with it, too. 'Can you blame Pete for being livid?' Nora was asking, as she sipped at her coffee. Maggie had been going over and over the things Pete had asked her, reliving the man's bewildered anger as he pieced together all the fragments of Georgie's departure.

The sense of intimacy among the three of us was palpable. Whatever way you cut it, it was as though Pete's misfortune and our own sense of shock had bonded us more closely together than we'd ever been before. We didn't voice it then, but I felt that night that the loss of Georgie was in some way a relief to all of us, in different ways. We could each be ourselves with the other, without any conflict of loyalty or expectation. None of us was anxious to please any more because none of us needed to be. I think that was it, or part of it, anyhow.

'Has Pete discovered any more clues?' I asked.

Maggie hesitated. 'He's not sure. It seems that she's pretty well covered her tracks. There was just one scrap of paper in between the liner of her wastebasket and the basket itself. It had a name on it.'

We looked at her expectantly.

'Well, go on then,' Nora and I both said at the same time.

'Pete thinks it might be significant. Either of you ever hear her mention anybody called Bob?'

'No,' Nora and I said in unison again. And Nora grinned at me. 'Why?' I continued. 'Has he reason to believe that she's run off with someone?'

Maggie shook her head. Then she stopped. Her face registered something I couldn't read. Then she went on as before, as though nothing had happened. I decided to let it slide, for now.

'No, no, no. Not at all. He's thinking along the lines of brokers, I think. He's already searching out all of them whose surnames are Roberts. I think he feels she might be trying to keep one step ahead of the law. He's on a hiding to nothing, though, I think. Those guys aren't going to release any confidential information, least of all to an angry spouse.' She lit another cigarette and apologized. 'Sorry, Claire – I really will go outside if you like.'

'Forget it,' I said. 'But I'm hoping we don't make a habit of evenings like this.' I turned to Nora. 'The happy parts, by all means, lads, but not the sort of stuff that drives any of us to smoke our brains out. Life's much too short.'

We called it a night soon after that. All Maggie could do was pace restlessly and smoke. There was a piece missing, she kept saying. A piece missing. Georgie would never be foolish enough to give anyone reason to come after her. Any legal or financial reason, that is. And all Nora could do was handle the photographs of Megan, already aeons removed from the drama of the absent Georgie. I felt tired and flat and encouraged the two of them to share a taxi home. They did, but not before they protested about wanting to help with the cleaning up. I waved them away and they finally left me to it, at my own insistence.

Maggie hugged me for longer than usual before she left. I had a strong sense that the breach between us was finally healed, that our future would be better than our past. I felt a surprising amount of gratitude to Georgie for having made it so.

'Take care of yourself,' she said, and then, as Nora opened the front door after her perfunctory embrace, she whispered: 'I thought you were very brave tonight. I'll call you in the morning. Maybe we could meet for coffee, just the two of us?'

I hugged her back. 'I'd like that. And by the way,' I said, 'you're holding back something. You'd better tell me tomorrow.'

Maggie looked over her shoulder quickly. Nora was just getting into the taxi. 'Our Italian supplier,' she whispered. 'His name is Roberto something or other.' She frowned. 'Like the film director, but with a different ending. I can never get it right.' Then her face brightened. 'Tarantini, that's it. Roberto Tarantini.'

'And do you think . . .?' I began.

Maggie shrugged extravagantly. 'Jesus, Claire, what do I know any more? He's years older, conservative as they come – and I found him terrifying. If there was anything between the two of them, they deserve an Oscar. Each.'

The taxi-driver sounded the horn. A brief, impatient summons.

'Gotta go.' She hugged me again. 'Thanks again for dinner. Talk tomorrow.'

''Bye,' I said. 'Take care. Sleep if you can.'

She waved over her shoulder and ran down the garden path, her high heels clicking. I smiled to myself. Despite Frank's well-meaning and often-repeated advice, no one could part Maggie and her stilettos.

As I loaded the dishwasher, some old memories began to nudge. A fragment of conversation here, a sideways glance there. Georgie at Trinity, not bothering to turn up if a more attractive opportunity presented itself, or two-timing Danny on the occasional weekend, or else just calculating the best way to get whatever it was she wanted.

I thought of the ways she'd always tried to sideline Nora, and how astonished she'd be at tonight's revelations. I felt sad as I remembered Nora's photographs: not just those of Megan, but the ones of Robbie's birthday party too. She'd brought them along to point out all the family resemblances for us – the dark hair and brown eyes; the sallow skin; the *handsomeness*. I had envied her her four children all over again. What's this the expression is: an embarrassment of riches? I wished, not the first time, that I had more photographs of Paul and me, ones that were more natural, less posed than was the fashion of the eighties.

It was as I was scraping the remains of the coq-au-vin into a Tupperware bowl – none of us had been very hungry – that I froze. I can still see myself standing there, wooden spoon in hand, rich red-wine sauce dripping on to the countertop in front of me. It made a pattern on the white marble, a shape reminiscent of the map of Australia. I had a sudden feeling of paralysed recognition, that moment when time stands still. As it began to recede, leaving the back of my neck tingling, it became a slowly satisfying click-clack of things falling into place. It was like the domino effect of hundreds of tiny pieces from the past twenty-five years, each knocking the other off balance, each tumbling after the one before it and finally settling in front of me into silence and to rest. I dropped the spoon, scattering New South Wales into Queensland, obliterating Tasmania completely, spattering the painted surface beside the stainless steel hob.

'Oh, good Jesus Christ of Almighty,' I said aloud.

10. *Maggie*

I like the feel of the air here because it's fresh and it's clean and it smells of newly cut grass in the mornings. In the evenings, there is the scent of turf fires and woodsmoke. It's a treat after the dirt and diesel of Dublin. I'll always be grateful to Georgie for helping me get my hands on this. My own cottage, views of the Curlews, miles and miles of peace and tranquillity. And it's just remote enough for me, tucked away safely between the hills of Leitrim and the waters of the Shannon.

My new weekend routine is very pleasant. For the last six months, ever since I found my refuge, I leave the shop as early as I can manage on Fridays so that I can beat the traffic. That means I get here by around half-five or six. The first few months were taken up with overseeing the renovations, making decisions about what to change and what to keep, and then cleaning up after the builders. I mean, they were all enjoyable activities in their own way, and Anthony, my builder, made sure that I felt in control all the time, but I was glad when they were over. I was impatient to start the fun stuff of decorating and buying and playing house. Anthony humoured me, and the man's response to every request was always, 'Yeah, that's possible. No problem.' Thanks to him, I felt a sense of excited ownership even while the interior was still a tip.

But all that has now come to an end. These weekends, as soon as I arrive, I light my fire and pull the curtains. In a couple of weeks' time, the clock will go forward and then I'll get another hour or so of brightness in the evenings. I'm looking forward to that. In the meantime, it's wonderful to close my own front door, to shut out the gloom and do something I haven't been able to do in years. I'm reading up a storm. All the books I've not had time for, the ones I bought and postponed for a quieter time, the Christmas and birthday presents that were never opened, but sat on shelves and bedside lockers waiting for their opportunity. Well, the opportunity doesn't come by itself, so why keep waiting for it? And I have discovered that quieter times are a myth. It's now or never.

And where is Ray, my husband of twenty years? Where is my family in all of this self-indulgence? My two lovely daughters are at university, managing their own lives and looking after their own flats. I have one young son about to spread his wings. In less than three months, a whole eleven and a half weeks, he will sit his Leaving Cert, and who's counting? We both are, that's who.

'You tryin' to get rid of me, Ma?' he asked me the other night when we were trawling the internet together, looking at student accommodation in Glasgow. But he was grinning.

'Kevin, I'm appalled you could even think such a thing,' I told him.

'That's a "yes", then, isn't it?'

We've been having this kind of banter on and off for a few weeks now. Part of me knows he's being the protective son, that he knows that when he's gone, the nest is definitely empty. He doesn't mention Ray, and I don't either. But I won't allow feelings of guilt or responsibility or duty to hold him back. It's his turn, his life. And oddly enough it's also mine. All we each have to do is take it. Then it's freedom for him, Glasgow, university life, fun, novelty and good luck to him. He doesn't know about 'Blue Heaven' yet. Nobody does, except for Georgie. But he will, in time. And until then, I'll continue to enjoy my solitary week-ends, my walks, my books.

My time. My life. The time of my life.

I get up about nine on Saturdays and walk to the local super-market for fresh bread and fruit. I like this kind of shopping. It's so much more enjoyable than the forced marches I used to have to the shops when the kids were small. I remember our student times, too, when Georgie hated grocery shopping even more than I did. Can't see the point to something that has to be done over and over again, she used to complain. A waste of our existence. And I agreed. I mean, at least when you shop for clothes you come home with something that gives you pleasure. And some-thing that *lasts*. But this leisurely shopping is different, this early morning stroll down the hill towards the village. It doesn't feel like a chore. Instead, it has become the way I choose to start my day.

I may well be the cause of some local gossip around Coillte, although people here are very polite. I have got to know Anthony of course, and through him, carpenters, painters, the owners of the local hardware store. I made it a point to bring nothing with me from Dublin. Everything I bought during the cottage's renovation was bought either in Coillte, or in the villages surrounding us. Everyone I employed was local. I'm not green enough to believe that you can buy acceptance, but I do believe that you can create goodwill.

When I finally arrived here last night, it was strange to feel that I was carrying on as normal despite the huge absence of Georgie. During other, previous lives of ours, even if we weren't in touch on a daily basis, we always knew we *could* be. Then, when we met, we just picked up where we'd left off, as though no time had passed at all. But this time things are different. I don't know where she is and I can't imagine her in her new surroundings. That makes me feel edgy, as though I have lost my bearings, although I am not the one doing the travelling.

And then, last night, I pushed open my front door to find Georgie's letter waiting for me. At a time like this, I felt that its arrival was significant in more ways than one. It was the first piece of post to come to me at my new address. Or should I say our new address? For legal and technical reasons, Georgie is the owner of my cottage because this is one bit of my life that Ray will never share. 'Blue Heaven' is not a name I'd have chosen for a cottage surrounded by so much green. Even the name of the village, Coillte, means 'woodlands'. But there you have it. Georgie thought that the name was so naff I should keep it.

'Hang on to it, Maggie,' she advised. 'It's just like a boat,' she looked all solemn and serious, 'bad luck to change it.'

And I have held on to it, just to please her. But I have my doubts.

I knew she'd get in touch with me eventually. I was just glad that it was sooner rather than later. It'd be hard to break a habit of forty years, even if you wanted to. It feels strange that she's only a week gone now and already we have all begun to adapt to her absence. True to form, her letter explained nothing and didn't try to justify anything. She knows that, with me, she doesn't have to. The envelope was postmarked Frankfurt, and that is all I need to have, to know that the one place in the world that Georgie has not fled to is Germany. And 'fled' is hardly the right word, either, I think. There is no sign of panic in Georgie's leaving. Quite the opposite. This was an orderly retreat, if ever I've seen one. I'll tell Claire about the letter at some stage, of course, but I'll have to let at least some time pass before I do. There is a role for her, spelt out by Georgie with her usual succinctness. But she's right, Claire might not want to accept it.

'Papers will follow by the end of the month,' Georgie wrote. 'You'll be able to see that "Blue Heaven" is yours for your lifetime. After that, I've set up the trust, as we agreed, and on your death, it passes to Eve, Gillian and Kevin. Your solicitor and mine will both be trustees, and they suggest that you invite one other person. Someone you'd be confident would make the right decisions on your kids' behalf. I think that Claire would be ideal, but you might feel differently. It could bring her into contact with Ray, and I don't know how either you or Claire would feel about that. There's no immediate rush; take your time and think about it.'

Trust; trustees; trustworthy. It was like a map of my life, pointing out the same destination over and over again, with me never managing to reach it. But at least I have this: something in my name, something that gives me independence and freedom, something that Ray cannot take from me, as he has taken so many other things.

There are a few shoppers here before me this morning. Not too many, as things tend to move slowly on Saturdays in Leitrim. Those who are here are recognizable by their uniforms of Day-Glo rainwear, deck shoes and, more often than not, small children with large life-jackets. I hope their boats are centrally heated. The March sky might be blue, but it's the blue that's forged out of of steel and wind and ice. I think of my oil-fired radiators back at the cottage and make a mental note to check the tank. It is an ugly-looking structure in the back garden, but Anthony did a good job of camouflage, by securing a trellis all around it. Once the soil heats up properly, I'll plant mile-a-minute-vine. There's no point in doing anything like that until the spring frosts have run their course.

My site – my site! – stretches to almost half an acre and I'm itching to get planting vegetables and flowers, some trees and shrubs. I bought myself a few coffee-table gardening books a couple of weeks back, off Amazon. I'm also watching every gardening programme that comes on TV. I heard someone remark recently that it used to be cookery, but now it appears that gardening is the new sex. I'll buy that. It seems to me perfectly reasonable that planting and tending, hoeing and digging, cutting back and nurturing something that responds is a lot less trouble for much greater reward.

I take one of the small wire baskets that lie just inside the supermarket door. Today, I buy fresh peaches, cherries and apricots. It's amazing the influence tourists can have on sleepy villages. I put two Spanish tomatoes into my basket. The tomatoes of Andalucía have to be the best in the world. For my breakfast, even back in Dublin, I copy what the local café in Mojácar used to serve.

I'd spent the whole summer there once I'd finished third year, polishing up my Spanish. Then, once I'd done my finals, I went back again. I was exhausted, unsure about my future, sick of the gloom of Dublin. I craved the light and the feel of sun on my bones. My mother had given me the proceeds of some insurance policy that had just matured, one she had taken out on me years back. I didn't need to think twice. I packed a rucksack, divided the cash into three small bundles and hid it in my socks and a money belt that I wore under my T-shirt. Then I took the cheapest flight I could get to Madrid, a train that took for ever to get to Almería and a series of local bone-rattling buses to tiny places like Agua Amarga, Carboneras, Aguilas, before finally settling on the village of Mojácar. Small and whitewashed and Moorish, with a string of empty beaches and blue water, it captured me the moment I saw it. I rented a tiny apartment up the hill from the beach and basically got lost for five months.

Georgie came to visit but the heat killed her. No matter how many fans we had, or how we positioned them, she couldn't sleep. And that was only June, long before the Andalucían summer really got into its stride. She went home after two weeks, fired up with plans for opening her own boutique in Dalkey. That was the time, though, that she told me she had made up her mind about Danny.

'He's out of control,' she said, one day while we were sitting on the beach under an umbrella. We were both sipping a *café del tiempo*, a delicious brew of espresso poured over ice cubes and wedges of lemon. It helped to cool us down. 'He's doing more and more drugs and lying about it.'

I wanted to be careful. I was hardly in a position to give advice about managing men.

'You think it's more than a phase?' I asked.

She grinned. 'It's a phase that's lasted more than four years. I'm not going to hang around to find out.'

'Do you still love him?' I asked. To me, it was always the only question that mattered.

She shrugged. 'What's love got to do with it?'

A lot, I thought. But I wasn't sure what I was supposed to say. 'Well, maybe you can work it out together, if he gets some sort of help . . .' I watched her expression.

She shook her head. 'You're too kind, Maggie, too trusting. Besides, I have ambitions, lots of ideas running around my head right now. I want to run my own business. How could I possibly rely on Danny?'

I wasn't sure what she meant. 'Do you mean he'd hold you back?' I asked.

She drained her glass. 'He stole from me, Maggie, about a month ago. A hundred quid. That's a hell of a lot of money.' She looked straight ahead of her. I don't think she even saw the bathers who dotted the shoreline, the toddlers screaming at the waves. Her eyes were fixed on something much farther away.

'Are you sure?' It was the only response I could think of.

'Well, it wasn't you and it wasn't Claire and I certainly didn't spend it. No one else has access to my bedroom. So yes, I'm sure. It's the last straw. I need to move on.'

And I knew that the subject was now closed. I lit a cigarette for her. We smoked together in silence. She left a few days after that and I missed her. But I knew that she needed to go home. I managed to survive the soaring temperatures, but that was only because I was doing nothing, not even thinking. I spent most of the day in the water.

Leitrim weather couldn't be more different from Mojácar, of course, but being here reminds me in so many ways of Spain. It feels as though I've been given another chance to live my youth. Maybe it has something to do with the newness of possibility after all these years in the doldrums.

Claire will love it here and I'm looking forward to inviting her. Georgie's absence has meant that Claire and I have moved even closer together. Our friendship has teetered on the brink of collapse, more than once, over the years. Now, at least I can feel that it has begun to pull back from the edge. Claire doesn't know this, but I knew about her abortion a few years after it happened, long before she told me. Keeping that secret from her was not easy, but Paul had made me promise not to tell. He confided in me the day of our father's funeral, and at the time, it made so many things fall into place. Claire's face at Nora's wedding, his running away to Australia, the suddenness of their split.

'I'm really sorry, Paul,' I said to him. 'It explains so much.'

We were sitting downstairs in our old home, having made sure our mother was settled in bed. My father had been ill for so long that I was sure his death would be a happy release for her. But the depth of my mother's grief had taken me by surprise. It just goes to show. You never can tell what goes on between two people.

We were both smoking up a storm. Paul had earlier produced a bottle of whiskey. Now he topped up my glass.

'Can't have a wake without whiskey,' he said.

I was glad everyone was gone. The house was now silent,

familiar. It was as though it had just let out a long sigh and settled itself more comfortably around us. I'd missed Paul, more
than I could have imagined. His abrupt departure to Australia
had left a gap in my life, a gap that had not been filled, despite
husband, children, friendships.

'I blamed you, you know,' I told him. 'For the split with
Claire.' I wouldn't have dared bring her name up. He did it for
me, asking where she was. I told him she had had to go on business to Dijon, although Claire's face as she'd told me made me
doubt it. She was never a very good liar.

He nodded. 'Blaming me might be more true than you
think.'

I waited.

'I was hard on her, Maggie. Probably too hard. But I was
young and idealistic and I couldn't handle it.' He stubbed out his
cigarette and then reached for another. I understood the compulsion. 'I told her it was because I couldn't trust her, because she
had lied to me.'

I looked at him in surprise. 'And it wasn't?'

'Not totally. In fact, hardly at all, if I'm honest. I was filled
with the Hippocratic Oath. I felt guilty by association.' He shook
his head. 'And she was tainted for me. I was a fool, Maggie. I'd
no idea then just how complicated life can be.'

I could see Claire's face swim before my eyes, watched her
pinched reflection in the hotel mirror as she repaired her mascara.

'And now?' I asked. I had the feeling that I was stepping on
to very dangerous territory, that something was about to give way
beneath my feet.

'I make the best of it.'

'Marlene? And the kids?' I knew I was prying, but I couldn't
stop.

'The kids are great,' he said. He drained his glass. 'It's not

Marlene's fault. I was looking to replace Claire.' He shrugged. 'Can't be done.'

I held out my own glass for more. What the hell.

'You sure?' Paul asked. 'Whiskey can give you one mother of a hangover.'

I just nodded. I didn't want to speak.

After a while, he said: 'It's all so black and white when you're young, isn't it? Anyway, that's between you and me. I don't want Claire to know that I've told you. Ever.'

So that the night in the restaurant when Claire confessed to the abortion, when she told me about her feelings of guilt and responsibility, I couldn't stop her, couldn't betray Paul's confidence. Instead, I had to pretend. It wasn't hard to appear surprised, to be overcome by emotion. After all, there was the incident with Ray to be got over, too. But at least I was able to comfort her on her childlessness. Or rather, I was able to attempt to do so without feeling compromised. All in all, though, it was a tough meeting for both of us, Claire and me. I have never told her of Paul's confidence. But it saddens me, that two people who could have made each other happy instead drove each other farther and farther away.

There's not a lot I can do about that, but I can now draw her closer as a friend. Georgie's absence has made that easier. I know that Claire's eyes will light up when she visits me here in Coillte and sees the size of the garden. I know how delighted she'll be that I want her to design it, and I think that she'll approve of what I've done with the interior of the cottage. I hope so. No fuss, no frills. Just open plan, white walls, solid wood floors. And maybe Nora would like it here, too.

After breakfast, I go for a walk. Sometimes the mornings are bright and cold and just right for walking, other times they can be a bit rough. It rains a lot here and the grey skies can make things look desolate. But as I am still a weekender, these changes in the weather mean nothing to me. I'm not condemned to 'a winter of discontent' – Georgie's words. Well, not hers specifically, just ones quoted by her. She reminded me that I can up stakes and go back to Dublin and cinemas and theatres and fancy restaurants any time I want. But the point is, I don't want. Not since the first night I was able to sleep here. Anthony had promised me that the cottage would be habitable, even hospitable by mid-January, and he was as good as his word.

Georgie came with me that weekend, to celebrate the end of the renovation. God, it was freezing. Sleeting. Snowing. We stopped off in Liffey Valley on the Thursday evening and bought a couple of duvets, bedlinen, towels, crockery – just enough to keep us going in case we didn't have time to shop once we got to Leitrim. Just as well we did, as things turned out.

Karen and her daughter had agreed to look after the shop. We all knew there would be very little business done. Georgie and I have never believed in January Sales, so there would be no stampede at our boutique. At the very most, we'd offer 10 per cent discount to select customers. That's how we've always retained our niche on exclusivity. That weekend, we'd told everybody who needed to know that we were taking a few days looking at premises in midland towns. Why not? Dublin and Cork and Belfast weren't the only places that women spent a fortune on clothes. Prosperity now runs in broad, deep channels from the coast down towards the dead centre of Ireland, irrigating all the places in between. It was natural that Georgie and I would be looking to expand again. Even Karen was convinced that that was what we were up to. So all bases were covered. Besides, mobile phones make it that much easier to lie, these days.

'Good luck,' Karen had called, as Georgie and I emerged together from the back room. I had gathered up the last of the cheques and the cash and Georgie had filled in the lodgement slip. We always went to the bank together on Thursdays and for a coffee afterwards. That's something else I'll miss, just another one of the small routines of our friendship.

'Thanks, Karen,' I said. 'Bring yourself and Dee out for a meal on Saturday night. There's an envelope in the till with your name on it.'

'Try out that new Indian in Blackrock, will you?' said Georgie. 'Then you can give us a report when we get back.'

Karen waved her thanks and called out, 'Drive safely.' I opened the passenger door of Georgie's car. She was rubbing her hands together as she sat in the driver's seat.

'It'll heat up in a minute,' she said. A Mercedes A140 – a recent purchase of hers, another new pride and joy. She'd told me in passing, very casually as I see now, that she had just insured Carla and Lillian to drive it. A perfect car for around town, she'd said. I remember being taken aback at that. It seemed a lot of car for two young women. Now I think I know what she was doing. Was a fancy car to be a compensation for her daughters? Georgie has always cared too much about money.

We sat for a few minutes until the windows cleared. She said, 'I feel like we used to feel at school when we mitched for an afternoon. Do you remember? That thrill of sneaking away while everyone else was in class?'

I looked over at her. Was it selective memory or did Georgie really not remember that punishment follows crime as night follows day?

'Yeah,' I said, 'I do. I remember getting caught, too, and being grounded at the weekend for a month.'

She laughed. 'Well, who's going to catch us this time?' She pulled out into the traffic. A swift, confident movement that made other drivers slow down for her. Georgie always drove like her personality. If that was me, I'd hesitate just a fraction too long, afraid to take chances. Then World War Three would erupt with blaring horns, flashing lights, shaking fists, all the component parts of Dublin road-rage.

It was about six o'clock when we pulled up outside the cottage, wheels crunching on gravel. Anthony was standing at the front door. He was lit up by our approaching headlights. Everything else was pitch black.

'Ah, shite, Georgie, the electricity must be off. Just our luck.'

'Is that your builder?'

'Yeah. You keep the lights going and I'll get out and talk to him.'

He was beside the passenger door by the time I had my seatbelt unfastened. 'What's up, Anthony?' I tried to keep my tone light but I was finding it hard to hide my disappointment.

''Evening, Maggie. Electricity went earlier this afternoon. I've put in a call, and they've promised to send someone.'

I tried to read his expression. 'Do you think they will?'

He grinned at me. 'Well, I think so. It's not just you, you know. It's the other cottages around here as well.'

'Do you think we'll be able to stay tonight?'

'Why not? Sure, haven't you enough wood for a fire? And O'Callaghan's is still open. I can nip down and get you some briquettes and candles, if you like.'

At that moment, Georgie spoke. 'Come on, Maggie,' she said, 'where's your frontierswoman spirit?'

I gestured towards the driver's seat. 'Anthony, meet my friend, Georgie. Georgie, Anthony.'

Anthony walked around the car and they shook hands through the window.

'We'll go,' I said. 'Maybe it'd be better if you stayed here? In case the repair man arrives?'

He nodded. 'Sure thing. A torch might be a good idea, too.'

'Okay, then, we'll see you later. Do you need anything?'

He patted his pockets. 'Matches wouldn't go astray. I've just used up the last of them.'

I got back into the car. 'Okay, Georgie, let's go. Back down the way we came from.'

Georgie reversed and then pointed the car back in the direction of the main road. All neat, economical movements. She said nothing for a few minutes. Then, her voice quiet, mocking, she said: 'How come you've kept him such a secret?'

I looked at her, surprised. 'Who, Anthony?'

'Yes, "Who, Anthony". He's a very attractive man, or hadn't you noticed?'

I sighed. Always the same, even when we were students. No, especially when we were students. And I'm sure at times in between then and now, although Georgie would never have told me if she'd had adventures. She's always been discreet, knowing as she does the way I feel about Ray playing away from home. 'He's a very nice man—'

But she wouldn't let me finish. 'Ah-ah,' she said, voicing her disapproval. Her tone was stern. 'We banned "nice" more than twenty-five years ago, don't you remember?'

I did indeed. 'Okay, he's kind and obliging and at least fifteen years older than I am. He's been very good to me but I am not interested. I'm also still married and I'm not interested. Right?'

'Right.' A pause. 'And is *he* married?'

I gave up. 'No, his wife died five years ago. The building and renovation firm is his son's business.' I listed things like a litany, ticking them off on my fingers. 'He doesn't work because he has to, he works because he wants to. He's got one son and two daughters. He lives about twenty miles away. Enough? And I'm *still* not interested, right?'

Georgie gave me a sidelong glance. I could see her turn, even though I kept looking straight ahead.

'Okay, then,' she said. We drove in silence for a few minutes more. 'Seeing as how you're not going to give me directions, I presume that this is the O'Callaghan's Anthony mentioned?' She pulled up outside the door.

'Yeah,' I said. 'Thanks. I'll be out in a minute.' I closed the door, harder than I intended. I was surprised at myself, letting Georgie rattle me like that. I just want to be left alone, I told myself as I walked up and down the shop's tiny aisles. Just left alone.

By the time we got back to the cottage, the repair truck was outside. My spirits lifted. 'Great!' I said to Georgie. 'Look!'

Anthony came towards us. 'Should take another hour or so. The fault is at the bottom of the road. It was flooded a couple of days ago.' He opened the door for me. 'Can I help you ladies in with anything? I found a torch in the van.'

I could feel Georgie's smile broadening. I was about to decline, to insist that she and I would go off for a drink and come back later, once everything was fixed, but she got there before me.

'That would be great, Anthony, thanks. If you and Maggie unload, I'll take care of lighting the candles. I can't wait to see inside. Maggie's told me what a lovely job you've done.'

I said nothing. I was just glad of the power cut. It meant no one could see my face.

As it happened, it took until nine o'clock to fix the fault. By then, the three of us were sitting around a turf fire, sharing a companionable bottle of wine. We'd emptied the car and Anthony offered to bring in the wood and briquettes from the shed and light the fire. I said yes. Georgie found her way around the kitchen, exclaiming at all the lovely things her candles illuminated. That helped to restore my good humour. That, and the dishes she had filled with nuts and pretzels. I was starving. I couldn't help thinking of the steaks in the freezer and fretted about them spoiling if the electricity stayed off too long.

Anthony and I had just finished telling Georgie about the setbacks in the renovation project, the delays, the problems caused by the discovery of an old well, when the lights came back on. The three of us sat, blinking at each other in the glare. It was as though a photographer's flash bulb had gone off. I was left with a vivid impression of Anthony's handsome face, his shock of dark hair threaded with grey, his large hands. Then the moment passed and we all stood up together, as though the lights had thrown a switch inside us as well, forcing us upwards and forwards.

'Oh, Maggie, this really is a picture!' Georgie's enthusiasm was genuine. She was looking around her, taking in details.

Anthony took that as his cue to leave. 'I'll let you ladies finish your grand tour in peace,' he said. 'But I might drop by tomorrow morning with more supports for the trellis, if that suited?'

'Yeah,' I said, 'that would be fine. And thanks for everything this evening. It's much appreciated.'

'Yes,' said Georgie, approaching us with her hand extended towards Anthony. 'Very nice to meet you. And congratulations on a lovely job. Bears no resemblance to the photos Maggie showed me six months ago.'

He smiled, all pleased. 'Thank you. I like getting stuck into a proper job like this,' he said. 'Makes a change from poky kitchen extensions and garden sheds.'

Georgie smiled at him. Her best, most winning one. 'We'll look forward to seeing you tomorrow, then.'

I came back into the kitchen to find her unpacking groceries. She turned to grin at me as I began opening cupboard doors. 'Don't say a word,' I warned her. 'Not even *one* word.'

And here I am again, after a momentous week. Last Friday at Claire's was traumatic, to say the least. I felt sorry for Nora, to have her news about Megan taken over by Georgie's abrupt departure, but she'll get over it. Watching her with her photographs that evening made me feel sad for her. What sort of parents would force that on their daughter? To give away their grandchild, just in case some snobby neighbours or sniffy clients might be upset? What a waste, I kept thinking. What an awful waste of all those years.

But Claire was right. She stepped in at just the right moment. I might have been about to get tearful. 'The important thing now, Nora, is that you have her back. *She* came looking for *you*. Have you any idea how lucky you are? That she wanted to know her mother so badly?'

Then it was my turn. I could hear the waver in Claire's voice all too clearly. Here was Nora, already with three sons by the man she loved and now she had her daughter back. I thought of all the losses in Claire's life – some of which she didn't even know about. I turned to Nora, handed her another tissue.

'She's right, Nora. Let's celebrate you and Frank and Megan.'

Claire stood up to go in search of more Prosecco. I wanted to keep her out of the room for as long as I could, to see if I could get Nora to put her photographs away, to change the subject, just for a bit. 'Claire, have you any sparkling water left, by any chance?'

'I'll have a rummage while I'm out here,' she called from the kitchen. 'Just hang on a sec.'

I turned to see Nora's face suffused with love as she continued to turn her photos over in her hands. I knew then I couldn't ask her to put them away. I couldn't ask her to do that, not without making everything worse.

Claire was brave that night, I have to hand it to her. I felt glad that Georgie had been the means of bringing us back together again after what had happened with Ray. Although at the time, I'd been angry at Georgie, once I'd realized how she had manoeuvred the two of us together when Nora wasn't around. Angry?

I was livid. Looking back, I threw a tantrum that was worthy of Georgie herself.

'What do you think you're playing at?' I almost spat the words at her. 'How dare you lie to me about tonight? How dare you try and put me in the same room as that woman?'

But Georgie just looked at me very coolly. 'You're here, now, both of you. The least you can do is listen to each other. I don't believe Claire has the remotest interest in your husband.' She lit my cigarette for me. My own hands were shaking too much for me to do it myself. 'Yes. Claire let you down badly. Once. Now let's take your husband. Would you like me to count the ways?'

That took the wind out of my sails.

She shrugged and put the lighter back on the kitchen shelf. 'Now she's in the living room, waiting. It's up to you, and she knows that. You say the word – *after* you've listened to her – and she's history. If you can't forgive her, neither will I.' She nodded towards the front door. 'There's a taxi waiting. If you say so, she goes. Immediately, once you've said your piece. You stay. Simple as that.'

I looked at her. I trusted what she said. 'Right,' I said. 'I'll listen to her. And then I'll let you know.'

She nodded, satisfied. 'And here's the last part of the deal, Maggie.'

I turned, my hand just reaching out to open the door.

'This is strictly between you and Claire. I don't need to know, I don't want to know. And Nora'll never know tonight happened, not from me.'

I didn't answer. My eyes filled and my throat felt hard and dry, as though it was choking on small stones. I opened the living room door and went in to Claire.

I think that she, Claire and I, now share an understanding that has made our friendship deeper, despite the secrets between us. We can trust each other.

I remember the night in O'Neill's when she and Georgie and I met for the first time. I've never told her this, but I arrived with every intention of freezing Claire out. When Georgie told me about her, I was immediately jealous. I remember that I warned Claire off that night, by telling her what good friends Georgie and I had been ever since we were kids. And then, to be honest, I backed off. My heart wasn't in it. Claire was so lovely and so open and so *vulnerable* that I felt ashamed of myself. I made it up to her afterwards, but I don't think she knew. Claire never sees badness in anyone. She's far too trusting, and that's what has got her into so much emotional hot water over the years.

Anthony will be back this afternoon. I called him about the leaking outside tap and he promised to stop by on his way to Sligo. His elder daughter has just had a new baby and he's off to see his latest grandchild – a little girl after two boys. I was embarrassed about having phoned when he told me. I didn't know what to say first.

'Anthony, that's wonderful news! Congratulations! And please, don't even think of calling here on your way. The tap is not important, it'll do next week or the week after. Any time you happen to be passing.'

'No, no,' he said. 'I have to pass your door anyway. It'll only take a few minutes to fix. Besides, visiting hour doesn't start till seven. I'll have plenty of time.'

There was no point in arguing.

I have promised Ray that I will not leave him. At least, not in the way that people generally do. I remember the panic in his eyes when I sat him down three months ago and told him that I had had enough. He looked stricken, that's the only word for it.

'Don't go,' he said, 'please don't,' before I had even begun to say what I wanted to say. I had rehearsed the words so often that

233

I was confident I wouldn't be deflected this time, that I would be able to keep on repeating my central message over and over again until he'd have no choice but to hear me.

'I'm not leaving, Ray, because I don't want that kind of upheaval in my life. But I am tired of living like this and I am going to make some changes. And the changes do not include you.' There, I had said it and the sky hadn't fallen. 'I am tired of giving you chances and tired of you breaking your promises.' He opened his mouth, about to say the words I had heard too often before, about how this time it would be different. 'Please don't say anything. Hear me out.' He lit a cigarette for both of us. 'I am not asking you to do anything, say anything or make any promises that you won't keep. This is about me and my life. I'll continue to live here during the week most weeks, but I'll be gone at the weekends. Every weekend and you will not be joining me.'

'But what do you expect me do?' He said it quietly, his tone more bewildered than sad, and I almost weakened again.

'Whatever you choose,' said my rehearsed script. 'You have your golf and your football.' Now stop, said my script adviser, her voice stern. Stop handing him solutions. Let him work it out for himself.

'Is there someone else?'

I looked at him, right in the eye. '*You* are asking *me* that?' His face flushed. 'You have no right to ask me that, no right at all. But if it makes you feel better, no, there is no one else, and *I'm* telling the truth.'

'Where will you be going?'

I didn't answer that one. Instead, I said: 'We can continue to do all the parent stuff together, Christmas, birthdays, whatever we decide. We can still be Mr and Mrs O'Grady to the outside world. But I can't be your wife in the way I have been for the past twenty years. I just can't do it any longer. I don't hate you, Ray, I'm just tired of being hurt.'

'They never meant anything to me, you know, not any of them.'

I knew I had to hold on to my temper, or all could still be lost. The time for anger had gone. Anger brought tears and fighting and promises and sex and reconciliation. Anger is brother to love in so many ways. It had sucked me back in before, purged my rage and shame and disappointment and then propelled me into the arms of this man that I still loved despite myself. I couldn't do it again.

'Do you think that makes it better, that they meant nothing to you? They meant a whole lot to me. They meant lies and deceit and promises made to be broken. That's what they meant.'

He looked at me as he spoke, his eyes sincere, his voice full of love. It was what I had fallen for before, over and over again, so I knew the drill. 'There hasn't been anyone, Maggie, not for the longest time.'

'Don't lie to me, Ray. Do not insult me by *lying* to me.' I stood up. 'Not only are you seeing somebody, you have been for several months. I even know her name. You should be more careful of what you leave in your shirt when you put it in the laundry basket.'

What a tired old cliché, I remember thinking, even at the time I found it. Letters and credit card slips: weren't these the usual shoddy ways that people found out about their cheating spouses?

I was ready for what was coming. I had already predicted Ray's reply and some detached part of me was interested to know if, after all these years, I'd finally get it right. I waited to see what he'd say next, how he'd try to put me in the wrong or, at the very least, doubt myself.

He looked incredulous. 'You read a letter written to *me*?'

I had to laugh. 'You have no idea how predictable you are.'

Then he got angry. 'I don't want your terms and conditions,' he said. 'Nobody dictates to me what I can and can't do in my own home.'

I picked up my cigarettes and my lighter. This was where the script ended, where 'exit stage right' was written at the bottom of my page. Pursued by a bear. 'Then you have decisions to make. We're all responsible for our own lives. I've made my decisions, now you make yours.'

And I left. My weekend bag was already packed and in the car. I don't remember the journey to Coillte, I just remember pulling up outside the cottage and being puzzled as to how I'd got there. I stayed in bed for the entire weekend. I shivered so much my muscles ached and my teeth chattered and there was no possibility of sleep. No matter how much I blasted the rooms with central heating, I still couldn't get warm. Finally, on the Sunday night I called Georgie.

'Where are you?' she said. 'I've been trying your mobile all weekend.'

'I switched it off,' I said. 'I'm at the cottage.' And I couldn't say any more.

'Something bad has happened. Tell me.'

'Ray . . .' I began, and then I broke.

'Stay where you are,' she said. 'Stay right where you are. I'm on my way.' And she hung up. I should have protested and said no, no, that's daft, it's a two and a half hour journey in the dark, the roads are icy, I'll be fine, just having a bit of a bad time, that's all. But I didn't say any of it. Because the truth was I wanted her with me. I needed her anger and the force of her convictions and her presence, more than anything else her presence, unequivocally in my corner. And that's what I got.

'Are you leaving him?' she demanded, before she even had her coat off. She was hugging me in the tiny hallway and I was weeping into her collar. 'Are you making the break this time?'

I sobbed and choked and hiccuped my way through my

script. She bundled me into the kitchen and put on the kettle. 'Have you eaten at all today?'

I shook my head and wiped my eyes with the wad of kitchen towel she handed me.

'I'm going to make us some food,' she said. 'Now, start again and tell me everything, right from the beginning.' She took off her sweater and grinned at me. 'Jesus, Maggie, it's like the orchid house in here. At least you know your heating is working.'

She stayed with me that night and the next. I heard her ring Karen and ask her to bring Dee, her daughter, into the shop for a few days. She said that something had come up and that we, she and I, needed time out to fix things. Then she rang Pete and said more or less the same thing. It was a brief conversation.

'You are doing what is right for you, Maggie. I don't know how you put up with it for all these years. It's time you had a break, maybe even a bit of fun.'

We were sitting in the living room, the fire lit, the curtains pulled against the bleakness of February. I felt exhausted. All of my energy seemed to have drained away, leaving my body listless and my mind blank.

'Fun?' I echoed. I shook my head. 'I just want a bit of peace,' I said. 'I'm tired of being tormented.'

'We all have our breaking points,' she said. 'Yours took longer than most. And that's because you've got great integrity, Maggie. I admire you.'

I remember I looked at her in surprise. Georgie was the woman of action, for the most part, not one for words, especially words about feelings. Maybe she was trying to tell me something. Maybe I stole her thunder that weekend in the same way that she stole Nora's on the night of Claire's party. Whatever it was, I'm sorry I missed the opportunity.

I don't care why Georgie left. I mean, I don't need her to give me any explanation or any excuses or anything at all except the truth. Her letter said that she'd be in touch again, when the time was right. I can trust her that she will. Until then, I have the business to keep me occupied, my children – or rather, my young adults – and this, my haven and my heaven, no matter what the colour. I can wait until she's ready.

And now I hear Anthony's car outside. He'll fix the tap and we'll talk and I'll ask about his granddaughter. Then, I'll make him a cup of tea and we'll sit together in my tiny kitchen. When he goes, I'll light the fire and read my book.

It's enough for now. I'm content.

Epilogue

Georgie

When I said the other night that I'd had no more nightmares, that is perhaps not strictly true. I had nothing as terrifying as the previous night's crashing aeroplane and salty drowning, but nevertheless, my sleep was disturbed.

I haven't thought about Danny Power in well over twenty years: I have no idea why his face visited me so clearly in the small hours of this morning. Perhaps when you leave one life for another, you have to revisit all the old significances before you can finally let them go. And maybe Danny has more to do with *now* than I'd like to think. Whatever the reason for his guest appearance the other night, I welcomed him. I even felt some sadness at the way in which I had cut him loose. I surprise myself these days with a new honesty. I no longer flinch from the truth about myself, now that I can leave that self behind.

Danny. Now *there* was an exciting lover for a young woman. He had that edge of danger, coupled with a confidence in his own attractiveness that made him irresistible. I can still see the look on Claire's face the first time she saw him. She couldn't take her eyes off him – it was as though she recognized something in him, a type of kindred soul. Luckily, she met Paul very soon afterwards, otherwise there might have been trouble.

Oh, I have to say that Danny adored me. There's no doubt

about that. But I think that beautiful people are narcissistic. They are drawn to their own likeness. I may have been striking, elegant, confident – all words used to describe me at different times – but I was never beautiful. Claire, on the other hand, could stop traffic. How could I have trusted Danny to resist had Claire turned her blue gaze upon him? Particularly given the amounts of dope he was smoking back then. I doubt that his moral standards would have been firm enough to repel that sort of temptation.

Ironically, it was Nora's wedding that made me realize for the first time that Danny was not going to be any good as a long-term prospect. I look at the words I have just written and I wonder was I really that calculating? I must have been. Because although Danny and I stayed together – albeit off and on – for another three years or so, I had already decided that my future lay elsewhere, that it *had* to lie elsewhere. I liked having him in my bed, enjoyed the fact that he was with me, loved the way that we made an arresting couple. What I did not like was the nebulous half-life of drugs and alcohol that he lived when he was not with me. But I bided my time, then as now. I didn't want to be on my own, not until I was sure that I was ready. I knew the time had come when I discovered that he was using me to finance his bad habits.

Poor, dim Danny. I don't think that he ever realized the fact that he had become a liability, and I'm not referring to his one foray into thieving. I don't think it ever occurred to him that what Georgie the student found delightfully irresponsible, exhilarating and fun, the twenty-something woman would begin to find tiresome. How could I possibly appear with Danny beside me anywhere other than that casual universe of college, inhabited by the terminally young? Danny had no gravitas, no *purpose*, no control over his future – or indeed, his present as it then was. That was not what I wanted, not what I was planning for myself. He was heartbroken when I told him that things were over between us.

'What do you mean, over?' His blue eyes were filled with injured incomprehension. I watched as he tried to struggle towards understanding, to make connections through the fog.

'We're not going anywhere, Danny, and I think you realize it, too.' I remember I tapped my pen impatiently on the table in front of me. We'd met at his pleading, in a restaurant of my choosing. I'd just signed the credit card slip, a signal that the meal was over. He who pays the piper calls the tune. I had decided not to mention the hundred pounds he had taken from the hidden drawer in my jewellery box.

One of those impossible arguments followed. The sort of arguments that have no resolution. He claimed that the dope, the cocaine, the ecstasy were all part of a passing phase. He could give them up, no problem, just like that. He even snapped his fingers to show me how easily he would adapt to their absence. He didn't need them. He just *liked* them, that was all: but he wasn't an addict, definitely not. All he needed was one more chance to show me.

I shook my head. 'It's too late,' I told him. 'Anyway, there's no point in doing it for me. You have to do it because you want to, for yourself.' I watched him wrestle with that. He tried hard to find a path that would convince both me and himself of his ability to change, even though he felt there was no real need to: he had things under control already. Whatever way he turned, he hanged himself. The irony of it is, perhaps, that a different woman – someone kinder than I, for example – might have stuck it out, supported her man, aided his recovery. But the truth was, I wasn't interested. At that stage of my life, I was ambitious to move ahead and Danny didn't fit the profile.

My father would never have given me my first premises in Dalkey had Danny still been hanging around. He made that quite clear, the night I approached him with a business proposition that Claire had helped me with. I have to say, I was surprised. I would never have thought that my father would bother to notice anyone in my life.

'Drop that young man of yours,' he said, looking at me over the tops of his glasses. 'He'll do nothing but hold you back.'

'It's over,' I said, angered by his knowledge, his presumption of parenthood after all the years of emotional absence. What I'd just told him wasn't strictly true, either: I had made my decision, but I still hadn't let Danny know his fate. He was ignorant of our split, on the night I spoke to my father. Or rather, on the night *he* spoke to me. Nevertheless, it was the unexpectedness of my father's assault that catapulted me towards explanation when I otherwise might have chosen an injured but dignified silence.

My father continued to look at me. 'Your mother and I don't like what this Danny represents,' he said. He uttered his name as though it were some form of swear-word: ugly, contaminating. 'And while that might be a matter of some indifference to you now, believe me, our disapproval will soon become significant.'

I remember the threat implicit in his words. Yes, Danny was history and needed to be told, for all the reasons I was already convinced of. Nevertheless, I was angered by the sound of his name in my father's mouth: but not angry enough to challenge him. He hadn't cared about me all that much since I was a teenager, now he was putting his oar in where it was least needed. But I swallowed my rage, and was conscious of doing so deliberately. I needed something from him, and was cynical enough to play his game. 'I said, it's over,' I repeated and met his gaze. Finally, he nodded. He pushed my folder towards me, across the squat, ugly, mahogany desk in his office.

'I like this,' he said, 'and I like your friend Claire's idea for the interior. That girl has a head on her shoulders.' He paused while he lit a cigarette. 'I'll finance this for you. You can manage it, stock it and work in it for the next three years. Then, we'll review it and see how things stand. You've got till you're twenty-five to prove yourself.' He shrugged. 'Don't know why I spent all that money on an English degree when all you want to do these days is sell clothes. You could have started four years ago, be ahead of the game now.' I said nothing. I felt a kind of savage gladness that he didn't know. Right then, I loved the gulf between us.

'Make a success of it,' he was saying, 'and you can expand, sell on, do whatever you like.' He stood up, a signal that our meeting was now over. 'For now, I'll own a twenty-five per cent share. We can discuss that in a year's time. If you've any sense, you'll take the minimum salary and plough money back into the company.'

I took the folder off the desk and shoved it into my briefcase. It was a far better deal than I could have hoped for, but I wasn't going to tell him that. Besides, I was filled with fury at his casual dismissal of me. It's been a useful emotion, over the years. Fury lights a fire, fuels a momentum that might otherwise burn itself out. 'Fine,' I said, any thanks I might have felt strangled at the base of my throat, killed by his coldness and my old, old resentment of having to ask him for anything, even to acknowledge my existence.

'You'll find a contract to that effect in the folder. I suggest you have a solicitor of your own choosing look over it.' He crushed out his cigarette in the cut-glass ashtray. 'Always pays to be careful,' he intoned. 'Even with family.'

I looked at him, wondering what that had ever meant to him.

'Especially with family,' he added weakly, attempting a grin.

I didn't respond to that, either.

'Get back to me early next week and let me know how you want to handle the renovations. Get your pal Claire to give you a hand.'

I wasn't going to tell him that Claire had recently landed a job as fashion correspondent for *Irish-Style*, Ireland's newest and trendiest glossy, already taking the market by storm. Even the hyphenated title gave a knowing, ironic nod towards the old Ireland, harking back to things like 'divorce, Irish-style', and 'abortion, Irish-style', while heralding the new and more fashionable, more right-on order. The last thing that Claire would have time for was overseeing renovations in a soon-to-be-boutique in the suburbs of Dalkey. I don't think that she even got to finish her first interview at the magazine: she was offered the job on the spot. I was very glad for her. Claire was in the right place at the right time, just where she ought to have been. She became a satellite of style as Dublin began to be the new party city of Europe.

Two years after I got Dalkey up and running – I'd called the boutique 'Oui Two' in the expectation of Maggie's future involvement – I decided that I needed to refine my stock even more. I wasn't exploiting my client-base cleverly enough. I wanted to import high-quality leather goods, shoes, silk handbags. Not the sort that every globalized street market now has to offer, but one-offs, quirky designs, originals by unknowns whose work I could promote – as long as they came cheaply enough.

I found just the man to help me. I met him at a trade fair in London about a year after I went into business. We had a fling that lasted for a whole, glorious weekend – but it was nothing that either of us wanted to make permanent. Besides, he was forty-something, already married, and I was a woman in a hurry. But Luis recognized a kindred spirit when he met one.

'We can do business, you and I,' he said, as he poured the champagne that room service had delivered. 'You are able to separate love and sex and work. That is an unusual characteristic in a woman, but an excellent one.'

I remember I looked at him as coolly as I could manage, given that we were still lying in his hotel bed, still tangled in sweaty sheets, the floor littered with our discarded clothes. 'If I didn't know better, Luis, I'd say that you had just managed to insult me.'

He roared with laughter. After he took me to bed for the third time that weekend, he told me of his Turkish contacts. I never inquired how hides of the finest leather made their way to his warehouses – and then to me – without attracting the attention of Customs. I never asked how shoes of such exquisite design arrived on my doorstep with a price tag that would make chain stores everywhere gag with envy. I never wanted to know how such intricately beaded silks turned up in otherwise innocent consignments of cheap handbags and unremarkable leather jackets – items I then sold on to the lower-end boutiques for their January sales.

Luis had already told me – pillow talk – that if I saw his bank statement I'd die of laughter. Mortgage, gas, electricity, life insurance: enough to keep the tax authorities off his back. Everything else was, he said '*dinero negro*' – all hidden, under-the-counter income. I didn't care. I stocked everything he sent me and sold them to the wealthy women of Dublin who made their way to 'Oui Two' in droves. I met Luis maybe half a dozen times during the following year. And at least twice a year since; every year for the next decade. It was no grand passion. But as I've said, we were kindred spirits. We stayed together in Paris, Milan, Madrid and Rome. He liked to claim that he was my mentor.

And then I met Pete. I was twenty-four, almost twenty-five. My approaching birthday was something of a milestone. I had decided that twenty-five or so was a good age at which to settle down, to acquire the trappings of marriage and possibly children. Pete was an investment banker, one of the many people Claire introduced me to. I liked his solidity. After Danny's flakiness and Luis's flamboyance, Pete seemed to me to be the perfect antidote. He listened gravely to my plans for expansion and made some perceptive comments. I told him about Maggie, what we could each bring to the other as partners, at some stage in the near future. I could see that he was impressed. Naturally, I was economical with the truth about my Spanish contact.

At the end of that evening in Claire's, he handed me his card. 'I think I may be able to help you,' he said. 'Why don't you give me a call?' I knew by the way he said it that it was an invitation to meet him again, not merely a request to do business.

So. I did call him. I hadn't known that I would, but Claire insisted. 'He's a good guy,' she said, 'and he's been brilliant for the magazine, when nobody else would touch us. He's not afraid of the stuff that comes out of left field, trust me. Besides, he likes you.'

I was intrigued. By then, as well as having my logical, intellectual decision in place about what I wanted to do next with my life, I had begun to realize that I was restless. I found all the old clichés coming home to roost. I wanted someone who was mine, in all the ways that Danny hadn't been and Luis couldn't be.

I was hooked. I was in love with love – or the idea of it. A dangerous, dangerous place to be. I could also hear the predictable ticking of the biological clock, stronger at that stage of my life than at any other time before or since. Six months after we met, Pete asked me to marry him. We'd had dinner in Patrick Guilbaud's – a performance rather than a meal – and I was feeling mellow, my natural spikiness soothed by the annual returns verified by my accountant that afternoon. Pete celebrated my success; it was a success that also reflected well on his judgement as an investor. We were both feeling very pleased with ourselves.

When he finally mapped out his life for me over tiny cups of espresso, I thought, 'Why the hell not?' And so I said yes, I would marry him. At that stage, we hadn't even slept together. It had been a curiously old-fashioned courtship, Pete a curiously old-fashioned man. I went home with him that night, and while he was a long way from Danny or Luis, I fell for his tenderness. Back then, it was something that I needed. And I must have been something that he needed, too.

And now? Well, now is now and now is different.

'Talk to me,' he has said on a few occasions over the past couple of years. And I am at a loss. About what? Why can't *he* talk to me? He is obviously the one with things to say, things on his mind that he would like me to listen to. I, on the other hand, am not: I have grown accustomed to the silences between us. There is nothing I now wish to share. The last few years have made me want to retreat from my life – or the private aspects of it at least – and be a completely other person. I was thinking recently about the fairy tale 'The Emperor's New Clothes' and I no longer know whether I am the little boy on the sidelines shouting about the emperor's nakedness, or whether I am the emperor himself. Either way, it seems that I have been parading bare through my surroundings, trying to gather enough cover to be invisible. And it hasn't worked. I have been exposed for what I am. So. I need a whole new wardrobe.

And yet, and yet and yet. I have been a good wife. A good enough wife. I have given birth to and mothered two daughters. I have been faithful, after my fashion. If I have strayed – and I am not claiming that I have not – I have done so discreetly, quietly, making sure that neither Pete nor my children have suffered. Until now.

And that's because this is different. If Pete is what I needed for the middle part of my life – the parenting, consolidating, conventional part – then this man, whose arrival I await with baths and perfume and eagerness, he is for the latter part. Or so I feel. Age makes sure that I qualify all of these assertions. I have learned that there are no certainties and no absolutes. Black and white continue to bleed into one another, muddying all the channels in which we live.

But these are the choices that I have made. At forty-four years of age, I know that all choices have consequences – something that at twenty-four, for example, I did not know, or did not fully understand. But I am prepared for that, for all that may come. And so I wait, surrounded by olive trees and vineyards and the hot gritty dust of Tuscany. *Toscana*, Luis used to call it, promising that we would go there some day. I liked its lilting cadence in Spanish, but knew that I could not wait for his promise to be fulfilled.

And so, I look out over my balcony and count the hours. Not since Danny have I felt such a feeling of anticipation, of danger. The unknown has me on edge, reminds me how alive I feel now after all the years of sleep-walking through my future. I have taken control again and I have to wait only three more days. That is all the time that remains. And I shall wait, patiently or impatiently.

One way or the other, it will pass.

And now to Nora.

I have been thinking about her, too, over the past couple of days. Not because I want to, God knows, but because it is inevitable. I never planned any of this, but nevertheless, this is how it is, this is how things are going to be.

I am enjoying the midday sunshine right now. The waters of the pool are glittering behind me. The sun brings warmth at this time of year, rather than heat, but it is the light that I love above all – the Renaissance clarity and purity of it. I have brought the small wooden table out of the shade and I am sitting at it now, with my journal. Before this, I have never been one for introspection. Maggie has called me 'Action Woman' on more than one occasion, given that I often speak my mind, she says, before I have even made it up. Perhaps I have operated on gut instinct in the past, or else that impulsiveness that has often brought trouble in its wake. I don't know, and I am no longer sufficiently satisfied to say 'Who cares?' as I have done so often in my previous life. I need to know, I need to understand what makes me tick. I have to find out how I have managed to allow my life to take me so much by surprise.

And so, shortly after I arrived here, I decided on the acquisition of a journal. It was a joy to buy. Its cobalt covers caught my eye at once in the Fabriano shop in Florence. Inside, the pages were of handmade paper and their quality was exquisite. I bought a pen to match and I sit out here for a few hours each day, writing. I have pinned my hair up, exposing the back of my neck to the sun. I love the way, to quote Maggie, that it makes my bones feel warm.

I decided – given that I had no fixed idea where to start – that I would begin my journal by trying to recall those events in my life that had caught me off guard the most. What I mean by that is, I would attempt to remember with honesty the occasions over which I was unable to exert any control. And 'with honesty' is the key here. I accept that for much of my life I have played games in order to get what I wanted. With my father, with Luis. With Pete. Sometimes, I have realized, I did so without ever having taken the time to find out what it was I really wanted in the first place.

To my surprise, given that she is so low down on the list of people that I care for, it was Nora who first came to mind. And I remembered, with almost painful clarity, how the woman had once managed to pull the rug from under my feet.

It was about three years ago and we were all having dinner at Maggie's one July evening, when Nora simpered her way in my direction. She started to handle the sequined hem of my jacket and I couldn't stop myself from moving away from her a fraction.

'I haven't seen this before,' she said. 'Aren't the little sequins a lovely touch?'

She was dressed in some hideous navy and white dress, with matching shoes that would have looked fine on Doris Day. Even her handbag was navy and white – a cheap and nasty plastic it was too, masquerading as leather, with the metal clasp already showing signs of tarnish. I remember I shivered. I couldn't help myself. Nora had once asked Maggie to design something for her, but Maggie managed to extricate herself from that nightmare with the combination of a little tact and a lot of kindness. She did not want to insult Nora by telling her that her large and ungainly frame did not suit the subtle numbers that we produced, or at least, that's how I should have put it.

Nora in white linen? Please. Or a cashmere and silk mix? It would have put the rest of our clients off for good. But I wasn't allowed to say anything to Nora in that instance, as in so many others. Maggie told me to leave it to her, so I did, albeit reluctantly. She told me afterwards, Maggie that is, that she had brought Nora shopping instead. She had even spent a whole day in her company, with one of those personal image consultants who help you buy the things that suit you best.

'What did you do that for?' I asked her. I couldn't think of anything I was less likely to do than spend that sort of time with Nora.

I remember that Maggie looked at me impatiently. 'You will never see anything good in Nora, will you? Sure, she has her faults, but then again, so do you, Georgie. So do we all.'

I wasn't sure that I liked her tone. But I wasn't about to fight with her, either. We'd had one row already over Nora, years back, and I didn't want to go there again.

'Sure,' I said instead. But I was careful not to shrug. 'Rather you than I, that's all.' And the inevitable happened, of course it did, after a year or so. I could have told her – I could see it coming. Once Nora had Maggie in tow, and her personal shopper to boot, she dressed well and stylishly. I have to admit, she made the most of herself for at least six months. But then she began to revert to type. And by the time Robbie's twenty-first rolled around, she had slipped back into all her bad habits again. I don't know how Maggie felt about that; I've never asked. I know how I'd have felt, but that's an altogether different story.

So that when Nora started tugging at the cuff of my jacket on that occasion in Maggie's, I was probably even more touchy than normal. 'Thanks, Nora,' I said, smoothing my sleeves. 'It's one of a new line Maggie and I are developing. It's the first time I've worn it.'

'Really?' she asked. Something in her voice made me look at her. Her expression was cunning, her tone full of false surprise. 'I thought I saw one very like it last weekend. And the woman looked awfully like you, too, from the back.'

I remember feeling bored already by the conversation. Nora always had that effect on me, ever since I was eighteen. 'Oh, yes?' I said, or something like it. 'Where was that?'

'In Castleknock.' And she kept looking at me.

I have to say that I was caught off guard. And particularly coming from Nora, I was unprepared. I put my hand up. After all, this is the time for honesty. Nevertheless, I think I was convincing. Either way, neither Maggie nor Claire picked up on what she was saying, so the situation never developed. It took a moment, but I regained my composure and smiled at Nora, shaking my head.

'Don't think I've ever been to Castleknock in my life,' I lied. 'Must have been somebody else.'

And that was that. But I felt her gaze throughout the meal that night. The irony of it is, it was she who had insisted, months beforehand, that we all foregather at her house for champagne and canapés to celebrate Robbie's twenty-first. Strictly a 'six in the evening till eight' invitation. I felt I could manage that, as long as Maggie and Claire and I arrived together and left together.

It was a pre-party party and we did all that was appropriate. We brought flowers for Nora, a bottle of wine for Frank – the same vintage as his firstborn – and a respectable amount of money from the three of us as a gift for Robbie. We all shook hands and kissed him and wished him happy birthday. I was designated to slip the envelope to him, away from Nora's and Frank's eager parental eye. Just this once, we felt, he ought to be permitted to be reckless.

There were all the usual stories to be shared – about how the four of us had, shortly after he was born, made a pact that we would keep on meeting, about how we had watched him grow, about how the years fly. You know the kind of thing. Nora was in her element and I was on my best behaviour, duly warned by *both* Maggie and Claire. And then it was photograph time.

'Let's have one of the four of us with Robbie,' Nora fussed, shooing us all towards the profusion of plants in the conservatory. 'Robbie, you stand there, in the middle.' I didn't like to tell her that the resulting photo would be sure to show a fig-tree growing out of the top of her eldest son's head. 'Claire, you go here, Georgie, you stand there. That's right, Maggie. Frank! Oh, Frank! Come and take our photo!' Robbie grinned good-naturedly. He raised one eyebrow slightly as we gathered ourselves for the photograph. I think he shared the joke. I ended up on one side of him, his mother on the other. That was not what Nora had wished – but Frank's word held sway. The composition of the photo would be far better that way, he kept insisting, much more *balanced*.

'A little closer,' Frank called. 'A little closer still.'

Robbie pulled his mother towards him. Then, he tightened his grip around my waist. His hand was warm, insistent through the fine silk of my dress. I cursed Frank for fiddling with light meters and lenses and flashes. Why couldn't he use a digital camera like everyone else, for God's sake? The pressure of

Robbie's arm was making me uncomfortable. He was too close, intruding into my personal space. I could see the beginnings of his five o'clock shadow, smell the subtle undertone of his after-shave. It wasn't that his presence was unpleasant: rather that there was far too much of it. Finally, Frank declared the photograph perfect and we were released. I turned to Maggie.

'Let's go,' I said. 'I don't want us to lose our table.'

She looked confused for an instant. There was no question of us losing our reservation. But she nodded. Given how I've always felt about Nora, she wouldn't have been surprised that I wanted to leave. But Claire had sensed something else, I know she had.

'You okay, Georgie?' she asked, as Maggie brought around the car. 'You looked a bit ill-at-ease in there. Not like you.'

I sighed. 'I'm sorry, Claire, I find it harder and harder these days to take Nora and Frank. She, in particular, makes me feel suffocated.'

Claire nodded. I don't know whether she believed me, but she didn't mention it again. The three of us went out to dinner together afterwards and reminisced. We also agreed how it never ceased to amaze us that a dry old stick like Frank and our Nora had managed to produce three such drop-dead gorgeous sons. We also agreed that Robbie was by far the most handsome and engag-ing of the three. And that was the end of that evening.

We all went home, duty done, and I decided to forget about it.

Some days later, I was walking down Grafton Street. I was head-ing for the Westbury for a meeting. As I was parking, I'd got a call on my mobile to say that Roberto, my Italian supplier, was running about half an hour late, having fallen victim to Dublin's traffic chaos. I didn't mind. It was one of those early June days when the city shows itself in its kindest light. I was reminded, bizarrely, of Noel Purcell singing about Dublin's being heaven, having coffee at eleven and all the delights of Stephen's Green. Talk about a blast from the past. But it was, as Claire was wont to say, a 'pet day'.

I decided to meander down the street, leaving behind the air of purpose that seemed to define everything I did in those days. How can I describe it? Apart from the glorious sunshine, it was one of those mornings when everything seemed right with the world. A good hair day. Warmth, cheerful shoppers and an unexpected half-hour's leisure to boot. Strangely, the combination of so many good things made me feel restless, as though something about myself and my life had now become hollow. I'd been conscious of that feeling for a while. A dissatisfaction that I couldn't pin down, no matter how hard I tried. It was as though something had started to unravel – a stitch at a time, but nevertheless.

Hadn't I everything I needed? A husband, a family, a career, friends, lots of money? What could possibly be missing? Such a sense of dissatisfaction had become, however, a nagging, insistent sense of loss – sometimes vague, sometimes heart-stopping. I can see that clearly now. But then, I never paused long enough to consider it. My response was to keep busy, busier. I think I might have been afraid to step off the moving staircase.

And so, when I stopped to look in the window of Richard Alan's that morning, it was as much for professional appraisal as for the pleasure of a momentary distraction. I was so intent on enjoying the dresses on display that I saw nothing of a figure hovering nearby. It was only when I broke my concentration by looking at my watch that I realized somebody was standing behind me and had been for some time.

Instinctively, I clutched my bag, pressing it closer to my side, and wheeled around to confront my stalker, shadow, mugger: whatever he was.

'Georgie? Georgie White?'

I whipped off my sunglasses, the flood of relief now beginning to make me feel angry. At least it was someone I knew. I wasn't in any danger. All this in the space of a second, before I recognized him. More accurately, I recognized the fact that I *knew* the man, but for the moment, his name eluded me. Context is all.

'It's me, Robbie. Robbie Fitzsimons.'

I stared at him blankly for another second.

'Nora and Frank's son?'

'Of *course*,' I said, feeling foolish. How could I not have known?

'This is a really strange coincidence,' he said. 'I was just going to call you to thank you for your very generous birthday present.' He hesitated. 'I know that "thank you" cards are more traditional, and I have written to you all as well, but . . .' and he shrugged. 'Well, your gift was nothing short of astonishing, and that's not something I felt I could put in writing.' He grinned. 'The folks might have come over all sensible, if they'd found out.'

I smiled. But I still felt put out. It was as though I had lost my sure-footedness and stumbled into the unexpected. 'Don't worry. Your secret is safe with us. I hope you can find something completely impractical to do with the money.' I settled my bag more firmly on my shoulder and felt the ground become stable beneath my feet again. 'Get yourself something beautiful to remember your coming of age.'

He nodded, considering this. 'I already have something special in mind.' He paused for a moment. 'I'm sorry if I startled you,' he said. 'I was pretty sure it was you, even from the back. But when you didn't turn around, I thought I must have been mistaken.'

I can smile now, at how his words were almost echoed by his mother, some three years later. But on that day, in the blue heat of Grafton Street, how could I possibly have known what lay ahead?

'Are you in a rush?' he asked. 'I mean, can I buy you coffee?'

I looked at my watch. 'I've probably got twenty minutes.' He didn't hesitate.

'Good. I know just the place,' he said. We turned right on to one of Grafton Street's many tributaries and sat outside one of the new cafés, its round metal tables gleaming in the sunshine.

'What would you like?' he asked.

'Espresso, please.' I waited to see how he would respond to this bit of sophistication, until I realized that for him, it was probably no sophistication at all. He had grown up with Dublin's café society, accepted it as normal.

'Two, please,' he said to the young waiter, who retreated, giving his tray a flamboyant twirl.

I remember that we talked about his birthday party, then his architecture studies, then his plans for the future. I was impressed. He was a single-minded young man, determined to succeed. Our conversation grew more serious, more intimate, until I realized that thirty-five minutes had passed. My mobile shrilled, making me jump. 'On my way,' I said to Roberto, 'with you in three minutes.' And I stood up to leave. I held out my hand to Robbie. 'Another Robert calling,' I said, laughing. 'I'm sorry, but I really have to go.'

He shook hands. 'Lovely to meet you again,' he said. 'I've enjoyed talking to you.'

'Me too,' I told him. 'And the best of luck for the future.'

He nodded, but there was something in his expression that made feel unsure of myself again. I left him and headed off towards the Westbury, conscious all the while of eyes burning into the small of my back.

Three, maybe four days later, just after the weekend, he called me.

'Please,' he said. 'I won't waste your time. But I'd like to speak to you. I *must* speak to you.'

I was intrigued. There was an urgency to his tone that I couldn't ignore. Was he in some kind of trouble? Had something happened that he couldn't tell his parents about? God knows, I am not the maternal type, but there was a need in his voice that compelled me to see him. That, and curiosity, I have to say. What could possibly be wrong in his life? Handsome, clever, articulate. Mature beyond his years. We'd all heard Nora's boasts over and over again.

We agreed a time and place for the following day. We met at a small café in Donnybrook, one of those local, hidden-away gems off the main street. He was waiting for me when I arrived, already drinking an espresso. I couldn't help it, I was amused.

'Hello, Robbie,' I said, as he stood up to greet me. We shook hands.

'What would you like?' he asked as we sat.

'Green tea,' I said. 'I've already had my ration of coffee. I'll be speeding for the rest of the day if I have any more.'

He ordered and we sat in silence for a moment. Then he turned to face me. Somehow, at that moment, I knew what was coming. My breath-catch was audible, I'm sure of it. I don't know where the knowledge came from, but it assaulted me, made me feel vulnerable in some inexplicable way. It was how I'd felt in Grafton Street the day he had appeared behind me; how I'd felt on the evening his father took our photograph. He passed a small box across the table after the waitress brought my tea. Gift-wrapped; gold-ribboned; full of hidden possibilities.

'This is for you,' he said. His expression was unmistakable.

The forty-one-year-old me said get up, go home now, no harm done. Be firm, no-nonsense. You are the adult woman, this is a love-struck boy. You can see it in his eyes, see it by the way he's looking at you. You know you can. He looks like Danny. Stand up and leave. Now.

But I didn't. It would be more accurate and more honest to say that I couldn't. My heart was racing and my mouth had gone dry.

'Open it.'

There was a knowingness to his tone, a wisdom in his eyes that made me think, 'He is all that you've said, Nora, and more besides. What a time to find out that you were right.' I wanted to laugh, I wanted to leave, but above all, I wanted to stay.

It took a moment but then I came to my senses, or thought I did. 'Robbie, this is complete madness. What on earth can you be thinking—'

'Open it, please.'

I shook my head and pushed the gift-wrapped box back to his side of the table. 'No. I don't know what you're feeling, but whatever it is, it's impossible. I'm leaving now.' And I stood – somewhat uncertainly, it has to be said, but I stood nevertheless and felt proud of myself. Behaving as an adult should. Sensibly, responsibly, firmly. But it didn't throw him.

'I fell in love with you the moment I saw you,' he said, as though announcing the weather forecast. I was conscious of other people in the café turning their heads. But it was a vague consciousness. They were local colour of some indeterminate shade, background noise to the main event. 'I know I'd met you before, over the years, but I didn't really notice you. Not in the way I saw you on the night of my birthday. Don't you want to know why?'

What woman could resist that? I should have, but I didn't. I sat, more heavily than I normally would, my knees having ceased to bend properly. I couldn't help it – I was watching myself from the outside, alarmed at how I displayed all the characteristics of a Victorian heroine. Shortness of breath, racing heart, perspiring palms. I even had to control the urge to faint. I rested my forehead in my hands, not looking at him. This, I told myself, is not happening. This is madness. Get a grip. It cannot be happening, not to *me*. I won't let it. I am used to being in control.

He leaned towards me. I could feel his closeness, feel the warmth of his breath, that tingling note of his aftershave again. 'Before you say anything, listen to me. I've grown up all my life knowing what love is. My father told me he fell in love with my mother the first minute she walked into his shop. He told me that if I was ever lucky enough to have that, no matter what the circumstances, I should never ignore it.'

I swallowed. Frank. Nora. All my derision, all my impatience, my cynicism over the years. Hoist with my own petard? I should think so.

'Robbie,' I said, my words slow and deliberate, 'my two daughters are only a few years younger than you are. You are a boy. There is nothing possible between us. This is a crush, infatuation – call it what you like. It isn't *real*.'

He grinned. 'And tell me, what were you up to at twenty-one? Were you a mere girl, an innocent?'

'Yes,' I said, firmly. 'That's exactly what I was. A girl. An ingénue.' An image of Danny loomed before me again. I could almost taste the intensity of his physical presence. I drove him away, back to whatever shadows he had emerged from.

Robbie's brown eyes were steady. 'You're lying,' he said. His voice was calm. 'And I understand why. And if you are so sure that I'm only a foolish boy, then why are you so terrified?'

Then I stood, with as much dignity as I could muster. 'I am not terrified, I am simply taken aback. This is ludicrous. I'm leaving now. Please don't call me again.'

And I left the café, hoping against hope that there would be a taxi to take me home. There was – and I fell into it and shut the door, just in time to see Robbie run out into the street after me, the glass doors of the café swinging to a close behind him.

But of course, he did call again. And again and again over the course of the next few days. As soon as I'd recognize the number, I'd switch my mobile off. He never left a message. Once, when I was having a coffee with Claire, I was taken unawares and answered without thinking. On that occasion, I was sharp to the point of rudeness.

'I want you to stop harassing me,' I said. 'Next time, I'll report you as a nuisance caller.'

'Then meet me,' he said. 'Just once more. Six o'clock tonight. Same café in Donnybrook. After that, if you still want me to, I'll leave you alone.'

If you still want me to. The arrogance of the young. Claire was looking at me, her expression one of concern. I did not want to have to explain anything to her. I hung up without responding.

'Is everything okay?' she asked.

I shook my head impatiently. 'It's only a nuisance call. I've had two or three of them recently. It's nothing.'

'It doesn't look like "nothing" to me. You've gone as white as a ghost.'

I tried to smile at her. 'It's no big deal,' I said. 'It's a bit of an irritation, that's all. And I really don't want to have to change my number – it's far too much of an inconvenience. They'll get fed up eventually and leave me alone.'

'Well,' she said, 'whatever you do, don't let it drag on too long.'

As soon as she spoke, I felt the rightness of her words. This had to be dealt with now. This boy had to be sent away. When Claire went up to pay for our coffee, I sent him a one-word text: 'Yes.'

I would meet him that evening and then that would be the end of that.

I arrived at the café at ten-past six. I gave Maggie one excuse as

I left the shop and gave Pete a different one by phone. But Maggie has never needed explanations from me and as I've said, my husband is not a suspicious man. I didn't feel guilty about my white lies, either, because I had no intention of doing anything about which to feel guilty, either then or later. Instead, I was angry. I wanted this to *stop*. And yet, Robbie's pursuit of me was flattering, at times even thrilling. There were days when the edginess of anticipating his calls and texts made me feel alive, vibrant, almost-three dimensional in a way I hadn't felt for a long time – not since Danny. Or Luis.

He was there before me, as I'd known he would be. I sat down opposite him. He met my gaze, no sign of embarrassment or uncertainty in his expression. I was nonplussed. It felt as though I were the twenty-one-year-old girl, and he the older, more experienced man. It seemed that neither of us wanted to be the first to speak. Eventually, I was the one who broke the silence. I kept my voice low and controlled. No histrionics, I'd promised myself – not that histrionics have ever been my style, anyway.

'Robbie,' I said. 'Please stop contacting me. You're wasting your time and mine and making me feel uncomfortable.' At least that last was true.

'I want you to open this,' he said, as though I hadn't spoken. 'I want you to keep it, no matter what you decide. If you don't take it, then I'll leave it here on the table when we go.' His tone was quiet, insistent. I believed that he meant what he said. I had to humour him. At least, that's what I think I thought at the time. The truth is, the moment I stretched out my hand for that gift I knew. There was no going back. Inside the box was a white gold Tiffany heart, studded with tiny diamonds. I froze.

'You told me to get something beautiful and impractical,' he said.

'*For yourself.*'

He leaned forwards and took the necklace from me. 'I did.'

He moved with speed and fastened it about my throat. As he did so, he leaned down and kissed the back of my neck. Lightning struck. I didn't trust myself to move or speak. Instead, I remember looking around the dimly lit interior of the café, searching for somewhere safe to stand. And I remember thinking: lightning never strikes the same place twice. I repeated it to myself, over and over again, like a mantra.

'I did buy something for myself. I wanted to see you wear it.' His voice was quiet. He sat down and leaned across the tiny table. I thought I could smell the sun on his skin again, the way I had the day we'd met in Grafton Street. But that was ridiculous. It was evening and we were indoors.

He took my hands in both of his. The pressure of his fingers reminded me all over again of how his hand had felt through the thin fabric of my dress. 'I don't know how, not yet, but I will.' His gaze was warm, confident. I sat looking at him, more and more immobilized as he stroked my fingers, kissed them one by one. 'It will probably have to be in some highly unconventional way. But you and I are going to be together. I'm sure of it.'

Even now, even as I write this, I can hear sensible people groan. Quite right, too, but I was no longer sensible, no longer sane. The only thing I was conscious of right then was the depth of my own madness. Because the words Robbie spoke had struck at something within me that responded, without my wanting it to. It was as if all the conflicting elements of my life had finally become fused. I could feel those disparate parts of me, the acknowledged and the unacknowledged, some present, some missing for years, all rushing towards this new centre like iron filings to a magnet. My thoughts became random, almost wild – but at the same time, I felt a stillness, a serenity, a sense of the rightness of things that I had never felt before.

My kingdom for a kiss? My life for a cliché? Was I about to

abandon husband, family, friends, business, to become a woman seeking to relive her life in the arms of a man half her age?

'Together? How can you say that?' I tried to pull my hands away. Even to my own ears, my voice lacked the strength of conviction.

He smiled and tucked a strand of hair behind my ear. 'Because I know it's true. And you know it's true. You knew it on the night of my birthday. We both did. That's why you ran, why you wouldn't look at me after the photograph.' He reached into the pocket of his shirt. 'Look.'

I looked. Claire, Nora, Robbie, me, Maggie. The photo had captured an instant I no longer remembered, illuminated a feeling I'd refused to recognize, then or later. I was caught in the act of trying to pull away from him, trying to pull back. I look stricken, unsmiling.

'See what I mean?'

'It's a photograph. It proves nothing . . . I often feel uncomfortable in your mother's presence.'

He grinned and tucked the photograph back into his pocket. 'Well, now at least you have good reason.'

I smiled. I couldn't help it.

Tomorrow, I told myself, I'd be sensible. Tomorrow, I'd deal with it.

For three weeks after that meeting in an ordinary café on an unremarkable June evening, I tried to resist. Despite what I was feeling, despite the discovery that I was becoming a whole new person, I resisted. I fought him daily with duty and with logic. We had twenty-one more days of phone calls, texts, even letters posted to the shop. If Maggie noticed, she never said. In all of these communications, Robbie was very measured and there was no sense of panic. He was simply persistent in the face of what he called the inevitable. Finally, I agreed to meet him somewhere private, so that we could talk. The novelty was thrilling.

We met in the flat of a friend of his. A small, clean and orderly flat above a motorcycle shop in Castleknock. It was the first of many such meetings. I was nervous, but exhilarated too. I remember I'd dressed with care and to make a point: a white linen suit, elegant, sophisticated, something that I hoped would emphasize the differences between us, make Robbie realize that I was no longer a girl. Make *me* realize that I was no longer a girl. That first day, though, one bit of me thought, why the hell not? I could use some excitement in my life, and Robbie'll get over it soon enough. I have to confess that I took even greater care with what I wore underneath my white linen suit. And that made an altogether different point. I'd splurged on silk, on lace, in shades and styles that were way more daring than anything I was used to. So yes, I knew.

He had arrived at the flat well before me, by arrangement. When he opened the door, he swung me off my feet, kissed me and handed me a glass of champagne. I was so taken aback at the businesslike way he did it, that I was speechless. It was as though to say, 'There, let's get that bit out of the way.' And it worked – instead of feeling awkward, we both laughed. He pulled out a kitchen chair for me.

'What on earth are you doing?' I asked. The kitchen was full of bowls, dishes, platters, all filled with bite-size portions of brightly coloured food. An ice bucket stood at one corner of the tiny table, beautifully folded napkins at the other. In between were wine glasses – none of which matched, each of which dazzled in the sunlight from the open window.

This is not real, I had to tell myself. But it was. It was authentic in a way so few things had been for so long. He caught me looking at the glasses.

'Victorian crystal,' he said, pulling something out of the

fridge. 'One of my mate's – Hugh's – passions. He's been collecting it for three years now. Says it's amazing the bargains you can pick up at junk sales and auction rooms.'

I nodded. What possible answer could there be to that? I felt more and more like Alice in Wonderland. This rabbit-hole was filled with young men, antique crystal and motorcycle repairs. As if I didn't have enough to grapple with already.

'I'm in my Greek phase at the moment,' he continued. His voice was cheerful, relaxed. I wondered how he could be so completely himself, so much without jagged edges. 'I like to cook,' he said. Then he glanced at me. 'Didn't lick it up off the stones, wouldn't you say?'

I couldn't answer. At the oblique reference to Nora, to my other life, I felt all at once filled with the panic of uncertainty. The loss of everything I had built loomed in front of my eyes, filling this small and spartan kitchen. What was I doing here? I wanted to flee, needed to clamber out of this tunnel before I did something that would make my old life disappear from view for ever. I tried to stand, but only succeeded in scraping the chair legs across the wooden floor.

'Are you okay?' he asked. The tenderness in his voice brought a lump to my throat.

To my horror, I could feel my eyes begin to fill. 'No,' I whispered. 'I don't think I'm okay at all.'

He wiped his hands very matter-of-factly and walked around to my side of the table. Without a word, he pulled me to my feet and put his arms around me. I could feel myself beginning to get drunk on the scents I already associated with him – sun, skin, maleness. We stood for what seemed like a lifetime, holding on to each other. My head rested comfortably against his chest. I was terrified that it felt so good there. The pressure I recalled from his embrace on the night of his birthday now became transformed into solidity. Gradually, I felt myself being grounded by it. That surprised me most of all. I had not expected him to sustain me.

He stroked my hair. 'I know,' he said, 'I know how strange this has to be for you. I'm sorry the way I sprang it on you – but I'm not sorry you're here. I'm in love with you, Georgie, and you're going to have to deal with that.' He kissed me. 'Because I'm not going to let you go.'

He pulled away and looked at me, his gaze unwavering. And then I kissed him back.

We've spoken many times since about that afternoon. About how in the end we each took the other to bed, about how we made love for hours until we were both exhausted, but still couldn't leave the other alone. Three times I got dressed to go home, promising that yes, yes, we would meet again, of course we would meet again. How could we not?

And each time, he undressed me once more, luring me back to bed. It was an irresistible combination of his hands on my skin, his words in my ear, the warmth of his laughter. Sometimes he teases me still, telling me what a pushover I was. All he had to do was cook *one meal*, he said, and he had me hooked. He made me laugh then, and he makes me laugh still. Somehow, the world became a lighter, kinder place that afternoon. And the strangest thing of all is, that instead of the strangeness I had feared, there was nothing but familiarity between us. Lying there in bed together, I felt as if I had come home, as if I had just woken from a long and dreamless sleep.

'"I wonder by my troth, what thou and I / Did, till we loved?"' Robbie was lying on his side, one hand on my thigh.

I had been about to say that now I *must* go, I really must. I couldn't delay any longer.

'"Were we not wean'd till then?"' he said, and kissed me.

I looked at him in astonishment. 'What on earth are you doing quoting John Donne?'

Then he grinned. 'Too much of a peasant, am I? No place for

the arts and the architect to meet?' I tried to protest, but he silenced me. 'I've done my homework. My mother said you were a meta-physical poetry nut. You see, I'm prepared to go to any lengths to snare you. Aren't you impressed?'

I don't think impressed was the word I was searching for. I pulled him to me again, feeling the first forty years of my life sheer away from me for ever.

And so we have been, for all of three years now.

Am I selfish and irresponsible, shedding a proper, orderly exis-tence for one that offers nothing but delight and danger? Absolutely. Insane? Probably. And yet it feels nothing like insanity should. Instead, it's all the old cliches of Maggie's songs. Soulmates, other halves. I've never found that sort of concept easy to understand before.

Robbie is a torrent of speech. I remember Claire telling me once, recently, that Ray had managed to seduce her with kindness. It struck me then, although of course I didn't tell Claire, that Robbie had seduced me with talk. Even in the most ordinary situations, he cre-ated intimacy where before I had only experienced proximity.

The first time he came to see me in Volterra, I was anxious. With nobody to hide from, with none of the thrill of imminent discovery to heighten our senses, how would we fare together? We talked, we walked. He saw Volterra with a different eye from mine. A trained eye. Where I was taken with the general, he was enthused by the specific. We spent the time quietly.

One night, we were in my kitchen together. He had cooked for us, while I read to him about the Madonna of Montenero at Livorno. We were due to visit the town the following day. He poured the last of the wine into our glasses.

'You going to ask her blessing on this accident of ours, or what?' His expression was serious, but his tone was gentle, mocking.

'Why not?' I said. Sitting there, across the table from him, I was conscious of the fragility of things in a way that the young cannot fathom.

'To continued happiness,' he said, raising his glass.

'To happiness,' I answered, hoping I could hold on to it for a little longer.

Because no matter what, I am a realist. Am I heading for disaster in ten years' time when I am fifty-four? Robbie will then, most likely, be an even more handsome thirty-four-year-old man in his prime. He teases me about this, says that as the years go on, I will no longer be almost twice his age. He performed some mathematical conundrum that showed the gap between us narrowing as we get older. Sleight of hand, I told him. You don't convince me. So, yes, disaster is probably where I'll take up residence in a decade or so, picking up the pieces of several lives.

But that's the future. I'm not worried about the future. It was the present I worried about as it galloped away from me, through one unchanging day after another. I am here. This is now, and I await his arrival. Full of expectation and with no regrets.

Tomorrow, I shall make my way into Volterra again. I like wandering through the shady, medieval streets, stopping for a coffee under the umbrellas of the piazza. I like the silence here at this time of year, before the tourists come. San Gimignano looms in the distance, towering out of the morning mist like a child's fairy-tale castle. I might wander into the workshops of the *artisani* again and watch the forms they have imagined begin to emerge as the alabaster is chipped away. I have always liked that idea: that in art as well as life the shape of something beautiful already exists and all you have to do is take away the excess. Discarding that which is no longer important.

My favourite part of Volterra, though, apart from the majesty of the Etruscan gates, is Le Balze. The first time I saw the way these cliffs had fallen away, clay crumbling under the pressure of sandstone, I was assaulted by vertigo. Their collapse left churches, monasteries and homes vulnerable to plunging into nothingness. Now, I feel instead a sense of companionship, of familiarity in the starkness of their presence. Robbie says it is because I, too, have discovered the joys of life on the edge. That what I have becomes more precious precisely because it can, at any time, slide away from me into the abyss.

Perhaps. All I know is it makes me feel exhilarated and present in the now.

The day after tomorrow, I'll drive to Florence to pick him up. He has solved the dilemma of Megan's arrival, he tells me. She will come and spend some time with him in Florence instead. Nora is less than pleased.

I couldn't help smiling when he told me, but I made no comment. There may be a time in the future when Nora is even less pleased than she is at present – but I'm not going to worry about that, not now.

Robbie will arrive and we'll live our idyll for a few weeks, a few months, and after that, we'll see. Whatever happens, we'll share the moment.

After all, it's the only one we have.